Dónal is a hotel manager living and working in North Clare, Ireland. 'Clíona's Wave' was a winner of the 2013 Irish Writers' Centre Novel Fair.

Dónal was shortlisted for the 2014 K Award for short fiction and is the founder and director of the of Doolin Writers' Weekend, Doolin Folk Festival and Doolin Irish Craft Beer Festival.

His other interests include reading, history, walking/hiking and bodyboarding. Married to Liz, they live in a cottage in the hills with a chronically overgrown garden, two kids Elsie Rose & Millie and a hyperactive puppy, Sally.

Clíona's Wave

Dónal Minihane

Indigo Dreams Publishing

First Edition: Clíona's Wave

First published in Great Britain in 2015 by:
Indigo Dreams Publishing Ltd
24 Forest Houses
Halwill
Beaworthy
EX21 5UU
www.indigodreams.co.uk

ISBN 978-1-909357-73-0

A CIP record for this book is available from the British Library.

This book is a work of fiction and, except in the case of historical fact, any resemblance to actual persons, living or dead, is purely coincidental.

Designed and typeset in Minion Pro by Indigo Dreams.
Cover design by Angie Crowe, craftycrowedesign.com

Printed and bound in Great Britain by 4edge Ltd www.4edge.co.uk
Papers used by Indigo Dreams are recyclable products made from wood grown in sustainable forests following the guidance of the Forest Stewardship Council.

Dedicated to all the women incarcerated in the
Magdalene Laundries,
my wife Liz, and my three Roses:
my grandmother Rose, mother Rose and daughter Elsie Rose.

The author would like to acknowledge the influence and contribution of the following people who have since passed.

Sr. Catherine Minihane, Connie Glanton, Catherine Cox.

May they rest in peace.

Clíona's Wave

Bealtaine

Bridget lay awake, taking in the dawn air, a sickly dread daubing her stomach. Fog painted the window but already she could hear stirrings on the pier below and imagined the scene. Men going about their business, mending nets, lowering lobster pots into boats. An engine murmured low and she followed it in her mind as it rumbled past the mansions perched on the hills of Glandore, out past the rocky outposts of the Adam and Eve islands and into the open seas beyond. She thought of her own father with his massive bulk and easy temperament, laughing with his mates on the deck of his boat somewhere in the vast oceans. How she missed him. She missed him more than ever this morning. He would never have let this happen. No, never. A pang of anger slipped into that dread.

This wouldn't have happened if you were here!

You should have been here to look after your little girls!

In his absence, the parish priest had gladly stepped into the vacuum and made all the arrangements.

The warm body beside her stirred and moaned. Bridget had felt the bump on her younger sister's belly during the sleepless hours of that night. It was five months now, beginning to show. It wouldn't be long before the neighbours noticed. Bridget slid from the warmth of the eiderdown and washed, the icy water in the basin giving her a start as she splashed it about her face. The priest was expected this morning. She put on her best dress, threadbare now at the shoulders. Her father had brought two dresses home during one of his terms of leave, one for herself and one for Neasa. How they had laughed as he recounted haggling with the Chinaman in the market in Singapore. Eyes pulled into slits, he mimicked the trader's accent and spoke of the sights, sounds and smells of the bazaar, strange animals screeching from cages, snakes rising to music from baskets, mountains of spices and rows upon rows of magical potions. So exotic.

Bridget left the room before Neasa woke. She couldn't face her this morning. She had no words to give. When she arrived downstairs her mother was at the range. More than ever she wanted to run up behind her mother, tug at her apron strings and be hauled up into her bosom for an embrace. Any warmth that had been in the house had long since receded. The bacon sizzled in the pan and the aroma filled the kitchen, but this morning, to Bridget, it smelled rancid. From that day on she'd associate the smell with an awful feeling of dread, no matter where she may be in the world.

When Neasa arrived downstairs, the three of them sat for breakfast in silence. Having a father in the navy meant they could afford such treats as this. Meat on a weekday. But this morning nobody tasted a bite. Bridget would gladly live on bread and water for the rest of her life in exchange for her father's presence this morning. She stole glances across the table. Neasa sat there stoically. She betrayed no emotion and chewed her food mechanically. Any traces of the girl she had once been faded over the last few weeks as her fate was decided by the parish priest, with no argument tendered by their mother. These meetings had been conducted over cups of tea served in the family china in the good room. Bridget caught snippets of the conversations through an ajar door: 'she'll be with girls in the same boat, Maeve', 'child will get a good home', 'best thing for her, Maeve'. Neasa was never present during those meetings.

This morning there was no conversation. Her mother stared blankly at her half-eaten breakfast, waited for the girls to finish, collected the plates and took them to the sink, her back turned to them once again.

A car pulled up outside on the dot of nine. It was a big, black Ford and reminded Bridget of a hearse. The parish priest stepped out, standing solemnly by the open door like an undertaker. Neasa's bag had been packed the night before and lay waiting for her at the bottom of the stairs. There was a sharp knock. Neasa rose from the table and walked to the door. Their mother remained at the sink, one hand clutched one side, her knuckles white, shoulders trembling, and from the other hand she dropped the plate she had been washing back into the water. Bridget made her way to the front door where Neasa was waiting, she searched her sister's face for a hint of emotion. Nothing. A brief embrace and Neasa left, carrying her own suitcase to the car.

She looked so tiny in the back of the big, black car. She didn't look back.

The car pulled off and Bridget followed with her eyes as it passed the pier and travelled down through the village. She lost it for a few moments in the turns of the road until it re-emerged and crossed slowly over the bridge. She imagined the bridge collapsing in its wake. A single gull dived from the sky, broke the water and surfaced. Prey dangling from its beak, it took its place on the rail of the bridge. Tears welled in Bridget's eyes. Neasa was gone.

Lúnasa

Glandore Harbour, from the Irish Cuan D'or, meaning 'harbour of gold' or 'harbour of oak' depending on who you talk to, is situated on the rugged West Cork coastline between Toe and Galley Head. The harbour begins with Adam and Eve, two little rocky outcrops of islands. They linger at the harbour's mouth, two jagged teeth peering inward at the busy boats, eager for company, disappointed when given a wide berth. They wait for their return in the evening.

Long ago the local fishermen mapped safe passage through the harbour mouth, and now, Adam and Eve's only hope lies with inexperienced sailors, the leisure types who frequented Glandore of late. So they sit and wait, guarding the treasure that lies scattered on the seabed. On calm, still nights, when the sky is cloudless and the sea like glass, the treasure glints and sparkles playfully in the moonlight, no good to anyone as the world moves on. The Drombeg stone circle, or 'Druid's Altar' as it is known locally, sits on the side of a hill on the entrance to the bay, erected thousands of years before Christ's time on earth. They must have been a wise people to pick such a beautiful spot for worship. Beside the stone circle is a fulacht fiadh, an ancient cooking pit. One could almost imagine the smell of the roasting meat, and the druids' chants drifting out across the water towards Adam and Eve. How lonely and beautiful it must have been without a house founded or a tree cut down.

Glandore Village nestles in hill and forest on the right-hand side as you sail into the bay. It is postcard-pretty with two Norman castles and a little Church of Ireland chapel, Kilfaughnabeg – its entrance hacked out of the rock on the approach to the village. The Marine Hotel sits at the bottom of a hill in the centre of the village, at its feet, a little cove protected by the harbour wall where punts and dinghies lie on their fronts like turtles. The village slopes upward following the contours of the bay, and houses squat cosily between road and sea. The waters flow to the right and fork underneath Poulgorm Bridge where the dense Myross Woods flourish uninterrupted down to the ocean's edge. Branches laden with evergreen leaves overhang the water as if prostrated in prayer and lend the sea its ethereal, emerald hue until it tapers off into silt and mud at the foot of the village of Leap beyond. The waters flow left into Union Hall, passing the pier of Kilbeg. A row of terraced houses stand guard over the moored boats. The woods behind tickle the backs of the houses, and peer out over the roofs at their brethren in Myross, wondering, I'm sure, how life goes there. The harbour ends at Union Hall, Glandore's poor relation. You'd hardly imagine it was the same mighty ocean that now simply laps at the village's toes, content to lie there like a dog fawning at its master's feet. The village either looks pretty when at full tide, or dirty when the tide is out, hence Union Hall's Irish name, Breantra or 'dirty strand'.

Bridget's house sits in the row of terraced two-up-two-down houses, second from the left on the pier in Kilbeg. Although she had never tried, she felt certain she could jump from her bedroom window and into the sea below.

Bridget dressed this morning with more care than usual. Today she was receiving her confirmation, and, nervous with excitement, she lingered more than usual in front of the mirror, pulling and scratching at her new, white dress. She was small for her age, slightly built, her fair hair hung in tight pigtails around her neck. Her face was a mass of freckles, which concentrated around her nose and cheeks. Bridget was often fearful they would all join leaving her with a two-toned face. She smiled at herself for encouragement, revealing an awkward gap between her top teeth. Neasa lay on her side in the bed, lazily watching, her head propped up with one hand.

'You'll have to take that dress off straight after mass,' Neasa said.

'It's my dress. I'll do what I want with it.'

'Just for today it's your dress. Mam said I'll wear it next year, and I don't want you ruining it on me.' Neasa was fourteen months younger, experiencing all the milestones one year later.

'Don't worry, Neasa. I promise I'll take it off after I help Dad clean the fish scales out of the boat,' called Bridget teasingly as she made her way downstairs.

Her father sat smoking a Players, a cup of strong tea at his elbow. He never ate in the morning. His big frame was bent over a book which looked miniature in his hands. The kitchen stood in a haze of steam and smoke in the morning sun, the sweet pungency of tobacco mingling with fresh bread not long out of the oven, and her mother whistled a little tune by the range.

'There she is now,' said her father, Seán. 'All decked out in her wedding dress. Aren't you a bit young to be getting married?'

Her mother turned from the range smiling, wiping her hands on her apron. 'Isn't she the little princess, Seán? Our own little angel.'

Bridget blushed, not used to all the attention. It was Neasa who typically led in the beauty and fashion stakes.

'Sit down there now,' said her mother, ushering Bridget to the table, 'till I get your food ready. You'll be needing a good breakfast in you for the big day ahead.'

Her father readied himself for his day's work, placing his oilskins into a sack, pulling the woollen cap over his head, covering the shock of sandy hair. His movements were rather easy and fluid for such a big man. He seemed never burdened by his bulk. Other big men could be cumbersome and clumsy but there was a touch of the dancer about him always, as if he moved according to some soundtrack, mournful and low, the kind of

17

music you'd expect to hear at a wake when the poitín, porter and pipes were gone and the sun was tentatively beginning to smear the night sky. His face though handsome told another story, a story both tragic and ancient. The story every warrior's face wore when the battles were over, won or lost. Lines on the forehead, lines around the eyes and mouth, a sadness in eyes that once burned with passion and conviction, a once powerful gaze now tainted with vulnerability and confusion.

'I wish you could come today, Daddy.'

'Now, we've talked about this, Bridget,' her mother said. 'You know your daddy never goes to mass.'

'But just for today.' Bridget pouted.

'He hasn't darkened the door of the church for years,' her mother said. 'He can't just turn up now like he's John the Baptist.'

'Era, I wouldn't give them the satisfaction,' her father said. 'Wouldn't Father Murphy love it, the whole village watching the return of the prodigal son. What a show he would make of it. And Kitty Collins, the old bag, wagging her tongue all over the village. I'm sorry, pet, I just can't do it.'

'Okay, Daddy.' Bridget's chin slumped to her chest.

Her father was about to make his way out the door. He stopped and bowed low to kiss Bridget on the cheek.

'Look,' he whispered, 'how 'bout we go out on the boat on Sunday, just me and you? We'll get Mam to make up a basket and we'll go out to Rabbit Island and pick periwinkles.'

Bridget brightened at the prospect of a whole day alone with her father.

'Well does that do it?' he said.

'I suppose it'll have to,' she said, unable to suppress a smile.

Maeve followed her husband out to the door. She was with child, but her condition was of no burden, and she carried it with grace. She looked young for her age, so that now, on her third child, she looked like a girl carrying her first. Her father often teased that as a baby she had been washed up on the shore of Union Hall around the time of the Spanish Armada and lay buried in the sand until one day they were picking shells and they came across a little hand poking up from the sand. Nobody knew where Maeve had got her looks, but somewhere down the family line there must have been a Latin injection. Perhaps some washed-up Spanish sailor from the Armada found solace in a lonely cabin with some Irish cailín, and the Spanish genes have been salsa dancing down through the generations since. Seán and Maeve hugged in the doorway. They were never shy about their feelings and often left the neighbours embarrassed, even scandalised as they touched and kissed like a courting couple.

She wants to visit her grandmother after the mass,' said her mother.

'Ah, love,' said her father, 'do we want that woman poisoning her mind against us?'

'She's my mother, Seán.'

'Era, some mother she is, girl. One who hasn't talked to her daughter in over ten years.'

'We all have a part to play in that, Seán, all that bitterness now, building up for years. Let's not pass it onto the kids. They want to know their grandmother. She's not all that bad. There's a lot of good she could teach them. Your parents are dead, so is my father. They've no uncles or aunts. She's the only link left.'

'We don't want any links left. That's what's wrong with this country, always looking back, carrying centuries on our shoulders.' He squinted, turned his face towards the sun, and rubbed the stubble on his chin. 'She'll turn her into a little free-stater, fill her with bullshit.'

'That's history now, Seán, and at least she'll get both sides of the story. What harm can it do?' Her mother rubbed the hairs on his arm and stared up at him with her big, chocolate

19

eyes.

'Jesus, girl, you don't stop. Well, I suppose it's better we at least know about it. When I wake one morning and find Bridget marching around the house in her Free State uniform, I'll know where she got it,' he said laughing. 'Now for God's sake, Pat is waiting for me below at the boat,' he said in mock exasperation, grabbing a handful of her bum before he sauntered off.

Bridget was wiping her plate with a cut of bread.

'Is your sister down yet?' her mother said. 'You'd swear she was the one making the confirmation.'

Neasa appeared in the doorway, still in her nightdress, stifling a yawn. Her black hair, straight and silky like a raven's feathers, fell around her shoulders. Olive-skinned with big, brown eyes, she was every bit her mother's daughter. A rare and exotic beauty, among the ruddiness and sunburn of West Cork.

'Are you not ready yet? We'll all be late.' Their mother ushered them both up stairs.

'Give us a look at you now,' she said to Bridget, holding her chin with one hand and going at her face with spit and vigour with the other. Bridget thought she'd scrub the freckles clean off her cheeks, so didn't complain. 'Put out your hands. Turn them around.'

She inspected her hands and nails for any trace of dirt that may have escaped the bath last night, or anything she may have picked up in the meantime.

'Now, we won't have your grandmother or that Kitty Collins saying that my girls aren't well turned out.'

'So I can call to Granny after mass then?' Bridget said

'You can, pet. But don't be carrying any stories to that Kitty Collins, you hear?'

'I won't, Mammy. Thanks.' And they sat together on the settle waiting for Neasa to reappear, the mother staring nervously at the clock.

Bridget knelt at the rail, her chin almost resting on top. Fr Murphy made his way along the line of boys and girls, dipping his chubby fingers into the chalice. He had massive hands, more suited to the farm than to the delicate duties of a priest. He offered the wafer to the children as if feeding a calf.

'Body of Christ.' His voice came from deep in his belly.

Bridget dared not look left or right. She stared straight ahead waiting her turn. She could smell him as he came closer, sweat and incense, overpowering.

'Body of Christ.'

'Amen,' she said, before taking the Lord, and was careful not to chew or swallow Him. She returned to her pew at the front of the church and knelt to say her prayers. The Lord was still on her tongue, melting now and sticking slightly. She rubbed Him off the roof of her mouth. She felt the eyes of the parish on her back as the Eucharist slid down her throat and the Lord came to rest in her belly. She left it a few minutes before she sat on her seat.

'This is it,' she said silently. 'I'm a big girl now.' She could look forward to joining the rest of the adults in the line at mass every Sunday. They had missed their communion because their dad held them back to spite the church, eventually he'd relented, but she'd had to wait until now, her confirmation day, before she could don the white dress and swallow the Lord. Neasa was certain to suffer bouts of ridiculous jealousy when Bridget and their mother went up the aisle and she, not yet in a Holy state to receive, was left behind in the pew like a little girl. At least for another year anyway.

'What's it like?' Neasa whispered. 'Do you feel different?'

'Be quiet,' Bridget answered, throwing her eyes to Heaven.

Bridget sat at the foot of her grandmother's rocking chair. The fire pitched shadowy dancers on the wall behind. The grate smouldered both summer and winter. The front room had little light and even on this fine day it was hard to tell the season. Bridget could hear the music of the post office counter, Kitty Collins chatting to the customers, the bell on the front door dinging every few minutes. It was pension day and busier than usual. The gossip that came in the door with each customer was traded back and forth over the counter like currency, keeping Kitty happily occupied and out of the way for the morning. Kitty ran the post office these days and looked after Bridget's grandmother since her health failed the last few years. She was a spinster who lived in the terraced house next door but spent all her waking hours with Alice and the post office.

Not a thing went on in the village without Kitty Collins knowing. Nosy by nature, running the post office had served to fan the flames of her insatiable curiosity and she thrived being in the centre of village comings and goings. It was even rumoured she steamed open the letters before forwarding them to the addressees.

With Kitty busy, Bridget wouldn't be cornered to listen to her today. She concentrated instead on coaxing Alice into storytelling mode. Her grandmother was the oldest person Bridget knew. She was a tough old character and had been through a lot during her life. Born in the shadow of the Great Hunger, the spectre of it perched like a raven on her shoulder throughout her life. West Cork was ravaged by the famine with one of the highest death rates in the country. It devoured Alice's family and she was brought up by her father who had been a hedge schoolteacher, poet and storyteller before Catholic Repeal. She gleaned her love of history, folklore and education from him. She lived through the Fenian risings, the Great War, the War of Independence and the Civil War. She was like a personal library for Bridget, her memories a chest full of sorrow and joy, a link for Bridget to the history of the land and the history of her family, a history her parents never spoke of. She looked up at her now from the foot of the rocking chair, the fire softening the old lady's features. She counted the lines imagining a story for each one.

'So your mother knows you are here today?' Her grandmother's voice was akin to the crackling of the log in the grate.

'Ya, I asked her this time. I didn't want to be sneaking around anymore. Someone would have told her sooner or later.'

'Era, better off altogether, that's a good sign, her letting you here. She might come herself someday.' She bent to pick up a piece of turf before dropping it into the fire. 'No sign of your father today? His eldest receiving her confirmation and still he wouldn't darken the door of the church.'

'He had to go out fishing, Granny.' Bridget knew her grandmother was only baiting. Her grandmother had a soft spot for her father however she tried to hide it down through the years.

'He's going to take me out to Rabbit Island on Sunday instead.'

'Such a stubborn man I never did meet. Your grandfather was the same in ways, God rest his soul. That's why they couldn't get on in the end, truth be told, and that's why your mother fell for him. She was always her daddy's little girl.'

'Why doesn't Daddy go to mass, Granny? Does he not believe in God?'

'Era, he does, I'd say, my dear,' Alice said softly, ''Tis the Church he doesn't believe in. There were times in his life he felt the Church betrayed him. The Church is only human and makes mistakes like the rest of us. We had God in this country long before the Church came, and we'll have Him long after the great churches they've built have crumbled to piles of rock. God is in here,' she said, placing her frail hand on Bridget's chest, 'and here,' her hand cold like worn leather on Bridget's forehead. 'He has no time for the church, but sometimes it is the non-believers

23

that are the most spiritual of us all. We are the Church, the world is your Church. Everything we need is inside us. There is no use blaming men or man's institutions for the bad that befalls us. We must accept it and make peace within ourselves. Your father may see this someday, too.'

Bridget's grandmother spoke like she had a great book inside her, one she'd long ago learnt by rote. She had a peculiar confidence about herself, seemed to know everything. She spoke to Bridget like an adult. Although she did not understand everything said, Bridget felt someday she might and stored it all away.

'How did the Church betray him, Granny?'

'It's a very sad story, dear, for such a happy day.'

'You told me I could ask you anything today on my confirmation.'

'You're stubborn, by God, just like your father and your grandfather. But I suppose it's your history. Maybe you'll learn from it. We're like the leaves in the trees and there is nothing we can do to stop the wind worrying us while waiting for autumn. Some of us will fall peacefully to the ground and some of us will be tossed and turned and blown to the four corners. Throw some more turf on the fire there. Fetch me my pipe and tobacco from the dresser and I'll tell you about your father and your uncle and the Church.'

Alice leaned forward to prepare her pipe. Bridget couldn't guess whether it was the chair or her grandmother that creaked – they were both ancient. She blew through the stem to clear it then dangled some loose strands of tobacco into the bowl, filling it to the brim, tamping it down until it was packed. The old woman lit a match, sucked on the pipe until it caught, inhaled deeply, exhaled, then relaxed back into the chair. The pipe belonged to her husband, dead all of ten years now. On the night he was buried, sick with loneliness in the post office, she had picked up the old pipe. She had always loved the sweet smell and, missing it in the house, filled it as she had done every night for her husband. Longing for a piece of him she brought the pipe to her mouth and sat there in the gloom smoking and, for the first time since he passed, allowed herself a tear. Bridget found the spectacle of the old woman dragging on the pipe beguiling. She had never known her grandfather, but Alice often brought him alive for her. The pipe had become a habit, a little comfort. Kitty Collins was scandalised and often passed comment that it was no habit for a lady, but Alice took no heed and with her sharp tongue told Kitty to mind her own business. Bridget didn't know how her grandmother put up with Kitty Collins, but that was her grandmother, she saw strands of good in the worst of people, even if she never let them know.

'Water off a duck's back,' she'd said when Bridget asked how she put up with Kitty rabbiting on and on.

'Now, my girl,' said her grandmother, 'it was over twenty years ago and the world was at war. Terrible times, but exciting times if you were young. There was a tension in the air, the same current travelling through young and old alike, stirring things up. Life was tough here as usual but now more than ever there was an expectation that something was happening. Everybody was mad about being Irish all of a sudden. You could hear the music of the old language on the tongues of the young again and the lost notes of the sean-nós songs seeping out under the doors of the public houses into the early hours of the morning. Home Rule was a whisker's breath away and all the young men had joined Redmond's Irish Volunteers. You'd see them marching up and down the village proud as punch, the young women looking on, hurleys over their shoulders in lieu of guns. Your father and your uncle Danny joined the Volunteers. Your father was nineteen and Danny seventeen. They were the best looking young men in the village. Great footballers they were, too, and very popular at the dances. When the Great War started, the Volunteers split in two. There were over three-hundred-thousand volunteers in the country at that stage. In Union Hall, the same thing happened as happened all around the country. Redmond called for volunteers to join the British Army. The hardliners and militant nationalists were outraged, the group split in two with the majority of the National Volunteers supporting Redmond. There was a surge in enlisting to the Irish Regiments in the British Army. Meanwhile the minority formed the Irish Volunteers. They drilled and trained away quietly. Your uncle Danny joined the British Army. He got caught up in the romance of it all and joined during the initial surge. Your father was incensed. He couldn't understand why Danny was fighting for the enemy, nor could he understand there was nothing here for Danny. They were farmers with only a couple of acres and your father was going to get the farm. Danny longed for adventure. He wasn't a realist like your father, he was a dreamer, a lovely young man. Your father's blood boiled in his veins. He was passionate about the cause. They fell out, and Danny went off to fight in the Irish Regiments in the war. Nothing was heard from Danny for two years until he returned in the summer of 1918, a ghost. At nineteen years of age the life was gone out of him. His eyes were dead, the colour of the bottom of St Bridget's well out by Trá Na Lan. Of course your father wouldn't talk to him, and most of the village shunned him. Things were heating up around here and he was seen as a traitor. He took to the drink, spent all his time in the pub, on his own, chain-smoking, lighting fag after fag, his hands shaking as he lit one off the other, seeking no company, uttering not a word, rings as dark as porter under his eyes. He could be seen staggering home from Nolan's pub in the early hours, a gauntly spectre walking the road by the lake towards Carrigilihy. One night, the men had been out on drills with the Volunteers and were coming home walking in single file through Kilbeg Wood, your father a little behind bringing up the rear. Suddenly the men in front stopped. He heard a bit of commotion at the top of the line, loud at first then whispers back the line. As he walked forward to investigate the men stood aside to let him pass. He saw a silhouette hanging from a rope. It was Danny, your uncle. Your father cut him down and tried to revive him, but of course he was cold and long since dead. He sat there on the forest floor, cradling poor Danny in his hands. The rest of the men stood around redundant, nobody daring to approach. They slipped away without a word, one by one, leaving the two brothers alone. The next morning he came out of the woods and carried the body home to your grandmother's house. Your father and grandmother pleaded with the parish priest to give him a proper funeral but the priest refused. Suicide is a mortal sin. His mother sent him to Cork to petition the bishop, then the politicians, but doors were shut in his face. It was a sweltering summer's day and when your father got back to the house his mother was on her knees by the bed praying, flies buzzing around his brother in the bed. The stench was a living thing. He had to bring him out in the middle of the night on the back of a cart and bury him in silence in the old *cillín* with the unbaptised children. Your father hasn't been to mass since, although really I think it's himself he blames, not the Church. It finished your grandmother off completely. The light left her eyes that day, God bless her. She died soon after. Her last wish was that she be buried up in the old fairy-fort beside her darling son in unconsecrated ground. Your poor old father had to make another trip up to the *cillín* in the middle of the night and put his mother into the cold ground beside his brother.'

Bridget walked out into the last flash of the evening sun. It was summer solstice, the longest day of the year. The rest of the year tapered off after today, days getting shorter and shorter, the sun dying earlier in the sky. She left the post office behind and took the road that skirted the sea down towards Kilbeg. Three swans glided a wing-span apart in the twilight, crossing the bay towards Glandore, a dull sheen on the water separating them, or perhaps holding them together, like the chains that bonded the

Children of Lir. Bridget had begun to wonder the source of what was wrong between her parents and her grandmother. She asked questions of her parents but was always fobbed off. She loved visiting her grandmother and listening to her stories and wished they would all make up. It all occurred so long ago, surely they could move on, but adults were funny creatures. She had the whole story now, poured down to her from her grandmother's mouth as she knelt on that floor. She ran the words over and over in her head, transporting herself back to those days, dropping herself into their story.

Her father and her grandfather John, her mother's father, had fought together during the War of Independence. John had been active in the Irish Republican Brotherhood for years. He enlisted Seán and introduced him to the top men in the organisation and while war raged in Europe they drilled, disciplined themselves and waited for their chance. It was around this time that Seán first began to court Maeve. He'd admired her from afar for years. John was the schoolmaster in the village and Seán often saw her helping her father in the schoolroom. He spent a lot of time with John and came to see him as a fatherly figure. On bad nights, while the wind howled out at sea and the fire hissed beneath the rain that seeped down through the old chimney, they'd sit around the hearth in the flickering light talking of the famine, the rising of '78 and of the time John spent in Frongach, the prisoner of war camp in Wales, where he was sent after the Easter Rising in 1916. Every now and then Seán would look up, searching in the shadow to catch a glimpse of Maeve who always made sure she was in the room doing something; darning, mending or making bread. Seán did everything right. He asked John if he would mind if he went walking with Maeve. John didn't mind as he thought of Seán as a fine lad. He might have been poor but he was well-respected in the village. There was a new optimism and confidence in the air and John felt that Seán was just the type of man the new republic would need. He was healthy and handsome, stayed away from the drink, educated himself well and always thirsted for more knowledge. Alice loved the boy. God blessed Alice with only one child and she had always wanted a boy. She fawned over him whenever he was in the house, frying up a bit of mackerel in the pan, darning his trousers when the knee was worn beyond use, always sending him off with a hot wedge of soda bread wrapped up under his arm. And of course Maeve adored him. She had ever since she'd laid eyes on him.

But the world became a different place for Seán after Danny died. Any softness in the chambers of his heart was burnt by fire and cooled to steel. He went on the drink, pouring spirits down his throat into the void inside. He'd go missing for days and would be found passed out over his brother's grave like a soldier lying over a comrade's body in no-man's-land. Other nights he would go on a rampage through the village waking everybody, screaming obscenities at the way his brother was treated. More than once the RIC took him in. He terrorised Fr Shanahan in the parochial house, often arriving in the middle of the night, drunk out of his mind on poitín. He would bang the door down or break windows with stones. Eventually Fr Shanahan, who was a frail old man, had to be taken away to a home, his nerves completely shot.

In all these months Maeve didn't see him, then one day he turned up, clean shaven and morose. He had not contacted the Volunteers either in all that time.

Things began to get serious. The Volunteers needed hard men, men who could go on the run weeks on end, living rough and hitting at the crown forces wherever possible. The war had ended in Europe and the British had sent a new force called the Black and Tans over to help pacify the countryside. Their name came about because of their uniforms; old army surplus, varying shades, a mismatch of tunics and pants that had been pulled off corpses on the Western Front. They were ex-British

Army officers. They were hard men, men who had survived the carnage in Europe, and they soon instigated a campaign of terror against the local inhabitants. Living in their barracks like badgers in their setts, they came out at night to hunt prey. Seán wanted to get back into the movement and John put him in touch with Tom Barry who was running the West Cork Flying Column. John had trained and drilled with the men and helped them on manoeuvres, but he wasn't a young man anymore, wasn't able for the rough nights sleeping in ditches, the cold and frost nibbling at his already arthritic limbs. Something had changed in Seán though. Alice noticed it.

There was a hardness about him, a hunted look in his eyes. He was restless and the boy had been flogged out of him. He was desperate for action, blaming everyone for Danny's death, most of all the British Army who had taken him to Europe and ruined him, buried him alive in the mud-filled trenches, massacring his senses, filling his nostrils with the stench of burnt flesh and rotten corpses, his ears with the echo of mortars and the screams of mutilated comrades, his eyes with visions of a hell worse than hell. Danny had come back a hollow man, the boy he had been, trampled underfoot and decomposing in some field in France, a corpse already before he ever swung from the branch.

Alice had begged her husband to keep him out of the fight, to give him money and send him away until it was all over, but John felt it was best for him to immerse himself in the cause, to try to forget about Danny. The bond between Maeve and Seán only deepened during this time. They began to see more and more of each other. It was all that kept Seán sane, he thirsted for her company, never sated.

Seán went on the run with the West Cork Brigade and they struck hard at the enemy, moving like ghosts through the hills and forests of West Cork, waiting under bridges like trolls, sitting on bough-tops like owls. Theirs was a world of shadows, a tapestry of black and white until they found their game, shattering the palate of the night with the glare of their guns, and leaving crimson stains on roadsides and bed sheets. They ambushed the British forces at Kilmichael and slaughtered thirty men in cold blood leaving no survivors. They killed RIC policemen and their families. They struck at informers and showed no mercy to them or their families. They attacked and burned the local barracks and Protestant landowners. They worked on their own and were a law unto themselves. They couldn't be controlled. John saw their tactics as underhanded and cowardly, guerrilla movements, attacking soldiers at night and shooting RIC men as they lay in their beds, sometimes witnessed by wives and children.

The men of the West Cork Brigade laughed at him and told him to go back to his classroom. In the last few months of the war, John had no contact with the men of the Flying Column. When Michael Collins negotiated a truce with the English for the Free State to split the country in two, there was a vote.

John voted for the treaty. Seán voted against.

The civil war ensued and John was promoted to Commandant on the Pro-Treaty side. Seán and most of the hard men from the Flying Column went back on the run and struck at the Pro-Treaty forces just like they had at the British. John and his men hunted them down all over Cork. It was around this time John forbade Maeve to see anymore of Seán but she ignored him. Though it pained her to go against her father whom she adored, the bond between she and Seán had become too strong. She knew what he would become if she left him, she knew she was the only force in his life that kept him sane.

The civil war was nasty and nowhere was it worse than in West Cork, brother against brother, neighbour against neighbour, men who had toiled together and who had fought together before the treaty now engaged in the most intimate and personal battle. The depth of bitterness between Seán and John grew and they became obsessed with capturing the other. Maeve was caught in the middle, and it was destroying her, all day and all night running scenarios through her head, Seán ambushing her father, her father catching Seán, Seán in front of the firing squad. Who would she rather come home? Seán or her father? She lay awake every night, all her senses fine-tuned, she'd wonder where they were. If she fell asleep, she'd dream, always the same dream every night, two men in the shallows of a river under moonlight, one cradling the other, weeping bitterly, the river stained red around them, like CuChullainn and Ferdia at the end of their mighty but futile battle. In her dream she could not see who had slain who. Downriver there were hags keening and wailing and washing bloodied cloths. Then her mother was beside her and she woke, realising it was herself wailing. Her bedclothes were all knotted up between her hands. She prayed to God neither of them would succeed. Seán was never caught and, when the truce came, he returned to the village. Maeve and Seán were married in secret and her father never spoke to her again. She'd picked her husband over her beloved dad. It was the first big decision in her life, the first one she'd taken on her own, and it ruined her. She always shied away from decisions thereafter, forever afraid she'd hurt someone again, always haunted by the image of her father collapsing after class in the schoolroom, lying dead for hours on the cold, flag floor before anyone found him. He didn't last more than a few years after the war. She could have made up with her mother after her father died but neither made the move, and the silence continued until one day Alice saw Bridget pass the door of the post office and called her in.

Bridget looked forward to every Sunday. Her father never worked Sundays and he would spend the mornings with she and Neasa when they returned from mass and before he went to Nolan's for a few pints of Wrastler in the evening. This particular Sunday was all the better as he had promised Bridget the whole day.

She'd have him all to herself. No competing with Neasa for his attention.

She envied her father who lay in bed free to enjoy the quietness of the house after they all left for mass. Bridget pictured him turning over in the warmth of the bed as the rest of the village walked like driven livestock up the slick lane to the church in the rain.

When they arrived back home he was up, washed and smiling, giddy as a child. They took the basket her mother had prepared and loaded it into the boat. The rains of the morning disappeared, the sun burst through the clouds like a dazzling debutante that had been straining to be let loose, and the sea shimmered in the sunlight as if thousands of diamonds had been scattered on its surface by the hand of a benevolent giant. Seán sat on the bench in the bow, the sun at his back. He cast a shadow over Bridget who sat opposite, his body blocking the sun, the muscles in his arms threatening to burst the sleeves of his shirt as he pulled on the oars. The boat lunged forward. He beckoned her over to sit between his legs, her soft hands resting on the roughness of his. He pretended she was a great help with the rowing.

There was nowhere Bridget would rather be. She was embalmed completely within her father's bulk, felt immortal under his restrained gasps for breath, his smell of tobacco and sweat, the stubble on his chin brushing the top of her head, the clunk of the wood on water and the creaking of the old timber as they lumbered along.

At the entrance to the harbour, Seán dropped the oars, pulling them back into the boat, they sat in silence as the waves lapped around them. She smelt the salt on the air and tasted it, toasted by the sun on her lips. They looked back into the harbour, the landscape soft and safe. They could make out little figures, ants on the pier. A small sailboat glided towards the bridge. They looked out to the expanse of the ocean before them, beyond Adam and Eve. Familiar and uncertain, exciting and terrifying, it seemed to Bridget they were sitting on a line between two worlds.

'Whist,' her father suddenly rose his fingers to his lips, 'do you hear that?'

'Hear what, Daddy?'

'Whist, listen.' He wrapped his arms around her shoulders and held her still.

Suddenly out of the repose, Bridget heard a low wailing. It built and seemed to ebb and flow in unison with the wind that gently rocked the boat. A stronger gust came and the sigh peaked to a mournful lament, a sorrowful keening as if the sea itself was pouring out its grief, penance for all the lives it had taken. Bridget had never heard such a melancholic sound.

'Do you hear it?'

'What is it, Daddy?'

'Tonn Clíona, Clíona's wave.'

'What's Clíona's wave?'

'Clíona was the goddess of love and beauty around the time of the first peoples of Ireland, the Tuatha de Danann. Her sweet song healed the sick and wounded, but she left the otherworldly island of Tir Tairngire to be Clíona with her mortal lover Ciabhan. They made love on the strand at Trá Na Wadla, and after, while her lover hunted deer in Kilbeg Wood she was wooed to sleep by magic music and taken by a wave. Now she is the queen of the sidheog, a banshee and her once-sweet song is an eternal wail.'

The keening reached its crescendo then faded and died with the wind as if never there. A gull swooped the boat, screeching, gave Bridget a start and made off with a scrap of bait from the stern.

When they approached the mouth of the harbour, her father picked up his rhythm.

'How do we get safely out of the harbour, Captain?' Seán

asked.

'Avoid Adam and hug Eve,' Bridget responded with a mock salute as her father veered away from the bigger of the two islands and kept close to the edge of Eve.

Out in the open seas the ocean became instantly more alive. It had been watching, excited at their approach, now unable to contain its enthusiasm, bobbing underneath them and worrying the sides of the boat. Every now and then, water splashed over the sides and onto Bridget's lap. Her father rowed on nonplussed. He thrust and pulled with gusto and the boat skipped over the waves. Beyond her father and beyond the bow lay nothing but ocean. Bridget squinted when suddenly from both sides of her father's back Rabbit Island began to appear. He didn't even have to look around for direction, he knew exactly where he was going and knew it by rote. Rabbit Island was a low island of less than twenty acres. No trees. It had turned its back to the ocean, steep cliffs facing out to the Atlantic. The island sloped down to the beach which faced Trá Na Lan only a stone's throw across the water. There was but one family living on Rabbit Island. The Driscolls, cousins of Bridget's mother. Because there were so many Driscolls in the parish, they were distinguished by occupation or where they lived: Paudie Driscoll, who lived on the island was known as Paddy the Island; Dick, who was a cobbler, was known as Dick the Shoe; and Miles, who worked in the local garage, was called Miles the Garage. Hearing her parents' talk of these characters when she was younger had always sent Neasa and Bridget into fits of giggles, imagining a man that looked like a shoe walking around the village. They saw Paddy now as they approached the island. He was rowing out towards Trá Na Lan on the mainland. A horse tied to the back of the boat, swam behind. Paddy waved, shouting across the waves in Irish. The phrases were caught in the wind and taken. It was only in the remotest parts now and on the islands that the old tongue was spoken, and Bridget strained against the wind to hear the music of the lost language.

They lay on their backs looking up at the sky. Tufts of clouds ambled across the expanse of blue, unhurried, patient. The grass was coarse but cushioned their weight like a sponge. They had eaten their lunch and their bellies were full.

'Can I bring back some periwinkles for Granny?' Bridget said.

'Era, she'd have no mass in them, pet.' Seán took a long drag from his cigarette.

'Why not, Daddy?' Bridget propped herself up on her elbow, and looked down at her dad's face.

'Famine food.'

'What do you mean 'famine food'?'

Seán stubbed the cigarette in the grass beside him and exhaled deeply. 'During the famine, families scoured the rocks and islands for shellfish. There was nothing else to eat with the potatoes gone sour. The coast was picked clean from Mizen Head to Toe Head. A lot of the older folk still fear the famine and either remember the hunger or have heard tell of it from their parents. The shellfish remind them of the bad times and the taste, to them, tasted of hunger and death.'

'Do you remember the famine, Daddy?'

'No, I was born much later, thank the gods, though it haunted my mother throughout her life.'

Bridget lay back once more and listened to the sounds of the ocean. The blunt force boomed into the caves and onto the cliffs on the other side of the island, a skeletal crunch as the waves broke against rock, a serpent-like hiss as it withdrew serving to warn that it would strike again.

'Do you love Neasa more than me?' The words were out of her mouth before she heard them, and she started, wondering from where such thoughts had come. And so, too, it seemed, did her dad.

'Bridget! What kind of a question is that?' Seán rolled to

his side to face her. 'You know I love you both just the same. You're my two little angels. Why would you think something like that?'

'I don't know.' There were tears in her eyes now. Where had they come from? Why did she have to go and ruin such a day? 'You're just different with her. You treat her different like she's a princess, and she looks like Mammy. I don't know who I look like. Everybody always admires her and says she's beautiful and ignores me. Nobody says that about me.'

'Ah now, pet, come here.' He held her to him.

She sobbed.

'It's true,' he said, 'I am different with you both. I love you differently but with the same amount of love. Your sister is like your mother. I see your mother in her, that's for sure. You are more like me. Every day I see more of myself in you, but I have been corrupted over the years. When I look at you I see all the good in me and all the good I could have done, like looking in a mirror and seeing the reflection you actually want to see. Your sister is softer than you and needs to be looked after more. You are well-able to look after yourself and though I worry about you I know you can handle what life will throw at you. You are independent whereas your sister needs me more. I know I shouldn't be talking like this to somebody so young, but something tells me you will understand.' He paused. 'Do you understand?'

'I think so, Daddy.' The sobs ceased. Bridget knew he was right and as always even though she was only twelve, he had spoken to her like they were equals. Her mother treated her like a child. Her mother was very much a class of child herself. She talked to Neasa and Bridget as if they were three sisters. She knew this was why she felt closer to her father.

'Do you know who you are named after?'

'Mammy said I was named after Saint Bridget because I was born on the first of February, Saint Bridget's Day.'

'When the Church came to Ireland they stole all the old pagan holidays, including Saint Bridget's Day. The feast was celebrated by the ancient Irish for thousands of years before it was called Saint Bridget's Day. They worshipped the goddess Bridget, and celebrated the festival of Imbolc to welcome the spring. Bridget was the daughter of Dagda the god of poetry, wisdom and healing. I like to think it was her we named you for. I'm surprised your granny hasn't told you. 'Twas she who taught me about all the old gods.'

'Granny told me about Uncle Danny. How come you never told me about him?'

A shadow fell over her father's face just as dark clouds move over the sea. 'That woman! She has no business filling your head with all that. Can she not leave good enough alone?'

'I asked her, Daddy. I wanted to know. She also told me about you and my grandfather John.'

Seán rose and brushed himself off. 'Look, Bridget. I can't stop you visiting your grandmother, nor can I stop you wanting to find out about your family and our past. Terrible things happened. I done terrible things myself, but it's over now and in the past and that's where I want to leave all. Talk to your grandmother as much as you want about it but don't bring it up with me again.' He walked towards the boat on the strand. 'Now gather up those things and let's get going. Your mother will worry where we are.'

Her father was quiet the whole journey back. It was cooler in the afternoon, a fresh breeze tussled with the waves and Bridget was glad when they were within the harbour and heading towards Kilbeg. A little figure stood at the end of the pier.

'Daddy, Neasa is on the pier waving at us.'

Seán looked over his shoulder without breaking his rhythm.

'She is indeed. What does she want with us?'

As they pulled in they could see Neasa was crying.

38

'Daddy, Daddy,' she said, 'Mammy is above in the house. She's screaming the place down. They sent me to get you to come quick. I think she's having the baby.'

With one leap he was out of the boat. The small vessel rocked frantically. Bridget clung to the sides.

'Tie up that boat and follow us up,' he yelled, and swept Neasa up in one arm.

Bridget waited for the boat to settle, did as she was told, then followed after.

She froze in the doorway. Screams. She had never heard such sounds before.

Mary from next door came down the stairs and handed her a basin. 'Go out and fill that with clean water. Your dad's lighting the fire. Heat the water in the pot and bring it right up to me. That's a good girl.'

Bridget rushed out to the pump to fill the basin. When she returned her father was sitting on the settee smoking a cigarette, Neasa on his lap, nuzzling into his chest. The fire had caught and Bridget lowered the water into the pot.

'Is Mammy alright?'

Another wail came from upstairs.

'She's fine.' Her father dragged deeply on his cigarette. 'The baby's coming, but taking it slow. She's in good hands. Didn't Mary deliver the both of you and half the babies in the parish?'

'Are you not going up to her?' Bridget said.

'Have you gone soft, girl? That's no place for a man.'

'Is it a boy or a girl, Daddy?' Neasa looked up into his face.

'We don't know yet. We'll know soon enough.'

'Well I hope it's a boy,' Neasa said. 'It would be nice to have a little brother to play with.'

'A boy would be nice,' Seán agreed. 'Too many woman in this house. We could do with another man to keep things in order.'

A ferocious cry came.

'Jesus, she'll have the whole village terrified. They'll think it's the banshee,' said Seán. 'Run up there with that water now, like a good little girl, and come straight down again and leave her be.'

Bridget took the stairs cautiously, afraid she would spill the water. Mary was at the side of the bed holding her mother's hand. Her mother's legs were parted at the knees, a cloth draped over her. Bridget crept closer until she was at the corner of the bed. Her mother looked like another woman, one of those she would see at the horse fair over in Leap, women with hard tough faces. Her brow was drenched with sweat and her hair plastered to her forehead, temples and cheeks. Something sat in her mouth and she was biting down on it hard as tears streamed from her eyes. Her mother turned her head Bridget's direction, looking straight through her.

'Leave that there for me,' Mary said. 'Go back down to your father. We'll call you again if we need you.'

'Will Mammy be okay, Mary?'

'Run along, pet.'

It was the early hours of the next morning when Bridget woke. She hadn't slept long. She lay awake most of the night listening to the cries, the cries of a stranger that had taken over her mother, the cries coming from the hard, tough face in the other room. Neasa lay beside Bridget in the bed, a wisp of dark hair caught at the corner of her mouth. Neasa slept peacefully, her face angelic, the corners of her mouth turned up in a little smile. She seemed so vulnerable and tiny curled in the bed and Bridget remembered her father's words yesterday.

Your sister is like your mother. I see your mother in her. Your sister is softer than you and needs to be looked after more.

Bridget resolved to do just that, to look out for Neasa more. She made her way down to the kitchen and met her father heading for the door.

'I'm going for the doctor.' He looked tired and worried and Bridget realised he must have been up all night. She pictured him smoking cigarette after cigarette by the fire, staring at the embers and wincing each time he heard a cry of pain.

'The baby won't come. Mary needs some help,' he said. 'Stay there now and look after Neasa and help Mary if she needs you. I'll be back with the doctor in an hour or so.'

Mary came down the stairs as Bridget put the kettle on the fire.

'Will you have a cup of tea, Mary?'

'I'd murder one. We've put down some night, your mother and I, God love her. Don't be worrying now, baby is just slow to come. It has to come out sometime, though. Better to get the doctor, just in case.'

Bridget caught the lie in her eye. Mary McCarthy lived next door and was Maeve's only friend and confidante. The other village women thought Maeve too high and mighty, but truth be told, were a little jealous of her fine looks. This troubled Maeve greatly and only served to make her feel more awkward around them, thereby widening the gap. Mary's husband Pat, worked the boat with Seán and the two men were the best of pals. Pat had been working on the buildings during the troubles and had only returned a few years ago when his parents died. They had left him the house and he had brought Mary, a local girl, and the four boys, all born in England, back home with him. He had missed the War of Independence and the Civil War and had no bitterness or chip on his shoulder as most of the men around the parish possessed. Seán found this refreshing and felt he could be himself around Pat. He didn't have to mince his words with him. The McCarthy's were very poor and always struggled to make ends meet but they were the most generous people in the village and the best neighbours you could wish for. Mary supplemented her income by cleaning one of the big houses in Glandore. She

41

would row across the harbour six days of the week, spend the day on her knees scrubbing and row back in time to have dinner on the table for Pat and the four boys. She was constantly exhausted and invariably dishevelled. She always had that thrown together look as if she were at the mercy of everybody and every element at all times. She was fervently religious but privately so, and never passed judgement on others. She treated Maeve like a little sister and was a little awed of her beauty. All the same she knew there was a vulnerability about Maeve, a want in her, she wasn't the same since her father died and she needed looking after.

Seán arrived home with the doctor. Dr Hosford had been reluctant to come, irritated at the summons. Seán possessed a degree of notoriety among the Protestant elite of Castletownsend. The Flying Column had terrorised their community during the War of Independence and was deemed responsible for the murder of a number of the doctor's peers, some of whose bodies had never been found.

'The baby hasn't breeched,' he announced, as if blaming Mary and Maeve.

His accent was of the parlours and grand halls of London society, even though he was born and bred in West Cork. Castletownsend was a Protestant village at the other side of the parish, the like of which you would find in England. A pretty little street that sloped steeply to the pier, curiously divided halfway down by two sycamore trees growing in the middle of the road. It was a favourite with retired naval officers and landed gentry. As a casual observer or day-tripper, one would wonder whether they had accidentally taken a wrong turn somewhere and ended up in Cornwall.

'I will need to turn the baby.' The doctor removed his jacket and rolled up his sleeves. 'Fetch me some hot, clean water and fresh towels.'

Mary scurried off to obey. When she returned he was still standing there at the foot of the bed, sleeves rolled up, arms bent at the elbows. Bridget waited outside the door peering in through a fallen knot in the woodwork, she wondered if he had even looked at her mother

'Good,' he said, 'now, stand over there, out of the way and please and be quiet while I work,' he said addressing Mary as he soaped his hands.

Bridget noticed his long delicate fingers. He removed his wedding ring, went to put it on the bedside table, then thought again, perhaps of his surroundings, and popped it in the top pocket of his waistcoat. He knelt at the foot of the bed, his head aloft. He eased his hands into Maeve. She winced at the touch. He looked at the ceiling as he worked his hands. Guided by memory and experience, he turned the baby so that the head was facing the right way. When he succeeded, he addressed Maeve for the first time.

'Do you think you can push now?' He did not disguise his impatience.

Maeve took a deep breath, and half in exasperation, half in anger at the way she had been addressed, she gave a series of almighty heaves. Sure enough the baby soon came clean, wailing into life. Maeve broke down in tears.

'It's a boy,' said Dr Hosford, cutting the cord and handing the baby over. He washed his hands quickly, returned his ring to his finger, drew on his jacket, and made for the door. Bridget stepped quickly out of his way as he came through. Her father stood at the end of the stairs, waiting for the verdict.

'Mother and baby are fine,' said Dr Hosford. 'It's a boy.'

Seán could not contain his elation. He whipped Bridget up into his arms and skipped with her over his shoulders back into the kitchen, pulling a jar from the top of the dresser, grabbing a fistful of notes and running back out to pay Dr Hosford. The doctor had already gone and was hopping into his motorcar.

'Doctor,' Seán shouted after him, 'please, how much do I

owe you?'

'Keep it!' said Dr Hosford.

'Ah, now, I insist. If it wasn't for you we'd have been in right trouble.'

'Aren't you lucky you left some of us alive then to deliver your babies? I thought there was no room for the likes of us in this new state of yours. Do me a favour, when your son is growing up and you are filling him full of all your old Fenian stories, be sure and tell him he and his mother were saved at birth by a Prod, will you?'

The doctor pulled the door of his car closed and made off. Seán's mood was such that nothing could faze him.

'A boy!' he said, puckering up and giving Bridget a big kiss on the cheek, chuckling as he turned towards the door. They made their way up the stairs to see the newest member of the family.

Bridie Keohane slipped from the snug of Casey's Bar, a bottle of Powers Gold Label tucked away in her basket. She hated this errand she performed for Fr Murphy. She knew they spotted her going in and out of Casey's several times a week and her cheeks reddened in shame when she imagined the talk. They'd believe the supplies were for her, that she liked a bit of a tipple. Perhaps they'd guess they were for Fr Murphy. Neither was preferred. And she didn't know which was worse.

She had been Fr Murphy's housekeeper for the past ten years and had been Fr Shanahan's before that until they terrorised the man. He had to be sent away. Fr Murphy was good to her. He was a simple man, didn't require much, and there were none of the unwanted advances there had been in Fr Shanahan's time. Lately though, Fr Murphy had been letting himself go, not looking after himself, acting a bit odd, perhaps drinking a little too much, but it wasn't her place to say. She tightened her shawl as she made her way up the gentle slope of the hill and out of the village, past the Black Field and up towards the church and the parochial house that was tucked in behind.

Fr Murphy slouched more than sat in an armchair by the fire. He was in one of his dark moods, staring deep into the flames. He was positioned directly in front of the fire, the armchair blocking the light so that the rest of the room was in darkness. There was no lamp lit, she could just make out his arm outstretched for the bottle as he heard her come in. She duly obliged. He didn't turn or offer a greeting. She fetched him a glass from the sideboard, scurried from the room and left him to his musings.

The priest poured himself a stiff measure and drank deeply. He sighed then filled the glass again. His dog looked up from her slumber by the fire, regarding him curiously for a moment then lay her head back down in between her paws. Fr Murphy petted the dog's head.

'Good girl, Delilah,' he said as he stroked her ears.

Delilah became the priest's companion when he moved to the parochial house ten years ago. He had been very lonely those first few months. It was a one-priest parish. All the other posts he'd held were as curate where he enjoyed the company of the other priests in the house.

Delilah belonged to one of his parishioners, a bachelor, who had died. Fr Murphy performed the last rites on the man. Delilah was just a pup and the dying man asked Fr Murphy to find a home for her. He had taken her home himself. He had always loved animals, was the second eldest of a family of big farmers from Michelstown, a town in the centre of the Golden Vale, an area famed throughout Ireland for its lush rolling pastureland. He loved the farm, the physical work, the satisfaction of an honest day's toil, the easy measure of progress.

He loved the ingenuity of the change of the seasons, the smell of the soil freshly turned, the independence and honesty of living from the land. He loved walking up the stairs in the evening, his body tired, mind at ease, anticipating a sleep that was deserved.

The eldest got the farm. There was no problem with that, it was always to be expected, but he had assumed he could stay on the farm to help his brother. There was plenty of work. He didn't mind taking orders and would do what needed to be done. His mother had other ideas. She had the notion he would make a great priest. Having a priest in the family would raise their stock enormously. He left for the seminary with a heavy heart. The books and ideas frustrated him. He liked to fix things with his hands, work his body physically towards a solution. He couldn't get his head around the more abstract notions and theories of the catechism and had trouble articulating and debating, so he remained quiet. His peers and his tutors took his silence for contemplation and devotion, thought him a deep and spiritual man. Fr Murphy did nothing to disprove this fact and the façade served him well, right up to when he got his first parish priest position.

He had a fine quiet parish now, good simple folk, nothing too taxing. He never felt comfortable dealing with problems or conflict and tended to run for cover when decisions or interventions were required of him. He didn't like to get involved in other people's business. Every morning as he buttoned up his soutane — thirty-three buttons and thirty-three barricades — he envied his parishioners. He would have liked to have moved among them, worked among them, elbowed his way to the bar counter among them, swapped yarns, help a neighbour mend a fence or plough a field, be involved in life and death rather than be a bystander, an observer, somebody looking from the outside in. He'd listen to the hurling matches on the wireless of a Sunday, hearing the crowds cheering and clapping after a score, imagining he was on the terraces with them, tucked into the warmth of the flock, rather than circling the fringes like a bird of prey, only swooping down when one of the flock were sick or dead.

The clock in the corner struck the hour, startling Fr Murphy out of his meditations. Nine o'clock. Time for evening prayers. He drained his glass and reached for the bottle again.

Seán woke in his own bed, his head a bevy of nails, his mouth as dry as a bag of sawdust. He sat up to get his bearings. Maeve was up already, sitting at the end of the bed, their new-born baby Seán Óg at her breast. Her look said it all. Seán went to the basin splashing cold water on his face.

'How's he doing?'

'He's fine, thank God,' said Maeve, 'not that you'd know anything about him and you out all night drinking whiskey.'

'Ah, I'm sorry, love. We were just celebrating. He's my first son.'

'You're a different man when you're on the whiskey. We've spoken about this before. You had the whole house awake last night when you came in.'

'Don't, Maeve,' Seán said, his head between his hands.

'You tried to force yerself on me, and only days after having a baby. Thank God you fell asleep before you done any damage.'

'Look, I'm sorry. We got carried away. You know I haven't been like that in a long time, not since Danny, and I promise I won't do it again.'

Maeve reached for his hand. 'Seán, you're a lovely man, kind and gentle and I love you, but when you get the whiskey in you, you're different. I don't know you.'

'I know, shur, I know.'

'Listen to me now. There are things inside you that you have buried, you have put them away for a reason. The whiskey

47

brings them all out again.'

'Shur, I know myself, 'twas just last night, Nolan put one up in front of me.'

'And shur you had to drink it of course!' Maeve's sarcasm had her sounding like her mother. 'And then you had to have another and another.'

'Jesus, woman,' Seán said angrily, making to leave.

Maeve caught his elbow. 'Sit down, Seán, and let this be the end of it. I won't mention it again. I know how much you wanted a son. Just remember your promise next time one lands in front of you.'

Seán kissed her hand. 'Can I hold him?'

With some food in his belly, he felt a bit better and called next door to Pat. He went through the front door without knocking. Pat was sitting at the table nursing a mug of tea. A slice of bread lay untouched on a plate. Pat wasn't a heavy drinker, but he had gone drink for drink with the bigger man last night. His eyes were blood shot and red-rimmed

'There ye are now, me auld stock,' said Seán.

'Not feeling the best, Seán,' he said. 'Been sick all morning.'

'Where's Mary?'

'Over to Glandore since half five, but not before she woke me to tell me what a fecking eejit I was.'

'I got an awful doing from my one as well. We were better off to stick to the porter altogether, and we'd be right as rain this morning.'

'Do we have to go out today?' said Pat. 'We had a great week last week. Should keep us going for a while.'

'Era, we'd better. There's good fishing today guaranteed, and there are plenty days for hanging around when the weather is bad.'

'I suppose you're right. I'll just get my oilskins. Better off being out of the house when yer wan comes back anyway.'

Neasa sat on the pier wall. She loved days like these. The air, the light, everything was soft. Even the lowing of the cows, like a baritone choir, complementing the day and saline scents from the sea, carried in as gifts to the senses from the ocean breeze. She was on her own, at a bit of a loose end, with her mother nursing the new baby, her father out fishing and Bridget up with her grandmother again. Neasa couldn't understand what Bridget saw in her grandmother. She was so old and just sat in the corner like a bag of kindle. Neasa had visited once out of curiosity and truth be told she found the woman a bit scary, sitting there wrapped in a shawl in the gloom of the post office, two eyes glowering in that wizened face. Neasa was sure her grandmother saw through her. She had asked Neasa once what she wanted to be when she grew up.

'I want to marry a nice man, just like Mammy did, and have lots of babies.'

'Is that all?' the old woman spat. 'You're more than just a piece of meat.'

Neasa had cowered at the sudden vehemence and cried.

'Your bladder is very close to your eyes. Don't be a cry-baby. I was only asking whether you had a bit of ambition.'

Neasa left the shadows of the room and went back out onto the village street to wait for her sister. She wondered what Bridget replied when asked the same question. She found out later.

'A teacher.'

Neasa sat on the pier wall watching the boys from next door playing football on the road. Overhead birds sat as spectators on the telegraph line, chattering away to themselves as if reciting the messages that flowed through their talons. She was only thirteen but was already aware of the effect she had on boys. They pretended they didn't see her but she knew otherwise. What had been a haphazard kick-around became a cup-final under her gaze.

Neasa came down from her throne and headed out towards Kilbeg Wood. She could feel eyes on her back as she left the boys to their devices and was sure the intensity drained from the game as she walked away. The woods were cooler and alive with the music of birds. She imagined herself as Little Red Riding Hood from the Grimm's book their mother used to read to them when they were younger, skipping along the path in the woods. She was a little lost, not sure what to do with herself today. When not at school she had spent most of her time with her mother. She would help with the baking or work in the garden. Sometimes her mother would let her dress up in her clothes and parade around the house pretending to be an adult, a mother, a wife. She'd wait for her father to come home of an evening and Seán for his part would play along, thrilling Neasa. He would dance her around the kitchen and sit her on his lap, then feign surprise when Neasa would tell him it was her.

'Oh, by God!' he'd say. 'You had me there for a minute. I thought you'd lost a bit of weight alright and were a few inches shorter, but I thought maybe 'twas from all the hard work and all.'

She sensed a presence behind her. She turned but nobody was there. She carried on but couldn't shake the feeling off. She stopped.

The gulls played above. The wind whistled through the trees, making the leaves shudder. A farm dog barked in the distance, calling for its master. The lonely call carried itself unanswered over the fields.

'Is somebody there?' The sentence came out lower than Neasa expected. 'Is there anybody there?' Louder this time. Was it the boys playing a prank? 'Paudie, Johnny, is that you? Stop messing. It's not funny.'

The farm dog continued to bark. Neasa could hear her heartbeat, it drummed in her ears. She turned back to make her way home. The dread stayed with her. She realised she was shivering. The forest closed in around her. Someone was following. Her legs moved faster. Behind her, a noise, what sounded like a cough, or someone gasping for breath, choking. Neasa broke into a run and didn't stop until she was back on the pier and her house was in sight. She looked for Paudie and Johnny and the boys but they were nowhere to be seen. The sun beat down, not a cloud in the sky, and she began to feel foolish. She sat at the end of the pier, legs dangling, and waited for her father to come in after fishing.

'There's the two of ye, thick as thieves,' Kitty said as she passed through the sitting room on the way back out to the post office. Alice gave her a look she wouldn't throw at a dog, a reproach for the interruption, and carried on with her story to Bridget.

It was late summer and the air hung heavy. Kitty heard a roll of thunder out in the bay and closed the door as the first few heavy drops of rain started to pour down, pattering on the dusty pane. She perched herself on her stool behind the counter and reached into her bag for her hand-mirror. She hadn't been a bad looking woman in her prime. More handsome than pretty, she had good strong features but her face had become coarse with the passing of time. The years spent alone with nobody to share a joke had tightened her face. Her lips were thin and drawn and her Roman nose, which had once been one of her best features, now seemed severe and pointed. She opened her romance novel, and cocked one ear to the conversation in the next room. They were on about the famine. It was always history, stories, legends or poetry with those two.

Kitty didn't like the fact that Bridget called around so

often. Alice had been alone after the old man died. She hadn't talked to Maeve or Seán in years and had no other family. Kitty had moved in with Alice to look after her. Her eye on the post office, she had helped Alice the last few years and received little thanks. Alice was a tough old bird and hard to please, but it would be worth it in the long run. Kitty had never married. She had been courted once and was besotted, but he ran off and joined the Navy. Over the long, lonely years, the Church had been the one constant in her life. She devoted herself to Jesus and could be seen in the front row of the church every morning, eyes fixed on the crucifix behind the main altar. She revered Fr Murphy, whom she took to be a very spiritual man and she often helped around the church and in the parochial house when the opportunity arose. There was a fierce imagined rivalry between herself and Mrs Keohane. She wished she could take her place as Fr Murphy's housekeeper. She often saw Mrs Keohane slipping out of Casey's snug and she let it be known around the village that the woman was fond of a drop.

'Mrs Collins, Granny told me to come in and get some humbugs from the jar.'

Kitty passed the jar down to Bridget. 'Take one for yourself and one for your sister.'

Kitty looked the young girl up and down. She wasn't the worst of them, Kitty thought. Rather plain looking, but quiet, polite and intelligent. No illusions of grandeur like her mother and that other one, Neasa, swanning herself around the village, turning heads already, and still only a girl. That one will cause trouble yet, she thought. She had always been jealous of Maeve and the attention her looks attracted. Even her own fella, before he ran off to the navy, had been struck dumb in Maeve's presence. Oh, she thought she was such a princess that one, high and mighty and she, married to that murderer who hadn't darkened the door of a church in donkey's years. There's a curse on that family. The O'Donovan's were always cursed. She

52

shivered as she thought of young Danny, hanging from the tree above in Kilbeg, never buried properly. She'd only been talking about him earlier with a customer, one of the Nolan's swore blind he'd seem him above in the woods one night and he all in black, the fires of hell burning from his eyes. Scared the living daylights out of him. It was said in the village that he walked the woods still, rope trailing from his neck, looking for someone to release him, for someone to take his place under the rope. Nobody dared venture there after dark for fear of meeting him. You can't turn your back on God like the O'Donovan's and get away with it. They'd get their comeuppance, Kitty thought, in this life or the next. In the meantime, she'd remain by Alice's side, wait for the time the woman departed and the post office would be hers.

Bridget walked from the village towards Kilbeg. As always after visits with her grandmother her head was in a swirl. She imagined the village of Union Hall during the famine, emaciated beings lining the streets, whole families lying in ditches, their mouths open, tongues and lips stained green from eating grass. She pulled her cardigan tight. The evenings were drawing in and a chill was beginning to assert itself in the breeze. Her grandmother's stories had really affected her. So much suffering and pain. What was the point of it all? She imagined her own family, her mother, father, Neasa and baby Seán Óg, crouched in a damp hovel, nothing to warm them, no food, no hope, the rank smell of death keen in their nostrils. She felt the pain, the desperation, the hopelessness. Granny said it happened all over the world all the time. The Irish didn't have a monopoly on suffering. It was happening right now somewhere else and would happen again and again.

'The human race has no memory,' Granny had said. 'It just looks forward all the time, grasping, desiring, chasing. That's why history is so important. Some of us must remember the past, chronicle it, guard it, teach it and ensure that future generations hear of it, otherwise it will all be for nothing, all of our lives, all of our suffering for nothing.'

The sun was beginning to sink over the harbour splashing a masterpiece on the horizon, the swansong colours of the dying sun almost volcanic in their intensity. Neasa's silhouette appeared framed in the sunset at the end of the pier, she sat there legs crossed, like a sacrificial virgin waiting for her fate, her hair flowing down her back onto the ground as rivers of black gold flow in underground caverns.

'Watcha doing?' said Bridget when she approached.

'Waiting for Daddy to come in.' Neasa stifled a yawn.

'I'll wait with you then.' She put her arm around Neasa's shoulder and Neasa put her arm around Bridget's waist.

'Do you know how the harbour was made?' said Bridget.

'It was made by the sea, silly.'

'Nope, that's not true at all. Did you ever hear of Domhnall Mehigan?'

'Is he in school with us?'

'No, you eejit,' Bridget said. 'He was a big chieftain thousands of years ago. When the Romans were trying to invade us he dug out Glandore Harbour and defended Ireland. They soon gave up and went over and invaded England instead. As they were leaving he threw massive stones at them from Crow Lane. When he was throwing the stones he sneezed and his handful of stones landed in a field down by Barty's Wood that we now know as the Drombeg Stone Circle.'

'Did Granny tell you that?'

'Yes, and lots more,' Bridget said.

'I'd like the stories, but I'm scared of her. I don't think she likes me.'

'Of course she likes you. You're her granddaughter.'

'Mammy's her daughter and she doesn't like her,' said Neasa.

54

'She does like her, of course she likes her.'

'Why doesn't she ever come to visit then, and why doesn't Mammy ever go to see her?'

'It's complicated. A lot of things happened down through the years involving Daddy and Mammy and Granny and Granddad, but I'm going to fix it soon,' said Bridget.

'Did you hear Daddy last night?'

'He woke the whole house up.'

'Why was he crying for Danny and Seán Óg?' said Neasa. 'I thought he wanted a boy, and who's Danny?'

'He was just confused with the drink. Danny was our uncle, Daddy's brother.'

'I didn't know we had an uncle,' said Neasa.

'We don't. He died very young. 'Twas him that Daddy was crying for last night.'

'I was scared when he came into our room. He looked different and his eyes were funny. He wasn't like Daddy at all, and there was a funny smell.'

'I know, he had a lot to drink. I heard him saying sorry to Mammy this morning. He said he wouldn't do it again.'

'I hope not. He was like the *púca* or something.'

'Sure, there's none of us perfect,' sighed Bridget.

The sunset had spent its grand finale, its radiance leaking out to twilight as the girls sat swinging their legs, the water darkening to mercury below them, lapping its tongue gently off the pier.

'Daddy should be home by now. We've been waiting here ages,' said Neasa.

'Maybe they got a huge catch, or maybe a mermaid got caught in their net.'

The mackerel hauls had never been so plentiful as that summer. It seemed all you had to do was drop in the net, pull it up and the bottom of the boat would be full of wriggling, glistening silver treasure. Seán was skipper of the boat and was making payments on it to Lynch, a publican in the village. He would soon own it outright. Sometimes they would have a crew of three but mostly it was just Seán and Pat. They enjoyed each other's company and could do the work of three people anyway. Seán always split the catch fifty-fifty after he had taken out the repayment for the boat. There's not many around would have done that and Pat was grateful. There wasn't a breath of wind as they left the harbour behind them. The two of them were still suffering from the night before and Seán constantly had his sleeve to his forehead wiping the porter sweat away.

'You can't beat the sea for the freedom,' Seán said.

'Aye,' said Pat, squinting high, scanning the sea for any sign of feeding.

'I spent months and years trudging around in the muck and the hills of West Cork, ambushing and drilling, fighting and killing in the name of freedom, and all I had to do all along was untie the boat and head for the sea.'

'I'm glad I missed all that, truth be told. I wouldn't have been able for it.'

'You were better off out of here, Pat.' Seán spat over the bow. 'You would have had to pick a side. There were no fences in West Cork during those years, and all in the end, for what?'

They pulled in the last of the mackerel, another great haul, and Seán sat on the side of the boat to catch his breath and light a cigarette. The sun had slunk behind the clouds and the sea, like a chameleon, changed, its colour tinted grey now in the shadow and textured like liquid steel. Seán wondered how many colours the sea could conjure. He'd spent a lifetime studying the waters and still she surprised, each evening mystifying him. There was no end to her mastery. Her repertoire was infinite. Colours that didn't even have a name, that couldn't be painted or reproduced by even the most talented of artists. And then there were her scents, and her moods that changed just as often. She was the ultimate conquest but though many men had tried none held sway over her, she answered to no one but the watchful moon. A gust of wind came in over the bow, shivering he pulled on his thick wool jumper that Maeve knitted. They had worked through the morning and they were both hungry. Pat lit the stove to heat their cans of tea and they unwrapped the soda bread they had brought for their lunch.

'Jesus, that woman of yours spreads the butter on nice and thick, so she does,' said Pat, looking at Seán's bread enviously. 'You'd hardly know I had butter on mine at all the way she spreads it so thin.'

Seán laughed, reached under the bench and pulled out a bottle of porter.

'How about a bottle of Wrastler to help wash it down?' He winked at Pat. 'That'll cure us'

They ate their bread in silence, taking turns to swig from the bottle. Seán thought on the catch and did sums in his head. If things kept well he might be able to start putting a few bob away. He knew Maeve would want Bridget to start secondary school in the autumn in Skibbereen and that would cost. He owed Lynch a bit on the slate but not too much. It would be nice to start looking towards the future a little.

'Have you seen the stranger around the village lately?' Pat said, interrupting Seán's train of thought.

'No. Who is he?'

'Era, I don't know, I thought you might have an idea.' Pat stretched back on a bundle of netting. 'I've seen him around now a few times. Tall man, wears a long, black coat, dark like a *fear gorta*. I'd swear I've seen him somewhere before, but can't place him. Something about him I didn't like. I don't know what came over me but I was walking home the other night, passing Kilbeg Wood and I saw him coming towards me out from the trees, gave me the shivers no end, I ran home to avoid him. Can't get him out of my head since.'

'Heard there was a yank home lately, one of the Deasys. Could have been him.'

The breeze died over the ocean as the two men lay down for a nap. Seán was warm inside his jumper and the bread and porter made him drowsy. It wasn't long before he drifted to sleep. Dreams found him. They had missed him onshore, where they hovered around his house at night, and sensing him sleep, travelled out on the breeze. They rested now, reunited with their maker in his slumber.

It always started with Danny, hanging from a tree with that expression on his face, like he hadn't meant to do it. A reel of faces followed, all dead. There was Cleary, an informer from the village, one of their own. They'd shot him up the back of Leap, put a hole in his forehead, his pleas echoing in Seán's dreams.

'Ah, lads, come on, for God's sake,' as if he was protesting after being fouled on the football field.

Next was the ambush at Kilmichael, the explosion as Tom Barry launched the grenade into the truck …

Boom!

Seán was blown out of his dream back to the land of the living, and was underwater. He surfaced and looked around in panic, ears ringing with the explosion. The boat was gone, bits of timber floated all around him, flames still licking at them above the water. Pat was twenty yards away, thrashing frantically. Neither could swim. None of the village fishermen could, for they thought it to be bad luck. Pat went under, the ocean smothering his screams before he surfaced again. Seán grabbed onto a piece of wood and, kicking his legs, tried to make his way over to Pat. His mate went down again.

'Pat! Pat!'

His friend resurfaced.

'Stop kicking. Just stay still. I'm coming for you.'

The water sucking at Pat was crimson. He must have

been hurt in the blast. That bloody stove! They had left the stove lit. A gust of wind. Newspapers. Then their fuel tank. Seán was covered in cuts and scratches, but Pat had fallen asleep close to the fuel tank. Pat went down again. With one hand still on the wood, Seán dived like a seabird and grabbed Pat by the neck. He pulled both of them up onto the plank.

'I have you, boy. I have you.'

Pat thrashed like a prized fish caught in an angler's net, spittle gathering at the side of his mouth.

Seán used all of his strength to put the plank between Pat and himself. Pat seemed possessed by a brute strength. It was wearing Seán out. All of a sudden Pat stopped and gasped frantically for air, then sighed and went limp. Seán shook him roughly.

'Wake up, boy. Wake up, will ya?' He slapped his face and pulled his head back by the hair. Pat's lifeless eyes stared out at him from the top of his head. Wide, frightened, questioning eyes.

'You bastard!' Seán shook Pat's head. 'Come on, Pat. For Christ's sake, come on.'

It was no good. Pat was gone.

The warmth drained from his friend's body. The sun was low in the sky and the water around him thickened. Seán shivered uncontrollably, his teeth chattering in his mouth. He had to start moving to keep warm. Reluctantly he let go of Pat. His friend's body rose to the surface. The explosion had ripped Pat's legs from his torso, his carcass lay like flotsam among the wreckage of their boat and slowly drifted away towards the sinking sun. Seán held tight to the piece of wood. He had to start kicking. If he got anywhere near the islands he might have a chance. The men never stayed out fishing overnight. His neighbours would know that. Boats would be launched from Kilbeg, the village, and probably Glandore. They'd search for him. Poor old Pat. Not a day's luck did he have in his life, and never would he have asked for luck.

'How are we picked?' he asked aloud. 'How do you pick us, you bastard? How did he offend thee?'

Seán kicked furiously.

Venomous thoughts coursed through the veins that pumped his legs. The sky grew darker. He lost the outline of the coast in the gloom but kept going, kicking, kicking, his thoughts adrift, flowing back to the good old days when he first met Maeve, before Danny hung himself, before he started killing people. The good times, the innocent times, when what went through his head was pure and untainted.

He met her first at the patterns in Carrigilihy. It was a bright summer evening, the sweet smell of fuchsia on the breeze. He could almost smell it over the water and it stirred in him a longing to see her again. He thought his heart would burst from his chest when she talked to him and then she smiled. He didn't know where to put himself. Every part of him had seemed to be in the way, awkward, big and heavy. Feeling her eyes on him, he wanted to put his hands up, to shield himself from her luminosity.

His legs were getting heavier, his breath laboured. He shivered constantly, sometimes violently. He was exhausted. He squinted, trying to make something of the darkness. Nothing. He hoisted himself up onto the plank, falling off and for a moment he let go of the wood. Panicking he flailed around madly, catching hold of it again, hugging it tightly, like he'd held his brother's stiff body in Kilbeg Wood. The cold was unbearable. He caught himself drifting off, out of consciousness and tried to shake himself. Not now, he thought, not like this, out here, on my own. But this is what I deserve. What goes around, comes around.

Not now, with my new son. Please, God, not now.

It was a calm night, hardly a ripple or a wave bothered the man drifting on the ocean. There were waves aplenty in Seán's mind. He lost consciousness and his dreams began feeding on him again, just little nibbles at first, then gorging on his rudderless mind. He was in Kilbeg Wood and there were two people walking ahead of him, their backs to him. The birdsong was loud and meddlesome. It bothered him as he strained to listen to what was being said ahead. The woods was dark today, full of shadows. High up in the trees there was movement, the wind tearing at the branches and leaves like a drunken sailor let loose in a brothel. He couldn't see the bay through the trees but he could hear the waves break against the shoreline with a hollow punch. He tried to catch up with the couple but no matter how fast he walked or ran they remained the same distance ahead. He couldn't make up the ground. He could make out one was a young girl in a red frock and one was a man. They were holding hands, their arms swinging between them. The forest track was worn out of the side of the hill. Trees shot upwards at right angles, solemn sentries guarding the way. On the ground in front of him he saw the frayed end of a rope being pulled along. His eyes followed it along the path and saw that it ended in a noose around the girl's neck, the rope trailing along behind as she walked. Seán picked up the rope and tugged gently. The girl kept walking. He tugged again. The man turned around. It was Danny, eyes malevolent.

'Leave her,' Danny said menacingly, his face gaunt and grey in the shadows, wolf-like he bared his lips, sharp teeth flashing white.

Anger burnt in Seán's chest. He grabbed the rope with both hands and pulled as hard as he could. He heard a sickening snap as the girl's neck cracked back. She swayed once forward and once back and fell to the ground. Seán ran to her, knelt over and looked into his daughter's face.

'Neasa!' he screamed.

61

Maeve sat by the hearth staring into the dying embers. She sent the girls off to bed, masking her worry. Now alone, it overcame her. She felt faint. Something was wrong, she was sure of it. They had never been out this late before. All the other fishing boats were in. She clasped the sides of the stool she sat on and steadied herself. Suddenly she was on her knees, hands folded in prayer.

'Please, Lord, do not take him from me. I need him.'

She wept. Maeve had never dwelt upon Seán's absence from mass, but now felt it significant. She blushed as she thought on the things Seán and herself did together. Others would have thought them shameful things, dirty things that no self-respecting Catholic would do. They were like animals together. They regularly savaged each other and could never get enough. Even now as she prayed, lust stirred in her as she thought of their lovemaking.

'I will change, Lord. Just please bring him back to me and to the girls and his new-born son.'

She had a primal urge to run down to the village to her mother's house. She would have words for her, comforting words, old words, words that would soothe and seal the soul. She pictured her own father, towering, glasses propped on the end of his nose, lowering his book, smiling kindly. Poor man, a thinking man in love with words, would rather read about the sea than swim in it. He had been lost in a world at war, a poet in the midst of fighters, a fifer steadfastly playing his tune while carnage unfurled around him. There was a lot in Seán that reminded Maeve of her father. She knew he was a deep thinker, but he would never let anyone know. He knew people would see it as weakness and he understood the practicalities of the world in the way her father never could. But there was a fire in Seán, an itch that could never be scratched, an imbalance he needed to work out. How would he have turned out if Danny hadn't swung from that tree? She cursed Danny for ruining her man, the man he had been when she first met him. Sometimes she dreamt of Seán doing unspeakable things. She'd heard rumours that he had killed many. She overheard once at a regatta that he shot young Cleary in a field up the back of Leap. When she dreamt she saw a figure bent over a body, crouched like a goblin. As she watched, he turned. It was Seán, his face and clothes covered in blood. She never asked about his years of war and on the run. He never wanted to talk about it and she didn't want to think on it. She pushed it aside and pretended it had never happened. Was God punishing them now?

'Mammy.' It was Neasa, and Bridget behind her. 'We can't sleep.'

Maeve sat up on the settee and patted either side. Her daughters jumped up and she spread her arms around them and squeezed tight.

'Is Daddy going to be alright? He's not home yet, is he?' asked Neasa. 'What's happened to him?'

'Your Daddy will be fine, sure, look at the size of him. What could possibly happen to that man? They probably just ran out of fuel. It's a grand night, nice and calm and they're all out looking for him now anyhow. They'll be home soon.'

'I hope so,' said Neasa. 'I was scared today in the woods. I think there was someone following me. I want to bring Daddy out there tomorrow to scare them.'

Maeve tensed at the mention of Kilbeg Wood. She'd stayed clear of it since Danny, felt there was something out there, felt that bad things had happened in the woods.

'Aw, there was nobody there, you were just imagining it,' said Maeve. 'Back to bed with ye now and I'll wake ye when Daddy gets home.'

'Can we sleep down here with you, Mammy?' said Neasa.

'Alright so, you big baby, run up and get your blankets.'

Neasa ran up to fetch the blankets.

Bridget turned to her mother. 'I heard Kitty Collins say to someone in the post office that Danny's ghost walked the woods, that he was damned for eternity and would have no peace until someone took his place.'

Bridget's words were like fingers of an icy claw up her spine. She managed to muster her words. 'Nonsense, don't be listening to that old biddy, she doesn't know what she's talking about.' She turned away and held onto the arm of the settee to stop her hand shaking. She knew Bridget was still there, standing behind her, she could feel her eyes on her back. She wished she would go away, didn't want to face her.

'What do you really think happened to Daddy?' Bridget said.

Maeve turned and looked down at the stony little face. Bridget was so old for her years. Even now, there was a calmness and wisdom in her eyes. It frightened her.

'I don't know, pet.' There was no point lying. 'I really don't know,' she said and let the tears flow freely.

The salt ship bound for Kilbeg came across him, draped lifelessly over the piece of driftwood. He was unconscious as they hauled him on board. It took three of them to haul him up and even then they couldn't hold him. They dropped him with a thud on the deck. The steamer came once-weekly to Kilbeg Pier to drop off bags of coarse salt to cure the mackerel. Three of them stood over the body, no sign of life. They turned him onto his back.

One of the men, a small bony specimen with a high-pitched accent said, 'Jesus, boy, that's Seán Donovan from Union Hall.'

'Who's he when he's at home?' said another.

'Who's he?' the bony one said indignantly.

'I'll tell you who he is, boy. Only Tom Barry's right hand man, one of the famous West Cork Brigade.'

'Jesus Christ, we better be looking after him so. Is there any life there?'

He put his ear to Seán's chest for any sign of breath. 'I don't think so.'

'Hold off a minute, boy,' said the bony one. 'Check by the neck.'

His fingers checked for a pulse in the neck. A faint beat, no more than a ripple of life. 'Ok, lads, we need to get him out of these clothes, *ar nós na gaoithe*. Wrap him up in fresh clothes and oilskins and get him in by the furnace.'

'Paddy,' he said to the other, 'make for Kilbeg Pier as quick as you can. We'll save this man yet for all he done for Ireland.'

Maeve must have dozed off a little before dawn. Mary was at her elbow now, gently prodding.

'They have him,' she said. 'They brought him in on the salt boat.'

'Oh, thank the Lord,' said Maeve, tears of relief welling at her eyes. 'And Pat? Is Pat with them?'

Mary just shook her head, and turned away.

'Oh, Mary! What did they say? What happened? Do they know?'

'They don't know anything yet. Seán was unconscious when they found him. They haven't been able to get any sense out of him. He's in a fever, ranting and raving all night about Neasa and Danny.'

'They'll find Pat, too.'

'There's boats out looking for his body now.' Mary looked out the window towards the pier.

'His body? Don't be talking like that. They brought Seán in, didn't they?'

'He's gone, Maeve. After I left you last night I spent the whole night praying to the Lord to bring him back to me. When I saw Seán on the pier just now, I looked into his eyes and knew

Pat was dead.'

A commotion sounded at the door. The women headed outdoors. Three men from the salt boat arrived with Seán on a cart.

'Oh, God bless you!' Maeve said to the men and she threw her arms around Seán. His skin was cold to the touch and he was barely conscious.

Bridget and Neasa appeared.

'Light the fire and put some water on,' said Bridget 'We'll get him a nice hot bath, get him back to his senses and put him into the bed.'

Seán was coming around, he opened his eyes and looked around him, confused. He looked from one to the other until his eyes rested on Neasa. She was staring at him, her beautiful brown eyes wide with fright.

'Neasa,' he cried, 'You're here.'

He opened his arms and she rushed into his embrace.

The funeral was a sad affair, sad and incomplete in the way a wedding without a bride, or a baptism without a child would be. Pat's body was never found and the whole occasion was surreal. Fr Murphy's deep voice droned as soft rays from the sun streamed through the stained glass windows and caressed the dust in the air. The stillness and stale air made Bridget drowsy. Her mind drifted out of the church and over the bay, over the waves and white-tops, ducked in and out of the inlets and coves. She pictured Pat's wasted body washed up on Squince Beach, and then on the rocks at Trá Na Lan. How could a body just disappear? And what of his soul? Where did the soul go? Would it lie on the waves and the wind? Would it join Clíona in her lament at the mouth of the harbour?

'Ouch.'

Neasa pinched Bridget's arm.

'What?' Bridget whispered irritably.

'Look. Poor Paudie.' Neasa tipped her head towards Pat's son.

Paudie sat across the aisle, his head in his hands. They couldn't see his face but his shoulders shuddered and they assumed he was crying.

Bridget longed for the service to be done. She worried about her father. After only two days, he left his bed and joined the search for Pat's body. He was out there both day and night. When the rest of the crews returned for the day, he would be out with a paraffin lamp checking along the coastline, walking along deserted beaches and coves, cliff-tops and headlands like a lonely Will o' the Wisp. After a week of searching he gave up. Of course he wasn't at the funeral today. He would mourn Pat in his own way. He would add the body to the heap he already had on his back. She had heard her parents talking this morning. Her father had no livelihood now, the boat gone, and no way of paying the money back to Lynch, no way of putting food on the table, no savings. What was to become of them?

'The Lord will provide,' her mother had said. 'We should be thanking the Lord for bringing you back.'

'You can thank the Lord,' her father spat back.

'Would you rather He left you out there? He brought you back for a reason, Seán. Can't you see that? You've been given a second chance.'

'And what about Pat, still out there somewhere? Did he not deserve a second chance? Surely Mary at least deserved a body to bury.'

'We cannot question the Lord. He has his ways. We must submit to Him and let life take its course.'

'There are no ways, there is no Lord, there is nothing,' her father shouted. 'Can't you see that? You are all fools. There is no rhyme or reason, no thought or pattern. We are all animals in a savage world.'

'Seán, please.' Bridget's mother pleaded in a hushed voice as if afraid God would hear them, but her father wouldn't be stopped.

'We are born into it crying and screaming, and our whole life we continue crying and screaming inside, in our souls, cast out, betrayed, cursed. We kill and are killed, destroy one another and the world we live in, trash and flail about, lusting after the flesh and foolishly re-creating one another, so that the same things can happen over and over and over again after we're gone.'

'Seán, you are tired, you don't mean this, I know you don't.'

'I'm off out,' said Seán. 'I want to be alone.'

'Seán, please.' Bridget's mother caught his sleeve. 'Come to the funeral with us, please. You don't have to come in. You can stand outside and look after Seán Óg.'

Her father hesitated, the hardness in his face softened momentarily at the mention of his son.

'I'm sorry, pet.' His voice scratched in his throat. 'I just can't.'

Bridget knew her father needed someone, someone to share the load he carried, the wrack of guilt tethered to his soul. Her mother couldn't see this, or wouldn't, she wasn't strong enough, she had her own guilt, her own regrets to attend to, sometimes Bridget felt her mother wanted Seán to carry those, too, to carry it all so that she could pretend she had no part to play in any of it. After the burial, Bridget went looking for her father. She checked all the pubs in the village and walked all the way out to Carrigilihy and up to Trá Na Lan. She doubled back up over the hill at Ballincola and down through the fields towards Kilbeg Wood. He was nowhere to be found. Back at the house, her mother was asleep with Seán Óg at her breast and Neasa was out next door with Paudie. Neasa had taken it upon herself to comfort Paudie in his mourning like one would tend to a sick puppy or a bird with a lame wing. Bridget decided to call on her granny. The sky had closed in with cloud, and a light drizzle came down, dusting the hedgerows so that they alone sparkled in the dullness of the afternoon. She let herself in through the post office. Kitty was behind the counter with her head in some romance book. She looked up when she heard the bell.

'Good afternoon to you, Mrs Collins,' Bridget said. 'Can I go through to Granny?'

'You can of course, dear. Work away,' Kitty said with a smile. 'Wasn't it very sad about poor Pat?'

'It was, I'm only after coming from the grave.'

'How is Mary holding up? That poor woman, she's a saint. And how is she going to bring up those four lads now?'

Bridget noticed a tinge of superiority in Mrs Collin's voice.

'She'll be fine,' said Bridget, with unintentional sharpness.

Kitty visibly flinched.

'God will provide, the lads will look after her, and she's got good neighbours.'

'Indeed, and you're right, my dear, and we're all praying for her. I'll be lighting a candle for her beyond in the church every day. Go on into your granny there like a good girl till I get on with my work.'

A pot of potatoes in their skins bubbled away on the range. Always potatoes, morning, noon and night, breakfast, lunch and dinner. Her grandmother ate them skin and all, smothered in butter. She cut them into quarters, rained salt down upon them and picked them off her plate with her fingers. The smell, mixed with lingering pipe tobacco, signalled this to be another realm. In off the street, in from the world. Bridget could leave things at the door, feel more grown up, and a little more grounded each time she journeyed back out again. Her grandmother sat in her usual chair, eyes closed, but Bridget knew she wasn't asleep. She snored when she slept. The room was peaceful. She had often come across her grandmother like this, her chest rising and falling gently, her breath rhythmic like the tide and the breeze, her mind elsewhere. Bridget sat at her feet and waited. Books were stacked in teetering columns around the chair, neglected, their spines coated with dust. Her grandmother rarely read anymore. Her eyesight was failing, and, she claimed there was nothing more books could teach her. Books were now a distraction, complicating things, looking for reason and patterns in life and finding reason where there was none. She did, however, encourage Bridget to read, but warned her to trust her own instinct, not take on the opinions of others.

'Books should give you an insight into how other people think so you can better understand yourself,' she would say.

Bridget marvelled at the wisdom of her grandmother, especially one who had never left the village. 'Did you not want to see the world?' she once asked.

'But I have seen the world,' Alice replied. 'I've seen it all here, passing up and down outside on the street. Had I never left this chair I would still have seen the whole world.'

'What about exotic lands and people, America or Africa, the things you read of in these books?'

'Agilly,' said Alice, 'when I worked in the post office the whole world passed through my hands. Letters coming and going from every corner of the globe. Without opening any of them I could have told you what they contained therein, behind the words and the letter and the bad grammar, the emotions straining to be let free. Homesickness, loneliness, fear, hatred, sometimes joy, sometimes sorrow, regret and jealousy thrown in for good measure. But all those letters had something in common, they wanted to share something. It was as if they had caught their coat on the door when they left home, and the further in time and space they travelled, more of the coat unravelled, till they clung to a mere thread for comfort.'

Bridget had not understood.

'Climb up on my lap, and don't be looking up at me with that open gob.' In a rare show of affection, she took Bridget's head in her hands. 'The world is in here.' She kissed her forehead. 'If you are sad, you will still be sad when you are two-thousand miles away. See that pot of potatoes on the range there? If you move the pot onto the settee, are the potatoes still in it?

Bridget nodded.

'When you move a pot from one place to another, whatever is in the pot remains. If you are at peace with yourself, it doesn't matter where you are. The only journey worth taking is in your head, it is the only journey that leads anywhere. The only thing you really have control over is your own mind. Some people are addicted to suffering. Once they get a taste of it they can't let it go. You don't have to be miserable, agilly, remember that. You can choose how to take the world, that's the only real choice you have. If you are content with what you are and what you have, you may never leave this village and you will never feel you have missed anything.'

Bridget smiled as she remembered those conversations, words typical of her grandmother. Always enigmatic. She would like to understand, but felt a little bit behind, always reaching but not grasping. Someday maybe, but still she wanted to travel, whatever her grandmother said. She sat in silence, her breath falling in with her grandmother's like feet in a sonnet melting into meter. She became aware only of the rise and fall of her chest. All thoughts fell away, her mind rested, every breath a drop of water falling into a still pond, rippling out to the edges and then dripping again. The chattering from the post office drifted across her consciousness like sounds from another world. She didn't know how long she was like that, but all of a sudden she looked up. Her grandmother was looking down, smiling through her eyes, radiating peace and wisdom. They said nothing for a while, just sat in each other's presence, allowing the world back in slowly.

Alice was the first to speak. 'How's your mother?'

'She was crying before the funeral. She had a fight with Daddy.'

'He wouldn't go to the funeral?' Alice reached for her pipe.

'No, he's gone off somewhere,' she said with a sigh. 'I went looking for him, but couldn't find him.'

'Leave him tonight, he has mourning to do. Go look for him tomorrow and bring him back home. The poor man, he's seen a lot of suffering. It would have ruined a weaker man, but that's often the way. The world burdens the strong for the sins of the rest of us. He'll be fine in a few days.'

'I hope so, Granny. He took me out to Rabbit Island the other day. We heard Clíona's wave on the way.'

'Ah, Clíona. That wan has been around a long time. Queen of the banshees, she was a maiden of the Tuatha de Danann. They say that she was the first banshee in Ireland and goddess of the mighty clan of the O'Donovans. I suppose your father didn't tell you of your lineage, did he?'

Bridget shook her head.

'I didn't think so. Your father is descended from the mighty Lords of Clancahill. If destiny travelled in straight lines, he'd be king. He can trace his line all the way back to Ivor O'Donovan, one of the first of the O'Donovans, descended from the Norsemen who took Glandore Harbour and all the lands in Carbery from the Normans in the twelfth century. All his descendants since are known as sliocht Iomhair or Ivor's seed and they ruled the area. The O'Donovans fell on hard times and had lost many of their lands by the seventeenth century but Clíona still wails when one of the family dies. She wailed for three days and three nights when the great Fenian O'Donovan Rossa died.'

72

Seán sheltered in a copse of hazel up in the old *cillín* on Squince Head. It was an old *lios,* the remains of an ancient ring fort that the old people believed was the home of the fairies. In recent history its story was rather more macabre, in that it housed the souls of unbaptised children, a graveyard for unfortunates not baptised before they died, making them, in the eyes of the Church, unfit to be buried with the rest of the Christian family, damned to spend eternity in limbo. Indeed Danny was buried here, too, and his mother. Lying with these tiny infant corpses was the body of a strapping youth in his prime. Seán imagined him out there somewhere in limbo, nothing but babies for company, wailing all around him. Seems more like hell than limbo, Seán thought, as he took another long swig of poitín. Serves him right, the bastard, he thought. What right had he to take his own life? It wasn't all his to take. He took a bit of the rest of us with him. Selfish bastard.

The night was bright and calm, the wind slumbered and lay flat on the ocean's skin. The full moon left a path on the still sea and painted up the boughs of the hazel trees so they looked like spectral limbs about to leap to life. An empty bottle lay at Seán's feet and there was another, half-full, in his hand. Cigarette butts were scattered in a semi-circle. The poitín was strong but had long since ceased to burn his throat. He drank it like water. He was tottering between unconsciousness and insanity, between rage and nonchalance. Every few minutes he omitted a low growl then slumped back into his stupor, muttering away to himself.

The ruin of a house stood between the *lios* and the sea, perched on the headland and bathed in the night's silver balm. Seán's mother used to come here to this house. They said it was a witch that used to live there. Long ago women would go to her for the potions and powders she kept, cures she pulled from the flowers, weeds and berries of the forest. That was before the Church ran her out and the parish burnt her thatch, and with it all that knowledge and knowhow up in flames.

Seán squinted in the glare of the moon. Movement around the ruins of the old cottage. He hauled himself off the ground and moved unsteadily towards it. The tails of a coat billowed at the corner of the gabled end of the house. The figure of a man. Tall, long black overcoat and black peak cap. He stood straight, motionless, looking out to sea, smoking a rolled cigarette. The tobacco smelt sweet and sickly, unlike any he had smelt before. Seán shivered, the night wrapped itself around him like a cold hug, the hairs on the back of his head rising like thorns and his breath billowing out in front of him as if it were a night in the depths of winter. He wanted to call out to the man but his voice was caught in his stomach, making him nauseous. His heart thumped in his chest, and his voice found a pathway.

'Hello,' he managed to croak.

The man just stood there, like he was not of this world, eyes fixed on the line where the lunar sky met the ocean.

'Hello there.' Seán fought to control the tremble in his voice.

Nothing. He inched closer.

'Hey, Mister.' Seán was drawn to this man, felt compelled to see his face. Nothing stirred. It seemed like the man was part of the night itself. He came right up behind him, the smoke from the cigarette sulphuric in his nostrils. His skin crawled with an army of goose bumps. Reaching out, he touched the man on his shoulder then recoiled in horror, the tips of his fingers burnt. Horror turned to anger as Seán made to grab his shoulder again from behind, but something held him rooted to the spot. He fought against it, but no matter how, he couldn't move an arm or a leg or even turn his head. He tried to close his eyes, but these too were fixed. He was completely helpless, at the stranger's mercy.

'Face me,' roared Seán. 'Face me you coward.' Tears borne out of helplessness streamed down his face, sulphur burning his eyes and nose.

And then, the stranger's head whipped around on his neck in one fluid movement, like a viper disturbed in his lair. He fixed upon Seán the most malevolent smile he had ever seen. Black teeth pared back grimacing. The eyes in hollow sunken sockets, ferine and demonic. For a moment Seán was arrested with the most acute sense of familiarity, perhaps recognition. Then he was drawn deeper into the stare, helpless. He mustered all his strength but he was being pulled into a great void, a deep black pool of despair. The stranger's hold was too strong. Seán felt himself tire, felt it hard to hold the stranger's gaze. He knew now it was a lost cause and felt himself slipping away and falling, falling into nothingness.

Bridget found her father slumped at the gabled end of the old cottage on Squince Head, a bottle upturned on the ground beside him. He snored like a donkey.

'Wake up,' said Bridget.

His face seemed caught in a grimace. She left him to his sleep, and wandered to the old *cillín*. She knew Danny was buried there. She knelt and offered a little prayer.

'May demons respect you,
Trouble neglect you,
The angels protect you,
May eternity accept you,
And the light of the heavens shine on your grave,
Amen.'

Afterwards she returned to her father's side. 'Come on. Wake up, you silly-billy.'

She shook him gently. Nothing. She shook him harder, grabbed his ear and twisted. She'd heard her mother giving out he was impossible to wake with drink taken. Still nothing. She sat down beside her father, pulled his arm around her and waited for him to wake. A lone ash tree grew through the roof of the old house, spilling over the walls, its gnarly branches deformed and contorted by the bothersome wind. Autumn was beginning to sing its lament and a leaf dropped from the tree, waltzing down onto Bridget's lap. She held the leaf in her hand a moment admiring the colours the season had painted on its palm. It was September and summer was coming to an end. Her grandmother had paid the fees for secondary school in Skibbereen and she was to start next week. She was very excited, but nonetheless she would miss those long evenings with her grandmother. She would have less time to visit her with travelling in and out of Skibbereen and all the homework and study expected of her. What a summer it had been, and all that she had learned in the half-shadows and dull light of her granny's front room.

Her father coughed and spluttered. Bridget moved from under his arm and stood up and it was just as well because he began to retch violently. His eyes were full of tears and when he wiped them clean and turned he spotted Bridget, half-staring at him, half-staring out to sea. Bridget ensured the stare he met was non-judgemental, soft and full of pity and compassion.

'Bridget, my love,' he said, his voice hoarse, as if he had swallowed a hawthorn. 'How long have you been here? How did you know to find me?'

'About a half-hour. I figured you'd be visiting your brother. Come on home now. We'll get you some hot water, clean you up and fix you some breakfast. Best thing in the world for you now. We'll take the back-way over the fields and we can pretend that we are the only people left in the world. How's that?'

'I haven't had such an offer since your mother got down on her knees and begged me to marry her.' He looked down at his filthy hands, wiping them on his soiled shirt before reaching out and taking Bridget's.

They set off through the fields. Neither spoke a word all

the way home, the silence broken only by the gulls that forayed inland from the sea, screeching like they were set on finding something stolen from them. Cows warily eyeballed the two as they passed, pensively chewing the cud as if pre-gustators for some great bovine chieftain. A dagger of swallows thrust themselves heavenwards, fencing some unseen opponent in the sky as butterflies danced a ballet of brilliant coloured wings around them. For a little while at least, it felt to Bridget like they were the only people on earth.

Maeve had the pan down, fixing some breakfast when they arrived home. They were all just happy to see him and happy to see him smiling. A surge of guilt threatened, but he pushed it away and whisked Neasa into his arms. He approached Maeve from behind and gave her a squeeze and a soft kiss on the neck, she smiled and winked at him, he felt heat stirring in his loins. It had been too long since they'd been together. He looked forward to getting her into bed that night.

'Sit down, now, the lot of ye, till I serve up some breakfast,' said Maeve. 'It's been like a mad house here lately, with all the coming and going. 'Tis time we sat down like a family.'

Later upstairs, Seán and Maeve were in bed, both lying on their backs, the light off and the rest of the house asleep. The child was breathing peacefully in the cot, sleeping the dreamless sleep of the innocent. Seán propped himself up on his elbow and with his other hand stroked Maeve's hair back onto the pillow.

'Well, have you drank enough? Have you it out of your system?'

'I do, pet, for now,' he said. 'I'm lucky to have ye. What would I do without my girls to look after me? Walking home through Kilbeg Wood this morning, holding hands with Bridget was the best half-hour I've spent in a long time. What could be wrong with the world when we have moments such as those? She's a special girl, that one.'

'She sure is. It's unnerving sometimes to look at her. She's so together for her age. Sometimes I think she can see straight through me. I wonder who is the mother and who is the daughter with the way she talks. She's like her grandmother.'

'Era, I've noticed. They're cut from the same cloth alright. At least she's one I won't have to worry about when I go away.'

'Going away? What's this? Going away where?'

'There's no work here and not a chance of any for the likes of me in this new bloody Free State. The only work the lads are getting around here is in the Royal Navy. I'm going to sign up.'

Maeve laughed. 'You in the British Navy? Now I know you're joking. Go away out of that.' Maeve caught his cheek between her forefinger and thumb. 'You bloody rascal, putting the fright up me like that.'

'I'm serious, pet. I'm joining up. How else am I going to support you and the kids, and help Mary next door? Not to mind paying the tick in Lynch's and paying for that bloody boat. I'll be away a lot, but the pay is good and it'll be sent directly home to you each week by telegram.'

'But you hate the British.' Maeve's voice exposed her panic. 'You spent years fighting them. It goes against everything you believe in.'

Seán sat up and lit a cigarette. 'I don't have beliefs anymore. Beliefs won't put food on the table or provide for my children. Whatever I believed in was just a mirage. The republic I fought for, the new ideal, where is it now? We're living under the tyranny of a church that is worse than any foreign government. We have no work and no future.'

'They won't let you in with your record, your history. You're notorious. They won't let you within a mile of a British ship for fear you'd blow it up.'

'I've an idea for that. I'll be visiting an old friend of mine in Castletownsend. He'll help me out, I'm sure of it.'

'Oh, darling, no.' Maeve wrapped her arms around his neck. 'How will I cope here without you? And Neasa and Bridget? They'll be devastated. You'll miss so much of little Seán Óg.'

'It's come to this, Maeve.'

She cried. 'How often will they let you home?'

'Era, a couple of times a year. It's not so bad.' He stubbed out his cigarette. 'Come here to me now and stop your tears. This is a good thing for us. We'll be better off than we ever were, and it'll be only for a few years until we get some savings, then we'll buy a little farm up in Ballincolla or out by Carrigilihy and live happily ever after.'

He kissed her full on the lips. She responded with hunger, grabbing him at the back of the neck and pulling him towards her, her tongue warm in his mouth. She bit his lip wantonly and reached for him under the covers. Then suddenly she checked herself, as if remembering something. The tension went out of her and the tightness in her body eased. She lay back as he rolled on top of her. He lifted her nightdress over her head and opened her legs, she lay there limp, turned her face to the side and whimpered as he entered her. There was no moaning or begging or dirty talk, the usual staples of their lovemaking. Usually she couldn't get enough of him, looping her legs over his thighs and pulling him into her, egging him on and scratching his bare back. Tonight, she just lay there, lifeless. When he finished she rolled to her side, knees curled to her chest.

Seán lay awake a long time that night. He thought he heard her sob in the darkness before she fell asleep. He got up and dressed, took his coat and went out for a walk. It was a mild night. He took a long draught of sea air through his nose, and he walked towards the woods across the short sandy beach beside the pier. There was a bright buttery moon, not quite full, a good sliver pared off the side. Just before the woods were some rocks that dipped their toes in the ocean, all topped with purple heather. It was there he lay down, on his back, his eyes heavenwards, counting the stars and making out the patterns in the sky, tracing constellations and mapping out his plans in his mind.

What would I do differently if I could go back to the beginning, start again? Oh there's much I could change, but who gets the chance? If there is no meaning in life, no reason, why fight it? Wouldn't it be better to go with the flow, to let the tide take me? It's time to stop fighting, stop fighting myself and fighting the world, time to live for others, for the girls and for Seán Óg. They don't have to be like us, don't have to repeat what we have done. They are our only hope. If they can be happy, maybe it will all have been worth it. Maybe everything I have done will mean something.

He mellowed under the stars' gaze, worries melting away for a time. Things seemed a bit clearer, now that he had made his decision. He resolved to try to take things as they came from now on, to think of his family first in everything. He put his hands behind his head and stretched his legs, letting out a long sigh. He took in the sea air again, perfumed with the montbriche growing between the sea and the woods. The woods, those same woods. Oh Danny, he thought, I shunned you, disowned you, practically put the noose around your neck, and for what? Joining the British Army. And look at me now! Irony is the gods' plaything. We could be brothers still, comrades still. What a fool I was. Will you ever forgive me? Then there was a smell he remembered, faintly, as if from a dream, as if someone had struck a match behind him. It took him a moment. He had almost dismissed his encounter at the old *cillín* last night. The memory was lost till now, mislaid in the murkiness of the alcohol and grief. He jumped up, scanned the edge of the dark forest. He shivered. He was cold. He remembered those eyes, icy, bottomless, a portal into the bleak corners of one's soul where you dare not look. Had it really happened? Was it a dream? Could there have really been a man? There was a lot of poitín drank. He could have hallucinated. It was known to happen with the stronger poitín. A rustling in the woods startled him, then the snap of a twig underfoot.

He scrambled away, over the rocks back to the beach. The sickly smell followed. His footprints remained, from when he had crossed the beach earlier, and a few paces away another set. Someone had followed across the strand, just as the smell followed him now. Seán ran, and ran on, not stopping, not slowing till he reached the house. He grabbed a bottle of poitín hidden behind the dresser in the kitchen, and took a long swig. The warmth of the spirit coursed through his body, melting the ice that ran cold through his veins. He went upstairs and checked on the girls and Seán Óg, relieved to find them sleeping peacefully. He returned downstairs to the poitín and sat a long time before the dying embers of the hearth, sipping from the bottle, waiting for the shake in his hand to subside.

'You know I won't be with you forever. I'm very old now and not long for this world'

'I know that, Granny, but I'll miss you,' said Bridget

'Era, what's there to miss? Only an old woman talking nonsense,' she said with a snort.

'I don't think it's nonsense. You know everything there is to know.'

'Anyone can talk. We're judged on our actions. You'll hear plenty of talk in your life, plenty of lofty words and ideals, but you won't see many actions worth remembering.'

Alice stared lugubriously out the window to the street. Her grandmother was different today, not her usual self. She seemed to be moving with the season. There was a touch of autumn about her, her skin jaundiced, her movements slow and languid, her words wistful as if she was waiting for a gust of wind to shake her free. Only her dark eyes still burned with vitality like two resilient summer berries shining from a withering winter's hedge.

'Listen to me now, girl.' Alice turned back to Bridget, her tone and expression stern. 'Don't you make the mistakes I made. Don't hold on to things. Let them go. Be good to people no matter what they have done. Remember all that we have talked about over the last few months, and when times are tough, don't forget I will be with you through it all. I will always be here.'

'Will you stop talking like you're already dead? You'll be around for a while yet.'

'Whist, girl. Will you listen to what I'm saying to you? Seek the truth always in life, speak it, live it, protect it. Keep a calm mind. The world was here long before us and will be here long after us. Heaven is here on earth if you want it, if you choose to see it. A wise man once said, "What hurts you blesses you. Darkness is your candle". You will suffer, you will feel pain, you will experience loss but it is how you react that will define you, the only thing that will define you, your only real choice in life. Don't try to put out a fire by pouring on more fire.'

Bridget had never witnessed a sadness so concentrated as it was in those eyes. Her grandmother bowed her head for a time.

'Oh, look now, how I go on,' she said lifting her head. 'I'm some example to you. Look at my actions. My daughter not living but a mile down the road and I haven't talked to her in years. What fools we are. Even when we know the road to peace, we cannot travel it for fear we'd get it.'

'I'll bring Mammy with me next time,' Bridget said matter-of-factly. 'I'm sure she wants to see you, too. I don't know why ye've left it so long all these years and nothing good to come of it.'

'Well, that would make an old woman very happy, if you could manage that.' Tears welled at the corners of her grandmother's eyes. 'I'd walk down there myself this very instant if my legs could carry me.'

'I'll bring her, I promise.'

'You're a special one, my dear. There's no doubt about that. Come up here to me.' She reached out to Bridget and held her tight. 'You'll make up for the lot of us, and all we've gone through down the years may have been worth it after all.'

The remnants of last night's whiskey throbbed in Fr Murphy's temples. He couldn't remember coming up to bed. The front of his pyjamas was damp and sticky. He'd had another one of those dreams. He'd once considered them an occupational hazard, an unpleasant but necessary side-effect of celibacy, but recently they visited more frequently and the guilt weighed heavily. They grew more disturbing, more bizarre. Last night's dream brought remorse and disgust so keenly it was like a cancerous lump in his throat.

A flame at his bedside flickered weakly in the light of day. He blew it out. Fear and anxiety had of late, rekindled his dread of the darkness, and each night he slept with a lamp lit. Delilah pricked her ears as she heard him rise and trotted to his side. He rubbed her ears gently.

He dressed, not bothering to wash, and went down to eat his breakfast. Mrs Keohane was in the kitchen, her morning smile wide on her face. The woman always thought the best of him, even knowing he was going through whiskey like his vows depended on it. He knew she hated ducking in and out of Casey's, saw the slight involuntary wince every time he sent her to the village on that errand, but she never complained, nor did she reproach him for his order. The woman was a saint, he thought, and she serving me. 'Tis I should be serving her.

'Morning, Mrs Keohane.' He coughed clearing his throat, dislodging and swallowing a good deal of phlegm. 'What kind of day is it at all?'

''Tis fine,' she said chirpily. 'Not a cloud in the sky, or a wisp of wind. You should get out after mass, get some fresh air. It's going to be a beautiful day.'

Maybe I will, he thought, pushing his breakfast plate away and opting instead for a strong cup of black tea.

He said mass, barely aware the words emptied from his mouth. They floated above the heads of the few veiled women that knelt before him and then seemed to rise, fading to nothingness, syllables settling like ash with countless others above in the rafters of the church. Afterwards he took Bridie's advice and donning his soutane, set off on foot, taking the road out towards Carrigilihy. When was the last time he had stepped out of his routine between house and church?

He always felt painfully self-conscious outside of these places, always aware that as a priest, he was expected to act a certain way, to behave in a certain manner. Did priests take impromptu walks alone in the countryside, he wondered. He walked, bent forward slightly, hands behind his back, Delilah trotting at his heels. It was a glorious day indeed. The fields were a patchwork of gold and green, the land pocked with the heads of rock peering through the pasture like subterranean creatures. There were a few good fields, tamed by some farmer's hand, but only a few. Nothing like the lush profitable farmland of his parish. Still, there was a prettiness about the landscape. It held a certain charm and he couldn't but have respect for the men that tried to make a living out of it. The hedgerows were laden with dainty fuchsia bells, and a striped orchestra of tuxedoed bees danced with the crimson damsels. The leaves on the trees were shot through with holes, yellows and golds creeping in, eating the green of summer. Swallows gathered in their hundreds readying themselves for their journey back to God knows where.

84

'Even the sparrow has found a home, and the swallow a nest for herself, where she may have her young — a place near your altar, O Lord Almighty, my King and my God,' he said, quoting from the Bible.

He picked a bulbous blackberry from the hedge. The taste took him back to his childhood: September days on the farm; rushing back from school to help his father in the fields; the days shortening as the month went on; a little chill beginning to creep into the evenings. He had always tracked with anxiety the retreat of daylight into the darkness of winter. This meant less time on the farm after school, less time with his father, and ultimately coming home from school in the dark with nothing to look forward to in the evening, stuck inside a stuffy house waiting for the darkness to retreat and for the days to lengthen again. He could understand now how it was for the primitive man, watching their god die slowly every year, waiting and hoping with all your heart that he would recover and rise again, bringing hope and salvation, just like Christ.

He reached the little bay at Carrigilihy. A stony beach curved off to the left. To the right was a little slip with rusty rungs from whence a web of ropes led out to the boats bobbing in the bay. The inlet was well-sheltered, steep hills on both sides and High Island lurked just beyond the entrance like a sentry or large rock that could be pushed to entomb all within. In its wake was Low Island jutting from the water, the fin of some sea creature following her mother. A lone boat was pulling up at the slip. Houses peppered the bay, but apart from the man in the boat, there wasn't a soul to be seen. Once a thriving little hamlet, Carrigilihy had been home to six-hundred souls before the famine. The main occupations had been smuggling and fishing. The tight little network of inlets around the West Cork coastline made it a paradise for smugglers, but now the bay had a sleepy quality to it. Most of the men were in the Merchant Navy or Royal Navy or working on the buildings in England. The water shone, still as glass, mirroring the deep-blue sky. Movement brought his eyes towards the slip where the man was pulling in his boat. Mackerel had come in and hopped frantically after the sprat. Gannets flung themselves from the sky into the banquet, the surface a splashing, splattering buffet, an orgiastic feast. His eyes rose to the slip from the spectacle, the man was standing there looking straight at him. Fr Murphy couldn't make out his features or discern an age, but noted the man was dressed in a long black army coat. Smoke rose from a cigarette held in a hand by his side and the scent of tobacco drifted across the beach towards him. The smell was like some forbidden thing. He let it waft over him and drank it in, the strength of it watering his eyes. A cloud passed over the sun, darkening the bay. The priest shuddered. His gaze remained fixed on the man who now appeared to be moving across the beach, not walking, not running. Gliding, yes gliding, his long black coat trailing along the sand like an oil slick, his path fixed towards the priest. A cold worm of sweat slithered down Fr Murphy's back. A bilious taste came to his mouth. He clenched his teeth and then his fists as the man approached, tensing as he caught a fleeting glimpse of the malice in the eyes. The man was mocking him, a twisted grin on his face as if he had seen into his dreams, as if he knew what a vile and disgusting creature he was. The man was approaching fast. He would soon be on him. Fr Murphy turned and ran, his soutane tripping him up on the road. He picked himself up again, not daring to look around. He felt the man's eyes burning into his back. He ran all the way home, passing startled parishioners on the way, not stopping to offer salutations. He continued until he was back in the parochial house. He sat down in his chair, reached for the whiskey and poured himself a large glass, all the time mumbling away, upbraiding himself, suffering a dark guilt as though he had done something terribly wrong and been found out.

Like many an evening the summer past, Bridget walked from the village down towards Kilbeg. She had spent the afternoon with her grandmother, and as always, meandered home in a dreamlike state, her head in a whirl after the new stories and the stirring wisdom. She could almost smell the brittle fingers of autumn on the light breeze that came in from the sea. It was bittersweet, holding all the memories of the summer now gone and the aroma of the unknown to come. Where would she be this time next year? Would Granny still be around? The doctor was a regular visitor to the post office lately, and last week Bridget had crossed paths with the priest as he exited the home.

'He's trying to tie up a few loose ends,' her grandmother had said when Bridget enquired after the priest's presence.

Bridget didn't feel any pang of dread or loss when she thought of her granny dying. She had told her she would always be here, always be around. Where could she go?

As she rounded the corner she came upon Neasa and Paudie. They were holding hands. Neasa had spent a lot of time next door since Pat died and had taken a shine to Paudie. Paudie had sunk into himself since his dad's death. Before, he had been full of the joys of life, always had a laugh or a joke for you, always in the thick of things, horsing around with the rest of the village lads. Now he cut a lonely figure, keeping to himself, shoulders hunched, hands bunched up in his pockets. Sometimes she'd see flashes of the old Paudie. He'd forget himself for a moment and a smile would light up his boyish features briefly before rotting on his face. Things were different this day. One of his hands ventured outside his pocket. She caught up with them.

'Hi there.' Bridget tugged at her sister's ponytail. 'Look at you two lovebirds.'

Their hands dropped to their sides. Paudie reddened and turned away.

'You shouldn't creep up on people like that,' Neasa scolded. 'It's not fair.'

'Era, stop will ya. I was only playing with ye.'

'I'm off,' Paudie said, making his way towards Kilbeg Wood, ducking among the trees and disappearing as if seeking shelter, fearing another blow from the world.

Bridget and Neasa continued to the pier. The evenings were pulling in and the setting sun boasted a fiery, orange glow over the harbour. The fishing boats were unloading their catch and gulls circled like Apache Indians, shrieking their blood-curdling war cries, making dashing raids for the plunder. On the pier, a line of women worked over barrels salting the catch. They wore colourful shawls and sang as they went in a tongue as vibrant as their scarves. The women were down from Donegal. They came every year to salt the fish, the fishermen eyeing them up and down as they came ashore after days at sea, leaning over the barrels, winking and cracking jokes. There was many a match made on the pier. Every year there would be one or two left behind waving the others off on their journey back north.

'How's Paudie coping?' asked Bridget.

'He's not good. What if he blames Daddy? I just want to make it up to him.'

'It's not Daddy's fault. It was an accident. Paudie knows that. He's always looked up to him. There's no point in you feeling guilty either. That won't help anyone.'

'I know,' said Neasa. 'But I can't help it. I should do something for him. That's why we were holding hands. I want to comfort him. I want to put my arms around him and squeeze him tight and tell him that everything will be alright.'

'It will be alright. It always is, eventually.' Bridget put her arm around Neasa and dragged her in close. 'You can't change what happened or make up for it, or take it on yourself. Paudie will have to work through it, but I'm sure you being there will help. Just stay beside him. He'll know why you're there.'

Seán lay in bed, staring at the ceiling, waiting for midnight to come and go. He ran through the plan in his head. It was risky but he trusted his instincts. It would work, he was sure of it. He knew men and this man wouldn't forget their last encounter. Maeve lay beside him, Seán Óg asleep at her breast. She had been strange ever since the accident. The night he had come back from the *cillín* she just lay there as he entered her. It had been no better since. She never refused him, but lately it seemed only one of them was involved. Thrown down passively, not resisting, but not partaking. She used to love it. Boy, she used to enjoy it so much. She was like a she-Devil. She was praying now, day in, day out, spending so much time in the church she might as well move in. Did I drive her to this? All I've put her through down the years. The last time he rolled off her, he felt as if he had violated her, as if his actions had been base. A man shouldn't feel guilty for wanting his wife. Why was she like this?

Tension had grown between them. Mornings had always been the best time, yet Seán no longer rolled over, cuddled or touched Maeve. He jumped straight out of bed and went somewhere private to relieve himself. There was an edge to their chat, the tenderness seeping slightly. Perhaps it's just a phase, something the time apart would cure, he thought, he hoped.

Seán left the bed, left the house, and made for Kilbeg Wood. The night was chilly and a westerly wind sang in the branches above and rustled the dead leaves around his feet. A half-moon gave some light but the westerly blew clouds across its face making the night full of shadow. He reached a wall in the middle of the woods and turned left following it until it joined another. At the junction he bent down and fumbled in the moss. He turned over a big stone and felt around in the darkness. His knuckles scrapped wood. He lifted the timber and reached down into a hole till he found a piece of string. He pulled until the bundle came up, and unwrapped the cloth from a parcel to reveal a wooden box. He opened it and took out his old handgun, held it up, checked the chamber and loaded it with bullets from the box. It was still in great nick after all these years. He didn't think he would have need for it again, but then he must have if he had thought to keep it all this time. He wrapped it up in the cloth again and stuffing it down the back of his trousers, bounded over the wall and made his way back towards the pier.

The wind whistled over the houses as he made his way up the main street of Union Hall. The street was dark and lifeless. Shadows moved over the rooftops, flashes of moonlight rippling along the dark slates. He thought of all the folk safe in their beds, dreaming their dreams, turning over in their beds as their minds, unleashed, took them on a merry dance through their hopes, fears and desires. Many a night he had walked silently through villages like this, sometimes with his men in the Flying Column, sometimes on his own on the run. Some nights he was on his way to pay someone a visit in their bed, to threaten them or warn them or even kill them. Those were years and deeds he could never take back. The world had them now, they were out there, permanently etched on the eternal Ogham stone of time and memory, and he suffered for them always. In the past on nights like this, he employed a routine to keep his thoughts in check, to keep him on track, to ensure he followed through. He thought of his childhood on the farm in Ballincolla, his father in the fields, sitting at the base of the hayrack, his mother coming towards them with the lunch, and bread and tea in milk bottles. Afterwards, his dad playing with them, rolling around, Danny squealing with joy as their father caught him and tickled him. He thought of regatta days in Glandore, football games and dances at the crossroads, himself and Danny with two girls down in Daly's fields, the awkward groping and tasting and the hushed conversations in bed as they wondered what it would be like to do it on top of them. Then, when all those memories washed over him in a loaded wave of almost unbearable nostalgia, he would think of Danny, hanging from the tree, face contorted, lips blue, and twisted in a grotesque smile. This would steel him and he would keep the image in front of him and he'd carry out his orders. Not this night. Instead he reached into his pocket for the little bottle of poitín and swallowed it in one go.

Seán knew Driscoll's boat would be moored just out from his house at Reen Pier. Driscoll wouldn't mind him borrowing it for a few hours. He pulled her in and soon he was rowing the short distance across the bay to Castletownsend. The retired admiral's mansion sat on manicured gardens that sloped down to the sea. Seán tied the boat up at a little jetty. He had pulled a boat in here on a night similar to this many years ago, been specifically chosen for the job. His order was to shoot the admiral in his bed in reprisal for a Black and Tan's atrocity. Seán couldn't even remember now which atrocity it was. There were so many back then. He wondered who would have been killed in reprisal for that job, had it been carried out. That night he had slipped in through a bay window. He had stood at the foot of the bed and cocked his weapon, his finger on the trigger. Adjusting his eyes in the gloom, he noticed a child lying between the admiral and his wife, a little girl, her thumb in her mouth, golden curls splayed across the pillow. Seán cursed silently, lowering his eyes, summoning images of Danny dangling on the rope, trying to stir up hate and bitterness. He cocked his weapon and moved closer to the end of the bed, raising his arm and aiming for the admiral's head. He hesitated, eyes drawn from his target to the sleeping girl, the gun shook in his hand. He turned back to face the admiral. He was awake, his eyes beseeching, mouthing a silent plea, motioning with his eyes towards the girl. Seán gestured with the pistol towards the door.

Outside, in the hall, the moment was gone. The admiral looked pathetic in his nightclothes, standing on the landing, his hands by his side, defenceless and altogether too human. Seán stared long into those eyes. The admiral returned the stare. Neither flinched.

'Have you got any rope?' Seán said easily, as if he was a

neighbour calling to borrow something for the farm.

'Outside, down the garden in the boatshed.'

'Let's go.'

The admiral led the way, gun pointed at his back. No words were exchanged. Seán tied him up and gagged him with a piece of old sail.

'Do you know who I am?'

The admiral nodded his head.

'Not anymore. You are to forget this face. I came here tonight to kill you. Those were my orders. When they find you, you are to say that a masked man came to your room, made to shoot you but the gun jammed. After that he hit you on the head with the butt of the handgun and knocked you out. The next thing you remember you woke up here in the boatshed, tied up. If you sway from that story, I will come back and do what I was ordered.' Seán left without looking back.

He was back at the bottom of that same garden tonight. He had asked the admiral not to remember him, but now he hoped the man would, and he hoped he'd be grateful for the mercy shown all those years ago. Men from the village wanting to join the navy for work required a letter of recommendation from the admiral. This night, he entered through a back door, made his way up the stairs and to the admiral's room. There he was in the bed, alone this time, his wife long dead and his family grown and living in England. The man was well into his eighties. He looked tiny in the bed, frail.

Seán left the gun tucked in the back of his trousers, sat at the end of the bed and grabbed him by the ankle, shaking him awake. The admiral woke with a start.

'You! What are you doing here?'

'So, you remember me, Sir.' Seán was surprised at his use of sir.

'How could I forget you? I have thought of you many times over the years, but I ask you again, what brings you here tonight?'

Seán explained.

'Well, I suppose you couldn't have come through the front door in daylight and made an appointment like anyone else?'

'It would have raised a few eyebrows, I'd say, Sir.'

'I've always wondered what type of man you were, and what type of man you'd become. So you are a family man? Then we have the same hopes, the same fears, the same worries.'

'Aye,' said Seán. 'It all changes, doesn't it?'

'If given the chance, would you change what you did in those years of war?'

'I would, Sir,' said Seán wistfully. 'If I could go back and do it all again I would. Oh Jesus, I would.'

'We do what we think is right at the time. It's a man's motives that count, not his actions. When I look back at my life I have many regrets. You killed people, sure. I commanded thousands of men who killed thousands of people. I am responsible for so many deaths. Why? I was following orders, fulfilling them out of a sense of duty. I had no motive of my own. I was acting on the motives of others.'

The admiral was lying awkwardly in his bed. Seán took some pillows and propped them up behind his back.

The admiral waved him away, rearranging the bedclothes himself. 'If I was to go back and change one thing, it would be this. I would act out of duty for myself and a sense of what I thought was right not trusting the motives of others, kings, prime ministers, generals, and blindly believing their morality to be correct. No, I do not regret the killing. I regret the motives. Tell me, what were your motives? Why did you kill?'

'It was my brother. I found him hanging from a tree. Every time I killed someone, I saw his face. Every time I pointed a gun at someone, it was my brother I was shooting, over and over again. It was never about Ireland really. I know that now, and we

93

were as much to blame for his death as the British. Probably more so.'

The admiral leaned to the side of the bed and lit a lamp, coughing as he blew out the match.

'Are you a religious man?'

'No, Sir, I'm not. I have no time for the Church, or priests, the sanctimonious, the self-righteous.'

'I pity you then, son. A man needs faith. Religion isn't about the Church, or the priests or the sanctimonious or self-righteous as you say. Religion is about what is in your own heart and your relationship with the world. It need not include anyone else. There is not a day goes by that I don't ask forgiveness from the world. These last few years I have great peace within myself. I realise I am a part of something more. We are all connected and we are all responsible for one another. I realise, like Socrates that I know nothing, and can never really know anything. The world will carry on regardless of what I think or do. This is my great peace. You, too, are a good man. I saw it in your eyes all those years ago.' He smiled, his kindly eyes sparkling in the lamplight, reaching for his reading glasses on the bedside table. 'Come now and we'll write you this letter.'

Samhain

Bridie Keohane bit her nails, her nerves were feasting on her. The floorboards above creaked and groaned with the weight of Fr Murphy pacing to and fro. A roar or a curse loosened every now and then, and the priest would return to mumbling incoherently. He hadn't left his bedroom in over a week, had refused to eat, drinking only whiskey. He must have had a stash somewhere.

He refused to say Sunday mass. Bridie had cycled to the next parish to inform Fr Keohane, a gentle man and a second cousin to Bridie's. Fr Keohane kindly returned with her and said the mass, then visited the parochial house for lunch. He had tried to talk to him, but Fr Murphy refused his company.

'I'll have to let them know in Cork, Bridie,' Fr Keohane said, sipping his tea. 'We can't let him go on like this.'

'But what will they do with him?'

'Era, the Church looks after its own. There are places priests can go for rest, away from prying eyes. He'll get good care and he'll be right as rain in no time. He's a good man, a good priest, very spiritual, a deep thinker. A lot of priests go through what he is going through, a sort of dark night of the soul, or crisis of faith. It's a very lonely vocation, Bridie. A break will do him the world of good.'

'Who'll say mass if he goes? Will you look after the parish?'

'Lord, I hope not. I have enough with my lot over in Leap.'

Now, Bridie waited for the car from Cork. There had been quietness, then the racket struck up again, first sobs and mumbles, then wails and a thump. She listened at the door. The smell of cigarette smoke hit her. But Fr Murphy didn't smoke. The strangest of smells seemed to waft out under the door, like there was something burning. It wrapped around her and made her tearful. She could hear him whisper excitedly as if in a conversation. Then the door opened. He stared out like a mad dog. Bridie fled to her own room, and locked the door.

The car arrived. Fr Murphy was taken.

Bridie allowed herself a tear and a cup of tea at the table in the kitchen. The metallic tick-tock of the clock on the wall behind, like an old friend. After her tea, she reluctantly pulled herself up and made her way to Fr Murphy's room to give it a clean. The replacement priest was due tomorrow, Fr Sullivan, a young priest from Cork City. When she opened the door, she gasped at the chaos. Empty whiskey bottles everywhere, clothes strewn across chairs, the bed, the desk, the window wide open and the wind tugging at the curtains trying to pull them out to his world. She looked around for cigarettes or butts but couldn't find any. There were bits of paper everywhere with scribbling. She picked up one, trying to make out the words, but she didn't understand the language. Tu es Nobis, Omnes ex Nobis, Omni tempore, Sumus responsible, Vocamus vos, scribbled over and over again.

Probably a prayer of some sort, she thought. Poor man, out of his mind like that. Such responsibility being a priest, such a lonely life. Thank God I was born a woman. She lost herself in her work, tidying and scrubbing. Before long she was humming away to herself, an old ditty her father used to sing when she was a child.

> 'Take heed, young eaglet, till thy wings
> Are feathered fit to soar
> A little rest and then
> The world is full of work to do
> A little rest and then
> The world is full of work to do
> Sing hushabye loo, low loo, low lan

Hushabye loo, low loo.'

Her grandmother was laid out on the kitchen table in the post office, toes pointing to the ceiling, feet cased in an old pair of Mary Jane shoes. Strange to see her in shoes. Bridget had never seen the old lady in anything but her boots. She had gone peacefully in the end, sitting in her chair in the corner.

Kitty had smelt burning from the shop counter. The pipe had fallen onto Alice's bosom and her cardigan was singed. At first Kitty had thought she was asleep. The little half-smile suggested peace, and she had grabbed the pipe and shook Alice roughly while she tried to get the cardigan off. By the time she succeeded, Kitty realised the old lady was dead.

Mourners streamed in and out of the post office all evening — sorry for your troubles — the line shuffling along steadily. Bridget could hear a constant stream of chatter, laughter and banter outside on the street, the grateful outpouring of platitudes after the plaintive words had been offloaded inside. It wasn't a serious funeral. The woman was old. It was her time. It was just a formality really, nothing anyone could protest or complain about. An opportunity for a chat with a neighbour or a bottle of porter in the middle of the week, a break from their everyday lives and tomorrow they would be back to their own affairs.

There was a huge fire in the grate but with the door left open the house had no choice but to welcome the cold from the street. Bridget hopped from foot to foot to keep warm. It had been one of those rare winter days, the brilliant sun blazing in azure-blue skies, but no heat, almost like a silent movie when there is laughter but no sound. The air so crisp and clean that you just wanted to bottle and store it, you'd feel like you could reach out and grab a fistful. Every breath fogging as it sprung from your lips offering itself heavenwards, tributaries feeding the sky above, as if your soul was rising out of you. Not a wisp of wind, a barking dog, a hammer on a nail sailed over in the pristine silence from the next parish. The full moon had hung in the sky all day, translucent, basking there like the Eucharist. Then towards evening, when dusk descended and the season's light leaked and the world crept towards the winter solstice, the hills, the fields and the forest softened and a mist crawled in from the sea, hugging the hills, laying down cover for a silent assassin, the otherworld coming to collect her grandmother's soul.

Earlier, Bridget sat on the rocks by Kilbeg beach, looking out over the bay. A tear had escaped her eye. She allowed the little accident, gentle waves lapping below her, winter finches chirping in the woods behind. Dusk came in gently, the sun slipping away for its long night's rest, passing the baton of duty to the moon who'd waited all day for the honour.

'*Slán go foill*, Granny. Don't go too far,' Bridget said, getting up and brushing herself down.

She walked back up towards the village, her mind uneasy. With her grandmother gone and her father going off to sea next week, she was losing much. Neasa had been spending more and more time with Paudie. She was the only one he would talk to. They would go for long walks together in the woods and over to Trá Na Lan and Carrigilihy. Bridget didn't know where Neasa was most of the time. Her mother hadn't been herself since her father came back on the salt steamer, had taken to praying morning and evening and was wearing a path up and down to the church. And there was something amiss between her parents. Sharp words, resentful glances and irritated shrugs replaced playful slaps and pinches and tickles. She winced every time she saw her father spurned, pushed away, hurt etched on his face at first before his features softened to a dull acceptance. Her mother had brightened somewhat at the prospect of a reunion with Alice but there was to be no grand ending. Time's mighty hand, the hand that writes the end of all stories, flourished his pen across

Alice's page and that was that, no epilogue or sequel, her life an epic, but even heroes seldom get to choose the timing of their own demise. Bridget knew, as she walked back through the village, pubs all closed and blinds pulled in the windows, the street dark in respect for the newly-dead, that her childhood was over. She was fourteen, but old for her years. She knew now that the family was her responsibility. Her mother would need her help, Neasa would need looking after. Her father would rely on her while he was away.

She inched past the line of mourners at the post office. The snuff was being passed down along the line. Everyone turned to let her squeeze in, the smell of the living keen in her nostrils, farm and field, sweat and porter, sour dinners on their breath, their good clothes failing to mask what was unwashed beneath. Inside, two old women were keening at the bedside, wrapped in shawls of black, two pairs of ancient eyes peering out from their cloaks, they leant back and forth over the corpse like two crows picking at a piece of bread. They had been childhood friends of Alice, two spinsters from Ballincola, never married, probably the last of Alice's contemporaries. Arriving out of nowhere earlier on, they had taken over, sending Bridget's father away to organise the coffin and Bridget up to Fuller's with a list: bread, meat, all sorts of food, jugs of whiskey, bottles of stout, pipes, snuff and tobacco. They had tried to coax Maeve into action but she had just sat there, sobbing and saying the rosary over and over. They took charge of the body, preparing her and laying her out, stopping the clock on the mantelpiece, turning the mirror to the wall. When Bridget looked at the body, she knew it wasn't her grandmother, knew it was a shell her grandmother had once used, now discarded.

Her mother sat beside the table, rosary beads in hand, shawl down over her face, chin on her chest, her breast heaving softly. The old rocking chair sat still in the corner. Bridget had never seen it empty. There was a worn patch on the seat and the

101

curved ends of the armrests shone like they had been waxed. Bridget was drawn to the chair, wanted to see the room from where her grandmother saw it, wanted to rock back and forth soothingly in its embrace. She slipped onto the cold worn wood, rubbing her hands along the smooth arms, feeling the ancient grain under palm, toeing herself gently off the floor. The old chair creaked into life. Her mother peered over her shoulder mid-prayer, looked back at the corpse and then back to Bridget as if she couldn't fathom what was going on. Bridget beckoned to her and she came and sat at the base of the chair, looking up at Bridget like a lost little girl.

'It's alright, Mammy. I'm here for you.' Bridget stroked her mother's hair. 'I'll always be here.'

This was Neasa's second funeral. She had been to Pat's. That was a sadder affair, given that he was young and there was no body to bury. Neasa hadn't known her grandmother at all really. She was upset that her mother was upset, and upset that Bridget was upset, but otherwise mustered no other feelings of grief. The new parish priest was presiding. Neasa much preferred this fellow to Fr Murphy. He was young and good looking, very clean and tidy and smelled of soap. He had come to the house yesterday to call on her father. The priest's older brother had been her father's comrade during the war years. They talked for an hour or so in the good room, and Neasa eavesdropped as they said goodbye in the hallway.

'Will you look in on the family while I'm away? It would put my mind at ease if I knew someone decent had an eye out for them.' Seán said.

'It would be my pleasure,' Fr Sullivan said. 'Wait till I tell my brother I met the great Seán O'Donovan. He's forever talking about you.'

'I appreciate it, Father. Great to see some decent men

coming out of the seminary for a change. Maybe there's hope for the Catholic Church after all,' Seán said laughing.

Fr Sullivan spotted Neasa, smiled sweetly, winked and left.

Neasa sensed someone watching her, she turned and looked straight into Paudie's eyes, burning with intensity. How long had he been looking at her like that? Paudie was changing. He was sensitive, more than usual. More than when his father first passed. He took offence at trifling words and stormed off. There were too many awkward silences. Last week, they had been up by the lookout, staring out towards Fastnet Lighthouse, its whiteness glaring in the winter sun. Paudie kissed her. His lips tasted of butter. It seemed to make him happy and he had smiled for a while. It was better than the silence. Afterwards, they sat together and talked. He was relaxed at least, if a little morose. Paudie raised his hand to his face to shield his eyes from the light of the sun.

'I can't look at the sea now without thinking of Daddy, somewhere out there,' he had said. 'I think of stupid things like whether he is still floating, or if he has sunk to the bottom. I think of him lying on the seafloor, cold and alone.'

'Oh, Paudie,' she had said, resting her head on his shoulder.

'Sometimes, then, I let my mind wander and I daydream that he's not dead at all, that he is washed up on some desert island somewhere and is living there quite happily, that he has built himself a little house. I see him with fishing line in hand or bent over a fire roasting a piece of fish. Isn't that stupid?'

'Not at all, Paudie. Come here.' She pulled him towards her, and not knowing what to say and wanting him to be happy, kissed him again. He responded with hunger, pushing her back on the ground, panting like a farm dog, one hand groping her breast, the other rooting in her skirts.

'Stop it, Paudie,' she'd said.

He didn't hear her, seemed to be possessed. She grappled with him and managed to push him off, getting back on her feet. She looked down at him on the ground, his head in his hands. He cut a pathetic figure, knew he'd went too far.

Back in the church, she turned her head away and tried to ignore him but she could feel his eyes eating into her. She'd liked the attention at first, and the kissing and cuddling. She was becoming a woman, her body had changed over the last few years. She was more aware of herself, beginning to become aware that she had a certain effect on boys, and liked it. Paudie was fifteen but built like a man. He did excite her, that was true, when they lay there outside the lookout, but lately he was more insistent, pushy. Where he was gentle before, he was now rough, pushing her hands back and holding them and touching her in places she hadn't been touched before. It still excited her but it was also frightening; a heady mix. She was a little scared of what she had gotten herself into but had nobody to talk to about it all. Bridget wouldn't know the first thing about boys and touching. She didn't seem to have any interest in the opposite sex. Her mother was ensconced in caring for the baby and spending time at the church. And Granny dying didn't help. She would have to deal with it herself.

The graveyard was mercilessly exposed to the elements. The wind came in strong from the sea. It was as if whoever had picked the site said, 'They are dead anyway, they won't feel a thing.'

'Twas sure and certain no cattle would graze there, no crops would grow there, and no home could be made there. The graveyard sloped down from the cliff edge and in the middle sat the ruin of an old church, the graveyard reclaiming it patiently. It was overgrown and sinking into the ground like many a headstone. Soon it would join the rest of the remains in the earth's eternal tomb. Storm clouds hung low over the land and the restless sea beyond was awash with squall whipping up whitecaps. Gulls were in from the sea, layering their screeching and crying and keening over the wind. To Bridget the wild and windswept graveyard seemed like a setting for the end of the world. The rain lashed down, dancing its staccato rhythm on the coffin top, the gale drowning out the prayers of the priest, making a mockery of the rites of humankind.

'May her soul and the souls of all the faithful departed, through the mercy of God, rest in peace, Amen.' Fr Sullivan sprinkled the coffin and the hole in the earth with holy water.

Maeve threw a handful of dirt. It tinkled on the hollow wood. Mourners began to leave. Bridget stayed beside her mother while men from the village took turns shovelling the earth, passing around the whiskey bottle until the hole was full. Neasa was at home minding Seán Óg and her father was organising things at Nolan's for drinks after the funeral. Bridget yawned. She had stayed up with her mother all night watching the body. In the wee hours Bridget poured her mother a drop of brandy and that loosened her tongue. She spoke about her mother and father lovingly, growing up in the post office, meeting Seán for the first time. All happy times. This was the first she'd heard her mother reminisce. It gave Bridget a sense of the girl her mother had once been. It saddened Bridget to see her now, a woman, but still a girl, ruined by the choices she'd made.

'It's a pity you never knew your grandfather, Bridget. He was a wonderful man, so kind and thoughtful. I miss him so much.'

'I feel I know him. Granny spoke of him often.'

'Oh, what are we going to do now, Bridget? Dad gone, Mam gone, your father going away on us.'

'I'll be here with you, Mammy, and Neasa and Seán Óg. We'll all look after each other and Daddy won't be away forever.'

Maeve put her arm around Bridget and squeezed her tight. 'You're like your grandmother, child, so calm and collected, like you know things the rest of us don't. No wonder the two of you got on so well.'

'She's not gone anywhere, you know.'

'Who?' said Maeve absently.

'Granny. She's not gone anywhere. She's still here and always will be. Where could she go? Where does anything go?'

'Maybe you are right, pet. Maybe you're right.'

The graveyard emptied and they stood there alone, like impostors in a hostile land.

'Come on, Mammy,' said Bridget. 'Let's go.'

They made their way along the gravel path, past the mound of whiskey bottles at the gate. It was bad luck to remove the bottles. Bridget took one look back in the half-light. There was a man in a long black coat standing over the fresh grave, his head bowed. There was something familiar about his profile. She was sure all the mourners had left. Where had this man come from?

'Mammy, who is that man beside the grave?'

But he was gone. A blackbird landed momentarily on the packed sod of the grave, its silky black fingered wings folded back, talons outstretched as if picking something up before alighting again in one swift movement and flying off over the ruined church into the storm clouds beyond.

Bridget would never forget Christmas of 1939. It was the last year that everything was as it should be, all the family under the one roof. The provisions of Granny's will saw to Bridget's schooling. She had missed the first term, so would need to catch up with the rest of the class, but was to start in the convent in Skibbereen in January. The family decorated the house with holly picked from Doctor's Hill, the brightest red berries Bridget had ever seen.

'As bright as the blood of Jesus on the Cross,' her mother had said.

Christmas Eve, all the curtains remained open and they lit candles with baby Seán Óg before he went to bed, tradition being that the youngest in the household lights the candle in the window so that the light would guide Mary and Joseph. Her mother and father seemed like their old selves, playing and joking. With her father's departure looming, intimacy between them seemed to have returned and she was glad. Bridget couldn't help thinking that her father's leaving had something to do with the way her mother had been treating him lately.

Her father walked them to early mass Christmas morning. They huddled close for warmth. It was still dark. Candles danced in all the windows bathing the street in half-light. He left them at the church and headed off to visit the grave of his mother and brother in the old *cillín*. Bridget stared after him awhile. He cast a lonely figure as he plodded from the village in the pre-dawn. He seemed like the last man on earth. Without thinking she broke from the rest of them and ran after him.

'Wait,' she said, 'I'm coming with you.'

'But what about Christmas mass?' he said. 'You can't miss mass.'

'Don't be silly, Daddy. God won't mind this morning. Isn't the whole world at mass? Besides, God is in here.' She placed her hand over his heart. 'And here,' she added, twirling her hands in the air. 'And he is above with your brother and mother, too. And wherever those men of the Church say.'

'Well, aren't you quite the philosopher.' He whisked her up in his arms. 'Away with us. You'll have the whole village talking. The apple doesn't fall far from the tree, they'll be saying.'

When they reached the old *cillín* Bridget let her father approach alone. The *cillín* was nothing more than a circular moss-covered mound of stones. Trees and briars grew all around but no one dared clear the mound for fear of the sluagh sidhe or the fairy folk. It was believed this was where the little people resided and they were not to be tinkered with. She left him alone for a time before joining his side. Dawn was breaking and a chorus of birdsong heralded the sun.

'It's so peaceful here,' said Bridget, 'compared to the other graveyard.'

'I don't think it matters much to the dead where they are buried in the end. It's only for us living, really, to have somewhere to go to feel close to them sometimes.'

'You can carry them with you. I feel Granny with me all the time.'

'I wish I could stay with you, you know. I'd love for all of us to be together. But I have to go, even though I don't want to.'

'I know, Daddy.'

'One thing's for sure and certain, this'll be my last war and I'll be home to you before you know it with my pockets full of sterling.'

The British Army was in need of men. Conscription had been introduced in the UK. This had expedited her father's call up and he was leaving for Cork on St Stephen's Day and catching the boat across the channel the following night. He was given a berth on the new aircraft carrier, HMS Illustrious. He was to be stationed in Lancashire for training until the ship was ready to join the fleet in the war against the Axis powers. The poor old admiral who had given her father his reference had since gone to meet his maker. Not long after Seán had visited him, he had another visitor in the night, a group of men from the IRA. With less compassion than Seán, they shot him in his bed. She'd went with her father to his funeral. He'd wanted to pay his respects. They'd certainly turned some heads. The admiral had provided many letters of reference for local men keen to join the British Navy. This, the IRA deemed as treasonous.

Bridget felt saddened for the admiral's demise, but her father had told her that he had his faith, that he was ready to go, wouldn't have been scared. Bridget wondered who had pulled the trigger. Probably one of her father's own men, men from his old brigade, men he had trained for such missions. Those men had not laid down their arms, and probably never would.

'You'll have to look after the others for me while I'm gone, you know.' Seán pulled Bridget up on to his knee. 'You're the toughest and smartest of the lot of them. I'm glad you'll be there to look after them.'

'Will you write to me, Daddy?'

'Every week, I promise.'

'And I'll write to you. How will I be sure you'll get them when I won't know where you are? And how will I know where to send them if you are constantly moving?'

'Tell you what. If you need to get me urgently, run down there to Trá Na Wadla with an empty glass bottle, put your letter in it and stuff a cork in the neck. Make sure you throw the bottle right into the current and say a prayer to Lir, the god of the sea. He'll make sure I get it.'

'Will you stop, you eejit,' she said punching him playfully in the stomach. 'Come on we'll be getting home.'

'Just a minute, pet. Wait with me one minute. There is something I want to say to you.'

'What is it, Daddy?'

'Remember that day out on Rabbit Island, you asked me about my past, and I snapped at you? Well I'm sorry. You can ask me anything you want. Anything, and I'll tell you.'

'It's okay, Daddy,' she said. 'I know everything I need to know. You are a kind and loving man and you're my daddy and I love you, no matter what.'

'But I've done terrible things. I have killed men, many men.'

'But you were at war, you did what you thought was right at the time. Who knows what we'll be called to do in our lives. Who knows how the world works? Maybe you saved lives, too. You are a good man, and that's what counts.'

'Where did you come from?'

Bridget saw tears in his eyes.

'Where we got you from I'll never know. I'll think of you every day, and my beautiful Neasa and little Seán Óg, and soon we'll all be back together, and the world will let us be.'

After Christmas dinner, they all huddled around the fire. They had eaten well. Neasa sat on her daddy's lap and Maeve cradled Seán Óg at her breast. Bridget read a book gifted to her by her granny, The Picture of Dorian Gray. The weather had taken a turn for the worse and the wind howled outside, its arm reaching down, tearing at the neck of the chimney. Rain lashed off the windows like an animal trying to get in. Seán twisted the dial on the wireless in search of the BBC World Service for King George's speech.

'Who would have thought we'd be sitting here waiting for the King's speech,' he said with a snort. 'If you'd have told me last year I'd be heading off to join the British Army, I would have called the men in the white coats for you. Life is a funny thing. Ha!'

The static crackled on the radio. The King's clipped voice came over the air, steady and clear, his words broadcasted to twenty-million people the world over. Bridget imagined families from all areas of the globe gathered like them, ears tuned to their wireless. Posh folk in parlours, sipping their sherry. Urchins in tenements huddled around meagre fires. Black, yellow, brown. All creeds, all colours, all scared, all uncertain, thinking of their loved ones away at war, wondering what would become of them and of the world in the year ahead. The King's words went out to them all. She felt as if it were the world itself talking to them, an ancient voice speaking to them from the bowels of wisdom, warning them of what was to come, what was to become of them, of what they were to unleash upon themselves. She felt his compassion and the gravity of his words. Tears stung her eyes. She turned, facing away from her family, watching Seán Óg in the reflection of the window. What kind of world will you grow up in, mo grá, she wondered. What will you see in your lifetime?

Oh Lord, she thought, please bring Daddy back to us again. The Christmas candle in the window had burnt down to the log. She stared into the dark night beyond. The radio fell silent, the speech over. What will the year bring for us, she thought? What has the world in store? She heard the words of the speech over and over in her head, the King's closing words echoing in her ears:

I said to the man who stood at the gate of the year, 'Give me a light that I may tread safely into the unknown. And he replied, 'Go out into the darkness and put your hand into the hand of God. That shall be to you better than light and safer than a known way.' May that Almighty hand guide and uphold us all.

'Amen,' she said quietly to herself, turning from the darkness and back to her family.

Imbolc

The bell sounded the finish of the school day. Bridget placed her books into her satchel, a bag now worn after nearly two years of use, a companion as she cycled in and out of Skibbereen twice daily in all sorts of weather. She collected her bike and took the road out of town. A cold wind blew up her skirt but she soon warmed. Was her father warm? Where was he? The Mediterranean? North Africa? She didn't know where. Bridget tried to imagine him on his ship, somewhere, somewhere far from here.

Every evening she turned on the wireless to the BBC World Service for news of the war, willing words of the Illustrious to be spilled from the announcer's lips, relieved however, when it wasn't mentioned. No news is good news, her mother would often say. Her father had been home during the summer, just before the Illustrious, or Lusty, as the men called her, was commissioned. They spent two weeks together, with so much to tell each other. Bridget, of all she was learning in school, the poems and books she was reading. They'd talk in Gaeilge, the language that was being discovered by Bridget anew. She loved to hear the old words rolling off her tongue. Her father, all about the ship and the men on board. The sheer scale of the ship amazed her. Ten times as big as their little village. Nineteen-hundred men on board, seven-hundred-and-fifty feet long, ninety-five feet wide, over one-hundred-and-sixty guns and forty aircraft. Surely the minds of men, their efforts, sweat and ingenuity could be put to better use. She wondered what her grandmother would have said about the whole thing. Two years had passed since she'd took her leave. Her grandmother had lived through the risings and the Great War. What would she have thought about this new war, these new methods of killing as many people as possible, as efficiently as possible.

Bridget free-wheeled down the hill into Union Hall. Passing the church and parochial house, she wondered about Fr Murphy and what had become of him. There had been no news of him since he went away to receive treatment for his illness. She'd heard his nerves were at him, he was away for a break, had been working too hard. She hoped he was alright. She had always thought him awkward and lost, as if he had woke up one day in a priest's garb not knowing how he had got there.

She left the bike at the gable of the terrace in Kilbeg.

'I'm home,' she announced coming through the back door.

'In here, Bridget,' her mother said.

They were in the good room, her mother, Neasa and the new priest.

'Hello, Bridget. How was school?'

Fr Sullivan visited regularly. A man in his late twenties, the priest took great pains in his appearance. His coiffure and dress immaculate. He looked more like someone out of a movie than a priest, perhaps like Cary Grant in The Philadelphia Story, the flick she and her sister saw in Crowley's Hall a few weeks earlier.

'Great, Father, thank you,' said Bridget feigning a smile. Her mother and Neasa were enamoured with Fr Sullivan and he enjoyed it just a bit too much. She noticed her mother was in her good dress again, hair tied up off her face.

'Father Sullivan was just telling us about Rome,' said Neasa. 'It sounds so amazing. I'd love to go some day.'

'Well, keep up the typing lessons and you might end up working in some swanky office in Rome,' Fr Sullivan said smiling over at Neasa. He smiled with his teeth clenched shut, his sensual lips sliding back over his brilliant white teeth, set into his gums like a rows of perfect milestones.

Neasa had gotten it into her head lately that she would

like to work in an office as a secretary. Their father had unintentionally planted the idea when home the last time, with his stories of all the office ladies in London, their glamourous dresses and hairdos. He had brought her back some fashion magazines that she'd leafed through daily until dog-eared.

Fr Sullivan had an old Remington typewriter. Neasa visited twice a week for lessons, dolling herself up each and every time. She'd be at her mother's powders, dusting her cheeks with rouge, dousing herself with scents from the perfume bottle. She thought nobody noticed at home, but hoped, Bridget was sure, that the priest did.

Bridget liked Fr Sullivan but was wary of the attention he splashed about. He called nearly twice a week, looking to borrow something, pretending he was passing, dropping in a book or conjuring any old excuse to call. She saw the way her mother looked at him. Neasa was worse. For a fifteen-year-old she was well advanced in the social graces relative to the opposite sex.

'Any news on Paudie next door?' said Fr Sullivan. 'How's he getting on across the water?'

'Good,' Maeve said. 'He's got steady work now in some munitions factory. He's sending money home every week, which is a great help to his mother. He writes the odd letter to Neasa.'

'I heard he had a soft spot for Neasa,' said Fr Sullivan.

'Aw, will ye stop. We're just friends.' Neasa's cheeks blushed.

'It wouldn't hurt you to reply to his letters now and then,' Maeve said. 'Poor young fellow over in London all by himself. Must be awful lonely for him.'

Paudie had only been gone a few months, and Neasa's new interest seemed an infatuation for Fr Sullivan. Paudie had been writing two or three letters a week, his last still lying unopened on the dresser.

There was a cry from upstairs. Seán Óg had woken from his nap.

117

'Oh well, no rest for the wicked,' said Maeve. 'Neasa can you give me a hand with Seán Óg for a few minutes.'

'Aw, Mam. Can't Bridget do it?'

'Your sister's just back from school. Leave her be.'

Reluctantly Neasa pulled herself up.

'Please excuse us, Father. We won't be long.'

Brigid and the priest were left alone. She knew the conspiring that was afoot, and was none too pleased with her mother for the dogged insistence. A life with the convent was not in Bridget's future. Not now. Not ever.

The room felt small for the size of the silence. Bridget shifted uncomfortably and made to rummage through her satchel.

'Do you miss your father, Bridget?'

'Yes, Father. Every day.'

'I think of him in my prayers every morning.'

'I pray for him, too, Father.'

'I've heard great things about you in the convent. Mother Superior says you are one of her most intelligent students.'

'Granny would have wanted me to work hard and get an education. 'Twas she made it possible for me, you know?'

'Tell me, have you put any thought into what you might do after you are finished? This is your last year.'

'I haven't really, Father, to be honest. I'm just trying to keep the head down and do the best I can. The future will look after itself if I do well.' She knew where this was going. Her mother had dropped all-too obvious hints of late.

'Have you ever thought about a vocation?'

'A vocation, Father?' She pretended to be taken off guard.

'Yes, Bridget, the religious orders. I think it would be a great choice for you. You are an intelligent girl, obviously a deep thinker. The religious orders are always looking for girls such as

118

yourself. You could continue your studies, travel. It's a good life.'

Bridget thought of Fr Murphy. The life didn't seem to be agreeing with him.

'Well, I'm flattered, Father. I'll certainly consider it,' she lied. Bridget received no enjoyment in the act, but a white-lie now and again didn't seem a huge sin. Her grandmother would agree, she was sure.

'I can arrange for you to meet with one of the orders. You could ask some questions.'

'Thank you, Father, but right now I'd just like to concentrate on my studies. I have very important exams coming up next week.'

'Right you are, Bridget. You have your wits about you, to be sure.'

She had no intention of being locked away in a convent. Not with so much to see and do in the world, so much to experience. Life, love, children. Maybe she would one day meet a man, someone like her father. Strong, independent, intelligent. Maybe she would get married and have kids, a house, all of it. Just because she didn't swan around like Neasa, fluttering eyelids, playing seductively with her hair, giggling at things boys said that weren't funny, did not mean she wasn't interested in men. Many is the day she stood above in the Black Field watching the lads. Did they think she was there to watch the football?

You could do God much more service out in the world than you could inside a religious cage. Her grandmother had told her you could talk to God, or have a relationship with God anywhere, anytime. Be still and know that I am God, the bible says. Don't they tell you he is omnipresent, infinite, eternal, and then in the next breath insist you can only access Him through the church, through the priests and the highfalutin language and rules and morality?

'How did your brother know my father?' Bridget asked to change the subject.

'They fought together against the Brits, and then again on the same side in the Civil War. Your father saved my brother's life, twice.'

'Twice?'

'Yes, twice. The first time was at the Crossbarry ambush in nineteen-twenty-one. About one-hundred IRA men from the West Cork Brigade, including your father and my brother, were encircled by one-thousand-three-hundred British soldiers. The IRA only had forty rounds of ammunition each. Your father persuaded them the only way out was to fight and break through. If they dug in they were sure to run out of ammunition. Would have been a major coup for the British to get the entire West Cork Flying Column in one go. The men were scared, but your father rallied every one them. John, my brother, was badly wounded and left for dead. The rest of the Column had broken through and were running for the hills. Your father fought his way back through the British line to John, picked him up, fought his way back out again and carried him ten miles to safety, on his shoulders.'

The priest paused. Bridget smiled. She was always rooting for her father. She could almost feel her daddy's big arms around her.

'The second time was when they escaped from the Women's Gaol in Cork. Nineteen-twenty-three it was. Towards the end of the war the British were running out of space for prisoners so they sent forty hard-line IRA men to the gaol on Sunday's Well Road. Many of them were awaiting death sentences so, for them, it was either escape or die. John had been on a hunger-strike for twenty-one days. He was weak, sick. Most of the men wanted to leave him behind but your father refused. With a knotted bed-sheet he tied him to his back and scaled the wall. The only time your father left John was when they found a safe house in Cork and knew he'd be looked after. Then he came straight back down here and joined the West Cork Brigade again.

John said he was the bravest man he'd ever met, and the most honest. All the men looked up to him.'

'Thank you for telling me. Daddy never talks about his time in the wars. I think he tries to bury it all.'

'Your father was on the losing side when the Civil War broke out. And the winners write the history. But without men like your father, there would still be British rule from Dublin Castle. Did you know the free-staters offered your father a government position if he came over to their side after the war?'

'No.'

'He refused.'

'I think my father is too brave sometimes. He listens to his heart instead of his head.'

'He's a victim of the times, Bridget. Look at him now, caught up in another war he should have no part in. These men are paying it forward. All this sacrifice has to have a purpose. Hopefully they're shaping the world for the years to come so that the likes of Seán Óg upstairs can live in peace.'

'Something good needs to come of it.'

'Ah, there ye are now,' said Maeve, coming back into the room. 'Did ye have a nice chat?'

'We did, Maeve, you have a very special young lady on your hands here. It's like talking to a professor. But now, I must be off to do my rounds. They say poor old Johnny Crowley is on his last legs and he'll be needing absolution. It was a lovely afternoon. I'll call again soon. Tell Neasa not to forget her typing lesson tomorrow.'

Seán ducked as a left hook raced at his head. He shot back up with an uppercut and heard the clatter of Barney's teeth rattling loose in his gob. Barney backed off, spitting bloodied enamel. They circled each other warily like two wild boars, stripped to the waist, a large body of sweating, shouting seamen cheering them on. The few Irish crewmembers were greatly outnumbered by the British. They were two beasts of men, Barney wider and younger, every inch of his broad muscled arms tattooed. He was a tough nut from Hackney, East End London. He had the swagger and menace of a pirate captain and had it in for the Irish. Barney ran things below deck on Lusty. That was, he ran things until Seán decided he had enough. The paddies were treated as second-class citizens, getting the worst jobs, the worst bunks, the worst food, sent to the end of the line for everything. Seán had kept to himself, trailing around like a bilge rat, chary of mixing with Irish or English. He lost himself in his work, every now and again allowing himself to think of home and the girls, of little Seán Óg. He was a stoker, shovelling mountains of coal into furnaces that never stopped burning, one of many feeding the fire of war the world over. Sometimes Seán stared deep into the flames imagining it was the world itself, engulfed in wildfire. Things had been coming to a head with Barney for a while. It was fine when they were on land but once at sea things changed. They ran out of space. Most of the Irish lads just sucked up Barney's ways, or avoided him. Seán took a stand.

Bang. Another jab caught him, bursting the skin under his eye. Seán stepped back, circled Barney again, waited until he went for another jab, ducked and caught him with a quick one-two, breaking his nose with a fine, straight right. Barney bent double, blood gushing from his cracked nose. Seán moved in to finish him. Barney tried to step to the right but Seán was too quick, in with a left hook and then a pounding right-hander to the jaw. Barney sprawled out on the floor. The crowd went quiet. Seán paced the circle of men searching for eye contact. Heads dropped. None wanted a part of what Seán just dished out to Barney. The circle widened as men shuffled back, silent now when moments ago they had bayed for his blood

'Anyone else want a go?' he roared.

Nobody looked up.

'I spent years fighting you bastards. The best years of my life, sacrificed trying to win freedom for my country. I wasn't fighting the British in particular, it would have been the same if youse were Russians or Chinese or Germans. I would have done the same. We just wanted our country back. Now we have it back, and still I've ended up here working on a British ship to provide for my family. I'm done fighting. I just want to do my job and go home. If doing my job helps stop Hitler and keeps my family safe, then all the better, but I'm done fighting the British.'

A few heads lifted. Mostly boys. A line of scared Dannys looked up at him

'Countries aren't worth fighting for. Kings rise and fall, borders change as quickly as allegiances. I fight for my family, that's the only thing worth fighting for. There is to be no more fighting here, no more enemies down here. We are in this together, equals. The enemy is outside. Irish, English, Yank, black, white, yellow, wide-eyed, slanty-eyed, all the same to me, all trying to get home to our families. Now leave me in peace to do my work.' He returned to the furnace, picked up his shovel and drove it into the base of a hill of coal.

To cool his boiling blood, Seán holidayed his thoughts to his last time at home, in the summer. God, he was missing so much. Seán Óg was a toddler now, not a baby anymore. Neasa had blossomed, now a woman. She reminded him so much of Maeve when she was her age. He would have to watch her closely, there would be a lot of lads in the parish sniffing around soon. Bridget, what a wonder! Wisdom beyond her years, and she flying it inside in the convent in Skibbereen, top of her class. Her mother had some notion of her joining the nuns. What nonsense. You don't lock a mind like that inside a convent wall.

Men drifted back to their work. Barney had picked himself up off the ground. Someone had given him a rag for his nose. From the corner of his eye, Seán watched the Englishman's movements. He started his way, ambling up behind. Seán swivelled, shovel in hand, ready to land another blow, but Barney held his hand out.

'Good fight, guv. Same time tomorrow?' His grin displayed a new gap between his teeth.

Seán laughed and shook his hand heartily.

The Illustrious was prowling the Mediterranean, escorting merchant convoys and attacking positions in North Africa as well as Italy. Seán didn't know when he would see home again. His last homecoming, sporting his British Navy Uniform, caused quite a stir. He was greeted with wide-eyed stares, even open hostility. Some of the Irish at home saw their own kind joining the British forces as wrong, even traitorous. The Irish were neutral in the war, one of De Valera's more popular decisions. They had endured enough hardships without involvement in a war, a war they felt didn't concern them. The war was referred to as the emergency. Although the Irish government cooperated secretly with the allies, the German and Japanese embassies in Dublin remained open during the war and airmen from both the allies and the axis shot down over Ireland were interned as prisoners of war.

Let those in Union Hall's streets say what they like, he thought. No boat and no livelihood. Were they going to keep his family from becoming paupers?

The shovel picked up pace. Sweat dripped down Seán's forehead, down his nose, down his chin. His shift neared its end. He would fall asleep before his head hit the pillow. Deep, peaceful sleep. No dreams tormented him on board this ship. Thank God for that, he thought, but he knew they would come back. No man could do what he had done and not expect retribution. The worst was Kilmichael in 1921, lauded as one of their greatest victories. Truth be told, it was a massacre, in cold blood. They had waited, lying in roadside ditches to ambush a British convoy. Tom Barry lay prone on the road in a British uniform. The first lorry pulled up and Tom had casually launched a grenade into it as if throwing in a sliotar at the start of a hurling match. The rest of them started firing from close range, slaughtering all the men in the first truck, blood pouring from between the slats, glistening on the road like an abattoir's yard. The next truck pulled up. The British soldiers held up their hands in surrender. They killed them all, finishing them with revolvers and bayonets. In the aftermath, when the gun-smoke cleared and the blood lust and adrenalin subsided, men lined the claret-stained road, some retching, some crying, others still like statues, dazed, numb. Tom Barry marched them back into the hills, drilling them relentlessly for hours lest they dwelled on what they'd done. Seán always remembered the lad he had finished with his bayonet, the whites of his eyes brilliant against his sunburnt freckled skin. A tattered comic book peeked from under his tunic, the characters and antics sullied with blood.

These men were the lucky ones, surviving the horrors of the Somme and making it home. This was supposed to be an easy assignment, to keep the Paddies at bay in their own backyard. They weren't supposed to die in Ireland.

Neasa stood before the mirror running the ivory comb through her silken hair. Her father had bought the comb in Africa, and brought it home during the summer. He had been different with her then, she thought, when he was home. He had been surprised by how much she had changed in a year and a half.

'By God, you're a woman now,' he had said, over and over. 'We'll have to keep an eye on you. You're not a little girl anymore.'

Neasa suspected he would have preferred that she remained a little girl, and not become the young lady she was developing into. Yet he was the same as always with Bridget, picking her up, placing him on his knee and messing with her. Perhaps because Bridget was still flat-chested, with a childlike face, and her interest lay with books. She and Bridget shared nothing in common. A shame. It would be nice to talk to her sister of things, to confide in her about Paudie and to speak of her little crush on Fr Sullivan, how she knew nothing would ever come of it and that it was wrong but it was oh, so exciting all the same. And then there were the notes she'd been getting lately. Left with no one to speak to of these things, Neasa daydreamed. She, he, a nice little house in the city, nice clothes, cocktail parties and restaurants, just like in the magazines, and Fr Sullivan on her arm like Cary Grant in the movies.

There was a note left on her pillow when she came home. He must have been in her room, known she was out, must be watching her. The handwriting was gracious and lazy, the note unsigned but promising to make her his queen. Each note would tell her where the next note would be. She would set off, her heart in her mouth, all the time thrilled, a clandestine treasure hunt. One was left for her behind the grotto, the next in a little cove called Trá Na Wadla under a piece of driftwood, another behind a loose stone in the lookout. All were vague, giving no clues to who her mystery admirer was, but it was clear that he was close and saw her often. He would comment on a particular dress she wore, or of a certain way she fashioned her hair, or insert a quote from a movie she had recently seen above in Crowley's Hall. He had even mentioned who she had danced with one night at the patterns, and said how jealous he had been. Who could this mysterious man be? The notes were always on the same parchment paper and scented slightly, the scent vaguely familiar but she couldn't place it. She convinced herself that it was Fr Sullivan writing the letters. It made sense. Anonymity. How could he possibly reveal himself? They could never be together, so this was his way of getting close, getting close to the forbidden. Such a shame to have all this excitement and nobody to share it with, she thought. Who could she possibly tell? Her mother? No way. Neasa noticed her mother had a bit of a soft spot for Fr

Sullivan herself. But her mother's curiosity possessed a religious undertone. She saw the priest in a messianic light, his good looks reflecting his inner purity and grace. Neasa picked the flowery oriental frock her father had bought her and put on her boots and overcoat. She longed for the summer when she could wear her light frocks and dainty shoes again. Hardly any point in wearing a nice dress when you have to cover it up in a coarse old overcoat. She stuffed the latest note in her box under the bed with the rest of them. This was the most exciting note yet. He wanted to meet her. Tonight.

Paudie hopped from the back of the lorry giving a thumbs-up to the driver as thanks for the lift. He blew on his hands to warm them then rummaged through the pockets of his overcoat for a cigarette. He had been travelling since yesterday, taking the boat overnight to Cork and the bus to Skibbereen. He had hitched a lift out to Union Hall and, although his mind was troubled and he hadn't slept a wink since leaving London, he was glad to be home and close again to Neasa. He hated London and the months spent there. His family needed the money but he'd had enough. Work in the munitions factory had been monotonous and boring. He was extremely shy and awkward, conscious of his accent and country ways, everything so foreign to him. Most of the other workers in the factory were women, with all the men away at war. He was not used to speaking to females, especially those who dressed so differently and were so forward. They wore smart skirts and nylons, lipstick and perfume, and tight sweaters drawn over brassieres and pert breasts. They sniggered at him behind his back, and he reddened whenever one passed as much as a word his way. He had digs with an Irish woman in Enfield. She kept four other men as well as him. She was a severe woman, a war widow from the Great War.

A picture of the King George V hung on her wall and she

warned the men, 'You'll not be coming over here to this civilised country with your Fenian ways. I won't have any of that in this house and my poor husband looking down on us who died for the King.'

She castigated the men daily for what she called their effrontery to remain at home while every decent man in the country was fighting. But still, she took their money. The rent was cheap and the food good so Paudie put up with the woman's sullen ways. It was only for a half-hour a day during the dinner. Paudie took to going with the men to the pub in the evening. He had never had a drink before London and he found he quite enjoyed it, and after a while began to skip dinner completely as well as the woman's dour words, going straight to the pub after work. He would sit at the end of the bar and drink pints of bitter, spurning any advance or company, leering at the other Irish drinking themselves into a stupor and singing the same bawdy old songs every night before stumbling out the door on their way to dingy lodgings. He wasn't an excitable drunk or a messy drunk. After the first few pints it was nostalgia, thinking back to the days he and Neasa had spent walking around the West Cork countryside, their first kiss at the lookout, she kissing him back, tasting so sweet and good, the way she looked at him at first, so tender and compassionate. Another few pints and a deep melancholy would set in, his thoughts travelling to how she changed, still the walks and the kissing, her letting him touch her. But the look had changed. She was just going through the motions, pitying him, treating him like a child. She had something he wanted but there was nothing she wanted from him that he could trade. Another few pints and he would lust, memories of her soft breasts, the warmth between her legs, she stopping him there.

Always then, at the end of the night, the bar closing, asking for one more and being refused, resentment would set in on the walk home. The bitch! Remembering her face when he had told her he was leaving, and expecting and hoping for tears, for entreaties, he saw relief.

'It's for the best,' she had said. 'Good for your family. We'll write to each other and you can visit.'

He had written letter after letter, three or four letters a week, and no reply. He tormented himself with visons of her lying in the grass by the lookout, another boy with her, doing things to her, both of them laughing, she pulling out his letters and reading them aloud, mimicking his thick accent and awkwardness.

That was London.

Lynch's was open. He could do with a drink before he confronted her A little Dutch courage. Mrs Lynch was wiping the counter when he entered.

'If it isn't Paudie McCarthy himself,' she said. 'Jesus, you look like an undertaker or a priest in those dark cloths. Where are you coming from? I thought you were across the water working.'

'Era, I was but I had enough and packed it in.'

'Must have been terribly lonely over there, you poor thing. Your mother will be thrilled to see you.'

He looked at his reflection in the mirror behind the bar, dark rings under his eyes, his face gaunt, skin stretched tight over his cheek bones. He hardly recognised himself.

'I'll have a bottle of Wrastler, Mrs Lynch, please,' he said, looking away from the mirror. The unfamiliar face staring back made him uncomfortable.

'Wrastler, now is it? The last time you were in here you were drinking lemonade. 'Twas your father's funeral, may the Lord have mercy on his soul, poor man.'

He went for his pocket to pay.

'Now, now, that's on the house. 'Tisn't often one of our own comes home. 'Tis more often now they'd be going away.'

Paudie knew she'd be hoping his pockets were full of

sterling and that he'd be spending it all there.

'You know Seán next door is gone off with the British Navy?'

'Ya, I heard as much.'

'People got an awful land around here. I mean, of all people, 'twas a turn up for the books.'

''Twas, I suppose,' he said, not wanting to get drawn into it.

'He came down the street here during the summer in his sparkling navy uniform, not a bother on him nor care in the world. There was a lot of people upset. I mean, there's lots of Irish men in the British Army, but they keep it to themselves and they certainly wouldn't wear their uniform at home.'

'Era, it's just a uniform, a few bits of cloth stitched together. What's the big deal? It wasn't like people didn't know he was in the Navy. The whole village knew, so why were they surprised when they saw him in the uniform?'

'Well, they felt like he was rubbing their nose in it.'

Paudie's anger rose. He took a swig of his Wrastler. 'Who felt that?'

Seán had always looked after their family when his father was alive, splitting the takings from the fishing equally even though it was his boat, always standing up for what he believed in and not afraid of anybody. Oh if he could be half the man Seán was he would have no problems with Neasa.

'What right have any of those hypocrites to say what Seán should and should not do, most of them sitting on the fence when the country's future was being decided, happy enough to let Seán do their dirty work? Seán doesn't have to answer to any of them.'

'Ah, don't be getting angry now, Paudie. Nobody meant any offence. It was just they were surprised with Seán of all people, that's all.'

'Were they now? Were they surprised when you told

them that half the money Seán is earning is being sent home to you, to pay off the loan he owed on the boat that sank? You have no problem calling in that loan did you, for the full amount and all, even though you and your family have plenty to spare, and you're quite happy to accept English money to pay for it? Aren't you? It seems that some people can afford principles, others don't have that luxury. Did any of those people with their noses out of joint offer him work or help after his boat went down? Did anyone offer him work after all he done for Ireland, all the sacrifices? You can tell those people also that he still sends money to my mother every week, still feels responsible for us after my father's death, even though it was through no fault of his. Who else in this village turned to help us when the family had no income? So curse this village and their hypocritical principles. They can all go to hell, and as far as Seán is concerned he can walk down the main street in a fucking dress for all I care. That's his business!'

Paudie swallowed the last of his pint, wiped his mouth with his sleeve and banged his glass back down on the counter.

'Thanks for the drink,' he said and walked out. That amount of words hadn't flowed from his mouth in years and it felt good. He would have one more in Casey's, he thought. He wanted to check in the post office also to make sure his letters had been arriving, just in case, then he would go find Neasa.

Bridget arrived home from school in high spirits. Top marks in her English exam, her favourite subject. She had been entertaining notions lately of becoming a writer. Often on the way home on her bike she would describe scenes in her head. Today's scene had been a pleasure, it wrote itself, no need to reach for descriptions, the world the way it was then. There was a light January snow falling like ash. The frost spun an edge on everything and the hedgerows shone, sharp in the pale winter sun. The landscape was like something out of a book or a cover of a Christmas card. Smoke drifted straight up out of chimneys. Stone walls were topped with snow and looked like piles of iced puddings. Unusually, the Friesian cows blended into the landscape with their white patches and even the dung on the road attained a sparkle.

Her mother and Mary were in the sitting room with Seán Óg who was playing with a pair of his father's old fishing gloves. As happened two or three times every day, Bridget felt a pang of loss when she saw something belonging to her father. His massive boots standing in the cupboard under the stairs, the smell of his oilskins every morning when she took her coat off the hook beside them, the rattle of his tobacco tin as she put away the dishes in the evening.

'Where's Neasa?' Bridget asked.

'Oh, she's away off somewhere,' Maeve said. 'She's taken to long walks recently, comes back all rosy cheeked and wide-eyed. Does her good.'

'Neasa going for walks?' Bridget said. 'Doesn't sound like her.' She hadn't seen much of her sister lately but when she did, Neasa seemed like one privy to some tantalising secret sitting always on the tip of her tongue, pursing her lips against the temptation to spill it.

'Well, Bridget, how did your exam go?' Maeve asked.

'Top marks, Mammy.'

'Oh, well done, pet. I knew you'd do it.'

'Well done, girl,' Mary said. 'We're all so proud of you. You've your granny's brains for sure. She was always the smartest woman in the village, and smarter than all the men, too. I hear you're thinking of a vocation. They'd be lucky to have a girl like you.'

'Actually, I'm making other plans, Mary,' she said. 'I don't think convent life is for me.' The words flew from her mouth before she could rein them in.

Her mother stared. 'Now, Bridget, that's not what's been discussed. We have Father Sullivan arranging it all for you and the mother superior in Skibbereen said you'd make a fine nun.'

'That's all fine isn't it, but nobody thought to discuss it with me, did they? I'm not for a vocation and that's that. You can tell everyone what you like, but it will not—'

'How dare you speak to me like that, if your father—'

'My father will support me in this. I know what you're up to Mammy. You hope to have this all arranged before Daddy has a chance to stop it, but I'm not going to let that happen. If you keep on about it, I'll leave. I'm nearly seventeen now. I'll find a job in the city.'

Mary hastily excused herself.

'Bridget, darling, where has all this come from? I thought the life would suit you?'

'Suit me? Suit you more like.'

'What do you mean by that?'

'It's your guilt, not mine.'

'Guilt, what guilt? What are you talking about?'

'Oh, come on, I know what you are at. Where will I start?' Bridget stepped closer. 'You want to give me to the church to make up for Daddy. You feel guilty for loving a man like him. I saw the way you treated him before he left. You feel guilty that you never asked him about the things he has done, the people he killed. How could you lie there beside him every night and not ask?'

Maeve gasped. 'Bridget—'

'You allowed him to bottle it up over the years, pretended it wasn't there, pretended it never happened. You made it a dirty little secret and you made him the man he is now.'

'You know that's not true. How could you?'

Bridget wasn't for stopping. Her voice high-pitched, almost hysterical, seemed to belong to someone else. 'I remember the way ye used to be, the noises that came from your bed at night. How could we not? We were right next door, Neasa and I. We used to giggle and laugh and mimic you both. I know that stopped years ago. I know you pushed him away, took the spark out of your marriage. I saw him when you turned away from him when he would come in for a kiss. I saw the hurt look on his face, not understanding, then blaming himself, thinking that no woman could love a man who had done such bad things.'

Her mother wilted before her, wincing at each word spat from her mouth as if she was slapping with an open palm. Where was all this coming from? Bridget couldn't even remember thinking those thoughts, but there you are, they must have been there all along.

'And all this, why? For God, for Jesus? I see you praying night and day, trying to be the person you think God wants you to be, living as they tell you to live, they who wouldn't know living or loving if either bit them on the arse. I heard you praying aloud the night of the accident. You think God brought him back because you promised you'd change. Then I see you swooning over Father Sullivan. Is he your new ideal man? He isn't half the man my father is. You drove him away, reduced the man to thinking we are better served by him being away from us, not tainting us. My father is more saintly than any of your priests or nuns or bishops. At least he lives by his heart. Now you want to give me to the Church to further assuage your guilt. You think it will count in your salvation. Well I won't go.' Bridget turned, breathless and flushed, and stormed upstairs throwing herself on the bed leaving her mother below in tears on the settee.

Oh, poor Mammy, she thought, she didn't deserve any of that. She is only doing what she thinks is right, struggling along like the rest of us, shuffling in the darkness, hoping for light. Her anger dissolved as quickly as the snow that had fallen in her palm on the way home from school. She made her way downstairs to apologise. The front door was open, her mother gone, Seán Óg left sitting on the floor still playing with her father's glove.

Maeve headed to the village, her pace quickening in the cold. She had left without her coat. She just had to get out of the house, her mind was falling over itself. Something drew her to her old home, the post office. She needed to be surrounded by happy memories, up on her Daddy's lap again, listening to a story from one of his big books, spectacles down on his nose, his kind, brown speckled eyes looking up from the page.

'Another?' he would say, the answer of course always being yes and yes again until she fell asleep in his lap. Vague memories of being carried up the stairs, wrapped up tight, a kiss on the forehead and, 'Sleep well, a chuisle mo chroí' he would say.

Oh Lord, was Bridget right? Did I drive Seán away? Why didn't I ask him about the things he's done? Why didn't I let him share his burden? Did he try? Did I change the subject, steering his thoughts elsewhere, because I didn't want to know, because I didn't want to be part of it? Yes! I let him find solace in drink, let him go up to the old *cillín* and wail at the moon instead of wailing in my arms. I wanted him to take the burden for all of us. Did I resent him for the split with my parents when all the time I could have resolved it? Did I blame him for my absence at my father's death? Have I heaped all my guilt on Seán and now doing the same with Bridget? And now who can I turn to? She's right about Fr Sullivan. She is. How could she see things so clearly? You know you have dreams in the night about him, dreams you shouldn't have. You forget them in the morning, push them aside, but you know deep down what they are.

She went in through the front door of the post office, shivering now with the cold, arms folded over her chest.

Kitty was behind the counter. 'Lord save us. You look like you've seen a ghost. Are you alright, Maeve?'

'Can I come in, Kitty? Inside I mean, into Mam's old room. I just … I mean I …' Maeve started sobbing.

'Oh, you poor thing. Come on in. We'll get you warmed

135

by the fire. What in God's name happened to you at all?'

Walking into the old room was like a kindly embrace from a forsaken friend. She had been here for the funeral but noticed nothing in her grief. Now she felt her way around the room, her eyes closed tight, stirring up old memories with touch, spines of books her father would have read to soothe her, tracing her fingertips on the worn skin of her mother's chair as if caressing the woman herself. Her fingers rested on an old photo frame, her eyes opened to the faded image, her father sitting in his chair, her mother behind, hand on his shoulder, Maeve sitting proudly on her father's lap. She longed to be that girl again. That girl was someone else, someone whole. She had lost the right to be that girl, gazing out from the photo into the future. Now she was just a vessel carrying around all the bits that had been broken inside her since, everything rattling in the emptiness, nothing fitting. For a long time she had ignored the rattle. The day would soon come when she might be re-united with her parents, but she would have to meet her maker first. She needed to be whole again, to put things right. She had hoped she was going about it the right way. Now she wasn't so sure.

Kitty came out with a cup of tea in one hand, a bottle of brandy in the other. 'Would you like a drop in your tea, love?'

'I will since it's going, if you have a drop yourself.' Maeve didn't know Kitty that well. She had heard Kitty once was a great old character, full of the joys of life, running around organising church dances, matchmaking at the patterns, the first to dive into the sea of a summer. Then she was besotted with a local lad, who soon became her fiancée. He had run off for no apparent reason a week before the wedding and she never heard from him again. She had changed after that, people said, became bitter. The fun went out of her.

'This place is much the way I remember it. You haven't changed much of it.'

'Era, what would I be doing with it at this hour of my

life. Anyway, I never feel as if it's my home, always feel I'm living in someone else's house. I'm terrified that if I move anything your mother, God rest her soul, would appear out of nowhere to berate me.'

Maeve laughed, surprising herself, the brandy and the familiar surrounds relaxing her that little bit. There had been a happiness here as a child, a happiness she had never regained. Just being here again made it seem possible once more.

'Truth be told, I miss the woman a lot. Don't get me wrong, she was no angel and not easy to live with, but she was kind to me in her own way. The house is lonely without her.'

'What was she like in the last years?'

Kitty didn't answer straight away. Maeve sat there feeling foolish, knowing she was in Kitty's power, waiting to be granted the words, her heart aching from having to ask a near stranger.

'Content. She loved Bridget visiting, really looked forward to that. The two of them would chat for hours, Bridget on the floor looking up at the old woman, highfalutin stuff. I couldn't make head nor tail of most of what they'd be on about, not that I'd be listening of course,' she added all too quickly, her eyebrows arching, her chin lifting, 'as I had plenty to be doing myself.'

'I'm glad Bridget got to know her. When I hear her talk I sense my mother's presence, like she passed through the child and left some of herself behind.'

The bell in the post office rang. Kitty excused herself. Maeve sipped on her tea, laced with so much brandy you could trod horses across it, and listened to the conversation drifting in from the post office.

'Ah, Paudie boy. Is it yourself? You're home to us again. The wanderer returns,' said Kitty.

'I want to know about the letters,' Paudie said, his words slurred.

'What letters, lad?' said Kitty.

'The letters I sent home to Neasa,' he spat.

'What about them?'

'Did she get them? Were they delivered? Was there any problem with the post?'

'As far as I know, she did. Two or three letters a week, wasn't it?'

'I suppose ye all had a good laugh over them, didn't ye? I suppose ye all think I'm the right fuckin' eejit, isn't that it? Well, fuck ye all, and that little bitch.' He stormed out.

Kitty hurried back into Maeve. 'Did you hear that?'

'I did,' said Maeve. 'Was that Paudie?'

'Twas indeed, he's home and he's drunk and wanting to know about the letters he sent to Neasa. He's in a nasty mood and I'd say heading to find Neasa as we speak. You'd better go and warn her.'

Maeve went for the door.

'Wait. Here, take this coat. It's freezing. It belonged to your mother anyway.'

But Maeve was in a hurry. 'Thanks for the tea.'

'Anytime,' Kitty shouted. 'I'm always here. You call around anytime at all.'

What a strange woman, Kitty thought, as she watched Alice's daughter tear up the road, her skirt and hair billowing in the wind, but I suppose she's had her own share of it down through the years. It can't have been easy married to West Cork's most notorious Fenian, his only family left the ghost of his brother haunting the woods behind them. All those years not talking to her own parents, both of them cold in the ground before she had a chance to right it. Turning up like that then out of the blue, no coat and perished with the cold.

'If you ask me, the whole lot of that crowd are a bit

touched. Your man in the Royal Navy, a Fenian one minute, parading down the street in his British uniform the next. Your wan Neasa thinks she's Audrey Hepburn with her magazines and typing lessons with that movie star priest above in the parochial house. That fella has a wandering eye, that priest. And then the other one, Bridget, head stuck in books, away with the fairies most of the time,' she said to no one.

The bell in the post office rang out again. She brought the cups to the sink and put the brandy back on the dresser before she went out to see who it was. She walked in behind the counter, still mumbling away to herself. With all the commotion she'd forgotten to light the lamp, the post office was in near darkness. When she looked up, there was a man standing there in the gloom, dressed all in black, his palms flat on the counter, a cigarette standing erect from between two fingers, the skin of his hands scaled and yellow. There were two dark holes where his eyes should have been, a rope hung in a loose noose around his neck. An icy paroxysm of dread coursed through her veins. She felt as if she were naked in front of him, her flesh licked all over by a cold reptilic tongue. She folded her hands over her bosom, lowering her head, closing her eyes, her only defence willing him away with all her being. She didn't know how long she stood there, not moving, not looking up. Tears weeping from her shut eye-lids fell in drops to the floor like blood seeping from a wound stitched shut.

In time the bell dinged and she felt the breeze from the street, before the door closed again. Still she couldn't lift her neck, or open her eyes, for fear it was a trick. When at last she summoned the courage, the man was gone. A stench replaced his presence, the smell of decaying flesh, the smell that wafts over the wall of a knacker's yard. She looked down at the counter where his hands had rested, the imprints of his bony fingers were singed into the wood. She rushed to the door, vying frantically with the lock before sliding to the floor, overcome with exhaustion and shame.

Bridget brought Seán Óg upstairs. She milled around her room, putting away her books and study things. Her mind busied like her hands, trying to catch up with itself, her hindsight pulling out of her. Sometimes she could be too honest, letting words fly before she'd time to run them through her conscience. She had spoken the truth to her mother but there were other ways she could have spilled it without hurting her so.

Seán Óg played under the bed, throwing pieces of loose paper from the shadows on the floor. Letters, letters written in a strange hand. She began to read one:

I saw you last night at the patterns, dancing a jig with the boy of the Murphys. I envied his hands around you. Did you know I'd be watching? Your hair was free and loose on the wind, your face flushed in the moonlight, it seemed that you alone moved with the music, that the music existed only for you, everyone else melted into the ditches and hedgerows and when the music stopped you turned in my direction and looked to the sky above me, drinking in the stars, your long slender neck arched, like a lone swan on a dark lake, a child of Lir, all the hungry eyes on the crossroads devoured you and mine no less, but you, you just watched a falling star and waited for the music to strike up again. I knew then that I would make you my queen.

Bridget reached for another, and another, each time the letter telling her where the next letter would be, each time the pick-up location different, each time the lines expressing more longing, more urgency, a piece by a composer climbing to a crescendo. The last one, dated today, simply said:

Trá Na Wadla at sunset, it's time for us to be together.

Oh, Neasa, you fool! You haven't gone there?

So these were her sister's walks. This was the secret dancing on her sister's tongue. If only Neasa had shared. Bridget promised her father she'd look after her younger sister. She pulled on her coat and boots, opening the door and stepping outside into the dusk. She looked towards the outline of the woods, a foreboding hung heavy over her as she traced her sister's steps to Trá Na Wadla.

'Neasa, Bridget, anyone here?' Maeve came through the door in a flurry. 'Is there anybody here?' Her call was swallowed by the darkness of the empty house. She turned to head back out the door when she met Mary coming against her, Seán Óg in her hands.

'Where's Bridget? Have you seen Neasa?' Maeve was panicked.

'Bridget said she was just going out for a walk, so not to worry. I saw Neasa go out about half an hour ago with her coat. Looked like she was going for a walk, too. Maeve I don't think—'

'You never told me Paudie was coming home.'

'I didn't know myself until a few minutes ago. He was just here, blind drunk, raving about Neasa. When he didn't find her he said something about heading to the lookout. That's where they used to go courting, I think. We'd best send someone after him. I'm worried what he'll do. He was raving.'

'I'll go for Father Sullivan. He'll know what to do.'

Maeve didn't stop until she reached the parochial house. She ran right into Fr Sullivan who was coming out the gate and onto the road. His cap was down over his face and his head bowed. She hardly recognised him in the darkness.

'Is it yourself, Father?'

'Maeve, is that you? What in God's name has you in such a hurry?'

Out of breath she explained to Fr Sullivan what had happened.

'I'll run up there after him and make sure nothing happens.'

'You've a light and all with you, Father,' Maeve said, noticing the paraffin lamp hanging by his side. 'Thanks so much for going to all the trouble.'

'Don't worry, Maeve. Paudie's a good lad. Hopefully he's away somewhere sleeping it off. He'll be red-faced tomorrow over all this.'

The stillness of the forest unnerved Bridget. The long, straight tree trunks loomed tall and close, her breath loud in her ears and billowing out in front of her like pipe smoke. Dusk was coming and the tide below caught its breath sighing gently to itself. Trá Na Wadla was a little cove eaten out of the coast, a bite taken from the land by a hungry sea monster. It was like a cave with a collapsed roof, overhung by rock on all sides, accessible only through thick scrub and a trek down a steep old smugglers' path.

Bridget had never been there and only knew of it through her grandmother's stories.

'Steer clear of it,' she'd said. 'At night time the sluagh sidhe come out to dance. You can hear their music coming over the fields, drifting out on the sea breeze. You'll drink the harmonies in, like honey poured down your throat, till you were drawn down and drowned in the melody. Many over the years were tempted by the music and mesmerised, caught in the net of the notes, following them to the other world, never to be seen again, taken back underground by the sluagh sidhe.'

The sluagh sidhe were the underground folk, the first people of Ireland, who had retreated below thousands of years gone. Bridget felt their presence tonight, as she stepped over the mounds beneath her feet, their existence just a whisper among

142

the leaves of the ancient forest. She remembered the wail of Clíona's Wave that came from Trá Na Wadla and hoped the banshee wasn't out tonight. No music hung in the air, just her footsteps snapping twigs like brittle bones. A sliver of moon above the water gave over a little light. She approached along a tight path, picking her way carefully through the narrow scrub until the steep shingle beach came into view. There was a dull sheen from the pebbles and cobbles in the moonlight as the ocean flowed in among them, worrying them. They cackled, then hissed as the tide withdrew. It was deserted tonight, no sign of her sister, no sign of the sluagh sidhe, just a lonely cove drinking from the dark sea.

She caught movement to her side as she came up from the beach. Someone was walking through the woods, tree trunks swathed in lamp-light. The shape of a man in dark clothing seemed to float through the forest, a lantern bobbing along in front, his shadow dancing behind. She cursed her grandmother for all her stories about the sluagh sidhe, tales about jack-o-lanterns and *púcas* who wandered the land leading travellers astray. She hesitated, made to follow, checked herself again. Then the light was gone, swallowed up by the woods, no wiser to the hand that held it and loathed to find out. Bridget nonetheless found herself scurrying off in its wake.

The cove had been deserted when Neasa found it. She'd stood on the beach her back to the ocean, facing the path, waiting for her admirer to reveal himself. She had expected him to be there, waiting for her, waiting in eagerness. The sun had set over the ocean and the sea had washed in the ink of night. Still she stood, waiting impatiently, expectantly. She suddenly recalled the last time she was there. There had been a note, left under a large piece of driftwood sitting atop a berm of stones beyond the rotting seaweed of the waterline. She clamoured over the shingle and reached behind and sure enough, there was a note.

I wanted to make sure you'd come on your own, that nobody would see us together. This night is to be ours alone. I'm waiting for you at the lookout. I know you'll come.

A ball of anticipation shivered inside, sending delicious tingles up Neasa's back and neck. It was like some tantalising movie plot, all twists and turns and she was only too happy to play the leading role. She always guessed the endings at the flicks in Crowley's Hall, always knew that things would come good, that the two were meant for each other, and would be together. She was sure the hand behind those letters was Fr Conor. He'd told her to use his first name. None of the boys in the village could write like that, none of them could thrill her like this. She moved like a fawn, picking her way gingerly through the branches and brambles, the darkness negated by the light she felt inside. The trees thinned about her and the lookout came into view perched up on the headland, a circular stone hut bathed in moonlight, squatting like a jilted lover gazing forlornly out over the ocean. The eyes of the lookout took in the whole coastline from Galley Head in the north to the Stags in the south. Once the mighty chieftains scanned the seas from here, watching for the Viking longships that struck fear into the hearts of their clans-people. Other times it was nefarious smugglers who signalled to their brethren from the clifftop or cut-throat wreckers guiding ships to their doom on the rocks below, murdering the sailors and stealing their cargo.

Now it sat forgotten and neglected, its grey stones piled like a funeral cairn on the clifftop, waiting to shelter the odd courting couple seeking refuge from the prying eyes and wagging tongues of the village. There wasn't a more beautiful spot to be on a fine day, but tonight it was eerie. There didn't seem to be any movement or light. She circled around it. Nobody. She looked back down towards the woods. Nothing stirred. It was still and calm and quiet, as if the world slumbered, resting under the cover of night. She approached the doorway of the lookout and peered inside. Moonlight shone through the windows opposite facing the sea. She took another step in.

'Is there anybody here?'

Nothing. It took a few moments for her eyes to adjust to the gloom. There in the corner, shrouded in shadow, was the outline of a man dressed in black, his back to her, facing the wall, smoke wafting over his shoulder.

'Father Conor,' she whispered, her voice wavering. 'Father, is that you?'

Shadows climbed the walls inside the lookout. Bridget stepped warily towards the door. A cruel laugh rang out, mocking the silence of her approach. She heard a struggle, someone crying out.

'No, please, not like this, not here, please.' It was Neasa

She was on the ground, in the corner, a man thrusting himself into her, the frock her father had bought her hitched up around her waist, the pale flesh of her legs white in the gloom. Her protests were muffled under the man's hand. Bridget opened her mouth to scream but it caught in her throat like a briar. She went to throw herself at him, to pull him off her sister, but something held her rooted to the spot, she was caught by some force, framed in the doorway, her heart running away with itself in her chest, beating madly in her ears. The man wanted her there, held her there to watch, to witness, as if he were some demon of the night, an incubus having his way, she tried to discern who he was but his form kept changing, one moment the figure of a dark broad-backed man, the next a pale-skinned youth, an old man with sagging flesh. It went on and on, a carousel of beings between her legs.

When it was over, the man, the thing, rose deliberately and buttoned himself up. She felt he knew she was there, felt he was mocking her, taunting her with his nonchalance, knowing she was powerless. The air was rank with a putrefying stink.

He started to turn. She ran, she didn't want to see who he was, what he was. She couldn't face him. She dashed rabidly through the forest like a hunted deer, a band of Fianna running her down. She tripped, grazing her face. Flailing madly she got back to her feet, imagining his icy breath on her neck, his cold fingers on her midriff, his mocking laughter ringing in her ears.

She didn't stop until she reached her house, bursting through the front door and straight into her mother.

'Bridget, Bridget, what's the matter?'

She threw her arms around her and squeezed her tight.

'Where have you been? Oh my God. Look at you, your face all scratched. What's wrong?'

'Oh Mammy, Mammy, Neasa, Neasa …'

'It's okay, pet. It's okay. Slow down, slow down, deep breaths. Now what's the matter?'

Oh God, what do I say? How can I tell her what I saw? How can I tell her I saw it all and did nothing and then ran and left Neasa under that thing, left her to that violence? Bridget broke down crying, her body shaking. Maeve put her arms around her, holding her tight.

'Hello, anyone home?' Fr Sullivan appeared at the door, the lantern hung from his hand.

Neasa was standing behind him. Was she waiting to be asked into her own home? The priest's overcoat was draped around her, sleeves hanging limp down her sides. She seemed to be staring at something beyond them like a ghost interrupted in haunting, as if she'd stepped in from another world, and now just wanted to step back out. Why? Why silent? Did I imagine it all? Am I going mad? How can she just stand there?

146

'Neasa—'

'Oh, Neasa,' said Maeve. 'Thank God. Any sign of Paudie in your travels?'

They were met by a fixed stare from a blood-drained face.

'No sign,' said Fr Sullivan. 'I found Neasa walking through the woods like a waif. She gave me a right fright, thought she was a banshee at first.'

'Is she okay? Did she come across Paudie?' said Maeve.

'She seems to have gotten a fright alright. Something has her out of sorts, but she hasn't said a word to me.'

'Are you alright, Neasa? Everything alright?' their mother asked.

'She'd no coat on and she was shivering with the cold, seemed to be lost.' said Fr Sullivan.

'Well thanks for bringing her back safe and sound,' said Maeve. 'Bridget was just in before you. She came running in the door awful upset. I couldn't make head nor tail out of what she was saying. Something tells me that Paudie has a lot to answer for.'

Neasa turned her head slowly looking at Bridget as if remembering something. Fr Sullivan was looking at her, too. She averted her eyes. Does she know I saw her? How could she? Why is she so calm?

'Well that's it then,' said Fr Sullivan. 'Your girls are home safe. No harm done it seems. I'll be off. I have the stations abroad in Skahane tomorrow. Need to set up for them.'

'Will you call next door to Mary, see about Paudie. If he hasn't turned up yet, she'll be at her wits end.'

'Of course. You look after your two and we'll find Paudie.'

'I will, Father, thanks. We've all had a hard time of it tonight.' She threw her eyes to heaven. 'A good sleep for all will do us the world of good.'

147

Neasa walked wanly towards the stairs, dragging her feet. Her mother called after her, but she continued trance-like up to her room.

Maeve turned to Bridget.

'What's going on? Something is happening here. There is something wrong, I can feel it. What were you going to tell me?'

Bridget hesitated, dropping her head to the floor as if looking down there for words. She searched for the right ones then realised there weren't any, they weren't there and never would be.

That night Bridget lay in the bed she shared with Neasa, the covers pulled right up to her chin, masts on the boats ringing out in the wind below on the pier. She stared at the cracks in the ceiling, she didn't want to close her eyes. Sleep wouldn't come to her tonight. Not a word had passed between the sisters.

Neasa was curled up in a ball. Her body shuddered now and again, just as it did when she sobbed before finding sleep. Regret fenced with reason in Bridget's mind. She thought she would go insane. Her temples throbbed, her brain burned. She didn't know what to do, or feel or think, she just felt numb and useless and guilty. What was it that held her back? What will we do now? Who was that man, those men, that thing? So familiar. Something familiar. Something from the past. What happens now? Daddy would know what to do. Mammy isn't able for this, she won't understand. She got up out of the bed, shivering in the night air. She sat on the windowsill a long time wondering what to write.

Maeve was up early. Seán Óg had a restless night and she hadn't had much sleep. She put on the kettle and cut some bread for the breakfast and some for Bridget's lunch. There was no stir out of the two girls, probably tired after all the commotion yesterday, she thought. Bridget's outburst, Paudie home looking for Neasa, and both of them out in those woods in the dark last night. Something is going on, she thought. Paudie had upset them. She'd have words with Mary about him. She resolved to have a chat with Bridget this morning and clear the air. There was a good deal of truth in what she had said yesterday, and if her daughter genuinely didn't want to become a nun, then she'd leave it at that.

The time was ticking and Bridget was going to be late for school, and Neasa late for her typing lessons. Maeve found Neasa bunched up in the bed facing the wall, and Bridget asleep on the windowsill like an angel housed in a grotto, a letter in her hand. Maeve eased the piece of paper free of Bridget's fingers.

Dear Daddy, We need you to come home, please. Come home as soon as you can. All my love. Bridget.

'Oh, you poor thing,' Maeve said, gently shaking her.

Bridget woke with a start, she looked up at her with surprise.

'Do you want to speak of this letter?'

Bridget started crying and put her arms around her mother, squeezing her tight.

'It's okay, sweetheart. It's okay. I know what's wrong and I'm going to go right up to Father Sullivan's this morning and sort it all out. Don't you worry.'

'You are?'

'You think I'm going to force you into a convent. I'll tell Father Sullivan to forget the whole thing and I'll write to the Mother Superior and tell her the same. How's that?'

Bridget just nodded.

When Maeve got back from Fr Sullivan's, Neasa was still in bed. The priest had seemed surprised to see her again so soon, standoffish. Maybe I shouldn't have called unannounced and so early, she thought. She had said her piece, and he had taken it well, even seemed a bit relieved.

'Wouldn't want to force anyone into doing something they didn't want,' he'd said. 'Is Neasa coming up for her lesson later? She's getting on well you know. We'll make a secretary out of her in no time.'

'I don't know. She went straight to bed last night and was still there as I was leaving. She really enjoys the lessons though, so we'll see later what way she is.'

Maeve brought Seán Óg to her breast and he latched on feeding hungrily. She looked down into the blue eyes looking up at her. Her tears fell on his face. She didn't know what well the tears were drawn from. Was it regret, loneliness, helplessness, wistfulness? Sometimes things just build up inside and need to be expelled, like sweating or sneezing or bleeding. She thought no more on it.

Maeve had enjoyed the visit to the post office yesterday, just being back in the house was a panacea, the once familiar surrounds like drinking deep from a goblet of some nostalgic elixir. She found Kitty, who was the gatekeeper of this nostrum, both hospitable and good-natured towards her. Kitty suggested she visit again, anytime, and Maeve thought she might take her up on the offer. She couldn't help feeling Kitty revelled in being gatekeeper just a little bit. She'd fed her titbits of information, but wasn't forthcoming with them. She'd waited for Maeve to ask and left her hanging awhile before answering, doling out crumbs from her mother's last years, holding some back, aware how valuable they were to Maeve. But Maeve hardly ever left the house anymore, and had very few she could call friends in the village. Mary next door was the only good friend, but she was too close to home, especially now that Paudie was making a nuisance of himself with her girls. That was the thing about being an only child. She didn't need friends growing up. She'd got all she needed from her parents. They'd been a unit, an island, self-sufficient until Seán came along, then he took over. Now she had nobody, they were all gone from her and she was like a child left behind after an excursion. She sat down to write a letter to Seán, a proper letter, not just the mundane clichés that her letters took the form of lately. She wrote to him from the heart, telling him how much she truly missed him, how much she wanted him, like before, asking him to come home, so that the five of them could be together again. The money didn't matter. He'd find something around here if he really tried. A man like Seán wouldn't be kept down. She put plenty of spice in the letter, telling him what she would do to him in their bed. It must be lonely over there on that boat, not a sight of a woman for months. Must be hard for a man like Seán.

She popped the letter into the post box herself to ensure Kitty's eyes didn't wander.

The birds woke Paudie, chattering and chirping like the women he worked with in the factory, carrying on with the business of the morning, disregarding him completely. He winced, his head caught in a whiskey induced vice, and he squinted through the pain. Where the fuck am I? Charily, he picked himself up off the cold earth, his clothes damp, body aching. An empty shoulder of Powers fell from his lap, smashing on the ground. The birds scattered, deserting their perches as if the elevenses bell had rang, leaving Paudie to the stillness of the frosted morning. The walls of an old ruin teetered over him, the roof missing in places, the winter sun streaming through the gaps, crows cawing in the high branches outside. He stepped to the rickety door, leant on the splintered frame, and spotted the *cillín*. He was in the old witch's cottage. How the fuck did I end up here?

Was it only yesterday he'd bounced along the road from Skibbereen on the back of a lorry, optimism rattling in his chest, shillings tingling in his pocket? Getting home was the goal, getting close to her again. He hadn't pencilled in a plan after that. What had he expected? Brass bands and dancing in the street? Neasa in her best frock at the bottom of Doctor's Hill holding up her skirt by the hem inviting him in?

The lorry ride was the zenith of his trajectory home, waking up in the witch's ruin the nadir, the memory of what happened in between like a ring dropped in a muddy pond. He blindly fished around for it longing for the familiarity to fit again. When he couldn't find it, dread began to pick at him from the wings. Oh Jesus, what did I do? With the whiskey anything was possible. I could have done anything. He knew he went looking for Neasa. Did I find her? Did I ruin everything?

He crouched back down in the corner of the ruin, his head in his hands, squeezing his temples trying to conjure a memory, anything, a flashback, a snippet, a clue. After the run-in with Kitty Collins all was black and silent. He'd stepped out of the post office into nothingness. He felt vile and worthless as if he'd been used, eaten up by the whiskey, his desires discarded. His despair only made him long for Neasa all the more. He could almost smell her soapy skin, taste the base of her neck, feel the softness of her milky white thigh. He reached into his pants calling up Neasa's image, his fantasies rushing his brain like an opiate, writhing himself into a frenzied longing until he had relief.

He tore up some dock leaves and cleaned himself up while considering his next move. His mother might have heard something, might be able to help him piece things together. He'd call on her first and then call on Neasa. Last night's clouds were migrating slowly across the sky, patchy pastures of blue opening up in their wake. Maybe all was not lost.

Bridget couldn't focus on her lessons, the ink swam on the page.

She gazed out to the bustle and business of the town. Bicycles and carts trundled by, neighbours stopped for a chat on the street volleying words back and forth as if a net sat between them and an audience around. A woman across the road leant wearily against her doorjamb, a jam-jar of steaming tea in her hand, ignoring for a moment the mill of children that pulled out of her skirts. Another violently beat a mat onto the path like it was a love rival at her mercy. She wondered about them, these strangers. What happened when the doors closed behind them, what regrets, fears, desires raptured them in the night? Was everyone a stranger now? Did everyone have ravenous secrets with curved beaks that pecked at them, regrets perched on their shoulders, digging their talons in so you wouldn't forget they were there? Perhaps not. Perhaps she was the only one. She sat, eyes downcast, arms folded across her chest as if nesting her secret under her top, something shameful she cradled.

The teacher droned on. Bridget heard the words but they fell into an empty space. The bell sounded, and soon she was pedalling away from town, the hustle and noise of the streets gradually giving way to the softer soundtrack of the rural dusk. A blackbird alighted from a roadside hawthorn and circled Bridget, then flew out in front leading the way. Bridget lowered her head, eyes on the road, thoughts with Neasa. She passed the landscape by where once she'd filled pages in her head with the journey's prose. If only her granny was still with her, she'd know what to do. How long would it take the letter to reach her father? She'd posted it this morning. And what of the distance between them? If he knew something had happened, he'd break borders, bend laws if he had to. She'd only written him two short lines. That's all it would take. He would come home. He would fix it. He was their only hope. How wrong her mother had got it this morning.

Bridget fed herself with the reel of yesterday's events. In slow motion she spooled them over and over in her head. Why had she been so powerless, unable to intervene, standing there like a helpless child letting those things happen to her little sister, and then running, as if she had some part to play in it, as if she was a co-conspirator? She hadn't said a word to Neasa last night, had left her suffering in the dark, sobbing in her sleep. She could have touched her, reached over and put her arms around her, told her everything was going to be alright.

It was dark when Bridget free-wheeled down the hill into Union Hall. She came out from under a canopy of trees on the hill and the sky opened up, blanketed with a frosting of stars. Again she thought of her father. Wherever he was in the world it was the same sky they looked at, the same stars. She noticed the blackbird was still with her, a sheen on its feathers distinguishing it from the darkness of the world. On they travelled.

Neasa sat at the kitchen table. Her mother sat on the settle nursing Seán Óg. Neasa was still in her nightclothes, her hands wrapped around a hot mug of tea. She looked up at Bridget when she walked in, but there was nothing in the hollow gaze, the same vacant stare as if last night's unwanted loving had poked out her insides. She hadn't bothered to dress, her hair fell dank around her face. It wasn't like Neasa. Bridget looked away.

'Your sister's still a bit under the weather this morning,' Maeve said. 'How are you feeling yourself?'

'Okay, Mammy.'

'I think there could be a tummy bug going around. She won't eat a bit and was shivering when I went to get her up. She's only out of the bed now. How was school today?'

'Fine. Exams are coming up soon, so I've a lot of study to do. I need somewhere quiet to concentrate,' Bridget said with a touch of irritation, though the tetchiness had naught to do with noise and study. 'I can't get anything done in this house.'

'Well, now, I was only over in the post office this morning and I got talking with Kitty Collins. I was telling her about your exams coming up and all the study you needed doing and she said you could go over there after school if you like and study away there to your heart's content, nobody to disturb you.'

'That would be good, Mammy.' Bridget couldn't look at Neasa. She needed to be somewhere else so she could think.

Just then, there was a knock at the door. Maeve went out to get it.

'It's Paudie, Neasa,' Maeve said. 'I gave him a good telling off about last night, but he doesn't remember a thing, do you want to see him?'

Bridget thought she saw a flash of panic behind the vacant stare.

'I don't want to see him. Tell him to go away.' Neasa's voice was throaty.

'Maybe it's best to see him, patch things up, or better still give him a piece of your mind and his marching orders while you're at it,' said Maeve.

'I don't want to see him. Tell him to leave me alone.'

'Okay, up to you. I'll tell him to come back later or tomorrow,' said Maeve.

'I don't want to see him again ever. Tell him to go away back to England and never come back.'

'My girl, what did that fella do? Did he hurt you, scare you? I'll go out to him now this minute and run him.'

Bridget felt nauseous. Was it Paudie up in the lookout last night? He had been out looking for Neasa. The laugh had been familiar and the movements, but the whole scene had been dreamlike. She felt she knew who it was but couldn't quite place him. Was it someone from the village, the school, someone she'd seen with her father, a travelling tinker, the priest? She tried to tack a face onto the familiarity but couldn't. She ran through the images from last night. Terror had seized her, she couldn't trust her eyes, they'd played tricks on her, she'd seen things that weren't real.

'I'll go, Mam,' Bridget said.

Paudie was smoking a cigarette. He turned and Bridget

155

saw the hope drop from his face. He had been expecting Neasa, had obviously rehearsed the smile, the feigning of nonchalance.

'Oh. Hi, Bridget,' he said, downtrodden. 'Neasa not feeling the best then?'

'She's in bed asleep, Paudie. Doesn't want to see you. Best to leave it.'

London hadn't been kind to Paudie. He was so thin, face drawn and worry-worn. It was obvious he hadn't been looking after himself. She left him standing there and closed the door. That fella has his demons, she thought.

'He's gone,' Bridget said.

'God, he looks terrible doesn't he?' said Maeve. 'Some of these lads let themselves go when they leave home, no mother looking after them. Let's hope you never have to take the boat,' she said to Seán Óg, playing on the floor.

'I'm going to get my things together and go up to the post office to study,' Bridget said.

'Bridget wait!' Her mother followed her into the hall. 'Is there something wrong, something the matter?'

'Just need some peace and quiet.'

'What about Neasa? She won't say a word about last night. You would tell me, wouldn't you if there was anything wrong?'

Bridget nodded.

'I wrote to your father today. I asked him to come home, told him we wanted him home. You were right in what you said the other day, I've a lot to answer for, I'm sorry.'

'I wrote to him, too. Let's hope he gets them soon.'

Seán rested on the deck of the Illustrious, his shirt open letting the balmy night breeze caress his tired muscles. They were somewhere in the Indian Ocean. Seán didn't know where, nor did he know where they were going or what their mission was when they got there. The top brass didn't share battle plans with the stokers. The sea was still his schoolmistress. Out here there were more colours, more smells, more sounds. Each day she was reaching into her repertoire anew, each day painting strokes from a new palate. He picked out the constellations in the sky: Pegasus, Orion, the Plough. They seemed to float over the ocean. He felt he could almost reach out and touch them. Back in West Cork, when he was on the run, he used to lie down in fields and look at the same stars, forgetting where he was and what he was doing, enjoying the insignificance they lent him for a moment. In his hand were two letters. One from Maeve. He read that first and how it had warmed his heart and stirred his loins. She wanted him to come home, wanted him again. Oh he could almost smell her heat and her hot breath panting on his neck. He nearly jumped off the bow. The other, from Bridget, stopped his heart, the fright it gave him.

Dear Daddy, We need you to come home, please. Come home as soon as you can.

He sprung to his feet, paced the deck. What a strange letter, only the two lines written in Bridget's florid hand. He stopped, checked the blurred postmark. Jesus! Posted three months ago, both letters on the same day. He paced again. What had happened? What was so bad that she couldn't even write it down, just a desperate entreaty for him to come home? The worry walked with him, building as he quickened his step. Up and down the deck he stomped, other sailors looking at him curiously. Already he was back in Union Hall running down the street to Kilbeg, bursting through the door to find them. I have to get home! He stopped, took in his surroundings as if noticing them for the first time. Damn this ship! The massive ship seemed tiny. He was trapped. He stared out over the vast ocean, once his freedom, now it hemmed him in. Something was wrong with his girls. Halfway around the world and he could do nothing about it. He made his way to his commanding officer's quarters, the letters held aloft in his hand.

He barked at the guard, 'Urgent message. I must see Sgt Stilton at once.'

The guard went to check on the CO and came back to usher him in. The CO was a third-generation naval officer from Lancashire. He knew of Seán, had heard of his now-infamous fight with Barney, had heard also of Seán's bravery when they were attacked by bombers east of Sicily back in January. They lost many men that night and suffered major damage. The sickbay and wardroom was set ablaze. Seán and Barney had come up from below deck, and under heavy fire had helped evacuate the sick men. They had saved many men that night. Seán and Barney had become firm friends. All the men below deck looked up to them. He had also heard a rumour that Seán was a former IRA man. It was just a whisper, but all the same Seán knew that Stilton had one of his men keeping a close eye on him just in case. Admiral Somerville, who had been killed by the IRA only a few years ago, had been his mother's brother, Stilton's favourite uncle. Seán had also heard that he had vowed revenge on those that carried out the attack. Seán was introduced into the room. Stilton was sitting behind his desk smoking. Seán wasn't offered a chair. He saluted and stood to attention before the desk.

'At ease, sailor,' Stilton said. 'Now what is so important that you had to disturb me at this hour of the night?'

'I received a letter from home, Sir, from my daughter, Sir. There's something wrong and I would like to request leave.'

He heard Stilton was a fair man and hoped he had kids of his own and would understand his predicament, it was a hope born out of desperation and now that he was standing in the officer's quarters he began to realise how futile his request was.

'What sort of trouble is it?'

'Well, I'm not quite sure, Sir.' Seán was aware he

sounded ridiculous.

Stilton rose slowly from his desk and moved to stand in front of him. 'You do realise there is a war on, sailor? You know we can't just let every man who gets a teary letter from home jump ship. There would be chaos.'

'I realise that, Sir, but this is different.' Seán tried to keep his voice steady.

'Every man on this ship gets letters from home, from their loved ones. Children get sick, babies are born, their women have affairs, life moves on without them. This is war. That is the burden we suffer with no choice.'

'Sir, with all due respect, I cannot stay on this ship, knowing something is wrong. I cannot.'

'Show me that letter.' Stilton's hand shot out and grabbed the letter before Seán could stop him.

Stilton paced as he read, and a smirk appeared, then a grin, and finally a burst of laughter. It was Maeve's letter he had taken.

'Is this the reason you want to go home?' He held the letter in the air, his voice thick with sarcasm. 'So you can get between your wife's legs again?'

He continued reading, sarcasm turning to condescension.

'How dare you barge in here in the middle of the night with this letter, this filth, and ask me for leave. I don't care if your whole family burns in hell, you Fenian bastard. You'll never get off this ship while I'm in charge.' Stilton scrunched up the letter and threw it into the wastebasket.

Seán went for him, hands outstretched aiming for Stilton's throat.

'Guards,' Stilton roared as he fell to the floor with Seán on top.

Seán's massive hands were wrapped around his throat, trying to squeeze the life out of him. The guards rushed in. It took three of them. Seán thrashed and flailed like a feral beast, but finally they got him under control and held him, his arms behind his back, out of breath, eyes wild. Stilton stood up, brushed himself off and composed himself.

'You don't understand,' Seán gasped between breaths. 'It's my daughter, my daughter needs me. I have to go.'

'Arrest this man for assaulting an officer. Lock him in the cells and hold back rations. Get that bilge rat out of here.'

'No,' Seán roared. 'Please no! I have to go. Please let me go.' The guards' hold tightened. 'You bastards, let me go. Let me go or I'll kill every last one of you.'

Solstice

The bell knocked Bridget out of her reverie. She'd been daydreaming, putting herself on Rabbit Island with her dad, lying on their backs staring up at the blue ceilinged sky. Her final exam was over. She'd finished with plenty of time to spare and fastidiously read over her paper not once, but twice. Every question was answered and she was sure every answer was correct.

That was that, she finished school. A dance was to be held tomorrow night. She wouldn't be attending. She kept to herself these days, losing herself in the routine of cycling to school in the morning, home to the post office in the evening, studying by candlelight late into the night until she was sure Neasa and her mother were gone to bed so she wouldn't have to see them on her return. Each morning she made sure she was up and out the door before they rose. School friends found her melancholy and withdrawn and she let them drift away, finding their conversations trivial and childish, preferring the company of her books and the sanctuary of the post office. She pined for a letter from her dad, pinned all her hopes on that. Every day on the cycle home she visualized a letter waiting for her at the post office, a letter telling her he was on the way. She didn't know what he could do when he got here, but even if he got here, if he was just here, things would be better.

She stepped out of the dull corridors of the school into the blinding sunshine. The summer stretched before her like a great trench waiting to be filled. She scrunched up her eyes, stood on the steps of the school, stalling the bike-ride home. The excuse was now redundant. No study. No need to be away from home. No need to be at the post office.

She had disowned it all, an absentee landlord, drawn a

sheet over it like the contents of an abandoned mansion, concentrated all her thoughts instead on her study and the hope of her father's return. It was all still lurking beneath waiting to be claimed as hers, dust had gathered on the surface but below nothing had changed, it sat there waiting to be dealt with. She'd thought about convent life many times over the preceding months. It appealed to her in a new way, as an escape, a life of prayer, penance and dedication to others wasn't as objectionable as it had been. There weren't many other options for a girl who wanted to travel, wanted to further her education, wanted to help other people, wanted to appease her guilt.

Her mother still had no idea what went on up at the lookout. Neasa hadn't said a word about that night. She rarely left the house, lost interest in her appearance and all the things that she used to enjoy, dancing at the patterns, playing with her mother's powders and perfume, teasing the boys while they kicked a ball around the road. Paudie had persevered for a time, now and again turning up outside the house at night, drunk, calling at the window for Neasa. Her sister sobbed and shook, pulling the covers over her head. Bridget would help Mary bring him in off the street. Eventually he went back to England. Neasa had stopped her typing lessons with Fr Sullivan. She hadn't been there since the night at the lookout. She no longer talked about the glamorous job in the city. Fr Sullivan still called to see Maeve, on occasion, to take a cup of tea, ask after Neasa. Neasa shunned all male company and didn't even ask after Daddy anymore or write to him, nor did she show any concern that he hadn't written. Seán Óg was her day. She fawned over the boy. Every night she cried in her sleep, curled up to the wall. So many nights Bridget wanted to reach over and hug her but she had left it so long now, there was a gulf there that she couldn't reach across.

Bridget dismounted at the post office instead of going straight home. She had no reason to, since her study was finished, but she couldn't face home just yet. The blackbird was with her

164

again and sat on the post office sign over the door like it was impatient for her to go inside.

'Hello, Bridget,' said Kitty. 'I didn't expect to see you today and your exams finished. I thought you'd be out in the fine weather celebrating. How did your last exam go?'

'Very good, thanks Mrs Collins. All went well. Do you mind if I stay here a little while?'

Kitty smiled in that strange kindly way that had been foreign to Bridget at first.

'Not at all, girl. You stay here as long as you want. I've a few bits and pieces to do out in the post office. You give me a shout if you want anything.'

Kitty had been very good to Bridget over the last few months, fussing over her, bringing her cups of tea and the odd bun. Many's the evening she had stayed with her for dinner and there were some nights when Bridget fell asleep in the chair. Kitty would drape a blanket over her, rather than wake her. Her grandmother had said that there was a good person in everyone just waiting for an excuse to get out. This may be the case with Kitty, she thought, but now Bridget believed that there was an evil person inside everyone, too, and more often than not they won the battle and wormed their way out.

'Your granny would be very proud of you today.' The bell sounded, announcing a customer.

Would she, Bridget thought. Would she?

Bridget sat in her grandmother's worn old chair and rocked back and forth. She picked up an old shawl from the ground and pulled it close. The pipe winked at her from the dresser. She put her hand on an old dusty volume of poetry and selected a page with a thumbed down ear. An ink-circled verse at the bottom of the page caught her attention.

Only a sweet and virtuous soul,
Like season'd timber, never gives;

165

But though the whole world turn to coal,
Then chiefly lives.

Bridget allowed herself a wry smile. Her grandmother's voice was preaching to her from beyond the grave. What would the old lady think of her now if she was here? What would she say to her? What words of wisdom?

'We're like the leaves in the trees and there is nothing we can do to stop the wind worrying us while waiting for autumn. Some of us will fall peacefully to the ground and some of us will be tossed and turned and blown to the four corners.'

There was a great stillness in the room. Bridget's heartbeat calmed. She sensed the old woman there with her, and closed her eyes and slowed her breath, recalling more of her granny's words, becoming aware of her chest rising and falling.

'The only journey worth taking is in your head, it is the only journey that leads anywhere. The only thing you really have control over is your own mind.'

Her head lightened and tension seeped from her body.

'What hurts you blesses you. Darkness is your candle.'

Her grandmother had been preparing her. This is what life is, this is what the world was. Her grandmother knew this.

'It is how you react that will define you, the only thing that will define you, your only real choice in life.'

Hadn't she told her that? She had been there for her all along, like she'd said she would be but Bridget chose not to see her. She understood her grandmother's words now, she knew what to do with them. What a fool she had been! She almost collided with Kitty Collins in her haste to leave. Outside she looked for the blackbird, but it was nowhere to be seen.

Bridget marched down to Kilbeg a new woman, breathing in again the beauty of her surroundings, the summer song of the birds, sweet scents from the hedgerows, salt carried in from the sea on the breeze. She filled the empty shelves of the pantry deep inside, with sights, sounds, smells, re-stocking her senses, replenishing the scullery of her soul. We can begin again today, rebuild, all is not lost. I will help my little sister. I didn't help that night but I can help her now.

She bounded up the stairs to their room, bursting through the door. She wanted to fling her arms around Neasa and hold her tight. Neasa was standing in the corner, in front of the mirror. With one hand she had her dress pulled up under her chin, the other rested on her belly. When she saw Bridget at the door she hastily dropped her dress and turned away.

'Go away. Leave me alone.'

Bridget counted back in her mind. Five months since the night of the lookout. She put her arms around Neasa. Her sister tried to push her away, but Bridget held tight. Neasa struggled again, but the fight collapsed, her body relaxed and tears flowed.

'It's okay. It's going to be okay. I'm going to look after you. Nothing's going to happen to you. It's going to be okay.'

The two sisters lay on the bed, Neasa's head on Bridget's chest, Bridget stroking her hair.

'I saw what happened,' Bridget said. 'I was there that night at the lookout. I saw it all and I ran. I've known all along, and I'm sorry. I'm sorry I didn't help you.'

Neasa's body tensed. 'What did you see? What are you talking about?'

'I was there, Neasa, I found the notes that evening under your bed. I went to Trá Na Wadla to find you. I saw a man in the woods with a light and I went after him. I saw you in the lookout. I saw what happened to you.'

Neasa said nothing, her face like whitewashed stone.

'I'm so sorry, Neasa. I'm so sorry.' It was Bridget's turn to cry. 'I saw the man, he was dressed in black. I thought I knew him but I couldn't make it out. Who was it Neasa? Who did this to you?'

'Don't, please. Don't make me say it.'

'Tell me who it was. I need to know.'

'Leave it. Please just forget it. I can never tell. Never.' Neasa sprung from the bed and sat in the corner pulling her knees up to her chin.

'Alright, alright. We'll leave it for now.' Bridget followed, squatted beside Neasa. 'How long have you known about ...' she inclined her head.

'About a month and a half. I wasn't sure at first, kept persuading myself it wasn't true, didn't want it to be true. But I suppose there's no hiding it now. I'm so scared. What's going to happen to me? What are we going to do?'

'We'll figure something out. It's going to be okay.'

'Do you think it will be alright, really?'

'You leave it to me, Neasa. I'll look after you now. Don't worry anymore.'

'I'm glad you're here, glad that you know. It's been so lonely. I thought about throwing myself off the bridge more than once. Everything is ruined.'

'Don't you ever do that. Don't you ever even think that way. We all love you no matter what. Mammy loves you and Daddy loves you and little Seán Óg needs you. What would he do without you?'

'Daddy doesn't care. I heard you and Mammy talking. You both sent him letters and he hasn't replied. He's forgotten about us,'

'Don't say that. He hasn't forgotten about us. He would never do that. It takes a long time for letters to get to him with the war on.'

'I wish he would just come home to us.'

'I'm going to write him a long letter telling him everything that has happened and then I'm going to tell Mammy everything, and then we'll come up with a plan, Daddy won't get the letter for ages so we'll have to sort this out ourselves.'

'Please, no. I'm so ashamed, and I'll never tell who it was.

Never! Promise me you won't tell them! Promise me!'

'We have to tell them. They have to know. It's not right. It doesn't matter who it was, it wasn't your fault. None of this is your fault,'

'You don't understand. Promise me, or I'll run away and none of you will ever see me again.'

Bridget hesitated.

'Promise me,' Neasa urged.

'Okay, I promise. But we can't hide the baby.'

The two girls looked to Neasa's stomach.

'Stay with me tonight, Bridget. Tell me one of those stories Granny used to tell you.'

That night Neasa fell asleep in Bridget's arms. She slept peacefully. Bridget lay awake running everything over in her head. There is a long road ahead for Neasa yet, she thought, but at least I will be there to hold her hand. Be strong now, she said to herself. Be strong like your granny taught you.

Seán blinked as he came out into the light, shielding his eyes. His time in the cell was up. It was more of a store-room really where the buffer kept bits and bobs. He had nearly gone mad, but one thing kept him sane for the three months; he had to get home to his family. He wasn't going to go under, let these bastards beat him. He had exercised daily in his small cell, push-ups, sit-ups, stars and squats, exercises he'd learnt at the naval base, keeping himself fit. It was harder to look after the mind, deprived of contact for so long, deprived of light for long periods, no daylight or fresh air in months. The first two months were hard. He trained himself for long periods to sit and concentrate, to close his eyes and breathe in and out, counting his breaths, aware of it, aware of the body, until the counting fell away and his mind rested, not thinking of the future or of the past but just being, completely in the present. He disciplined himself and allowed an hour in the morning and an hour in the evening to think of home, the girls, Seán Óg and Maeve. They kept him going. Now his mind was fresh and clear and focused on one thing only, and that was getting off this ship and getting home to Ireland, by any means possible.

The guards returned his uniform, and with a bar of soap and a razor, led him to a shower. He washed up and shaved. He was leaner than when he went in but still in good shape. He put on his clean uniform and was led back to his quarters. He knew something was wrong the minute he met his bunkmates. They welcomed him back but wouldn't meet his eye. Barney hopped down from the top bunk where he was reading what seemed to be a smutty magazine, cigarette hanging from the corner of his mouth.

'Welcome back, guv,' he said, giving him a big bear hug and lifting him off his feet.

'You look good, like you've been away on R and R instead of in the hole.'

'What is it Barney?' Seán said.

'Come for a walk with me, guv, I've news for you. Let's get you a bit of fresh air.'

They went up on deck. Seán took a gulp of the fresh ocean air and it damn near burst his lungs, it was so good.

'Get it into you, guv, me ol' mate. You can't knock the sea air.'

Now that Seán was out, tributaries of relief, hope and impatience flowed into one great lake of restlessness inside him, he took one look out over the ocean as if acknowledging an old friend in a crowd before turning to Barney who shifted nervously from foot to foot beside him.

'What is it Barney?'

'You've had another letter from home while you were inside. It's not good. I hope you don't mind I opened it, in case it was a death or something. Figured you'd want to know straight away. I would have. Anyway nobody's dead or anything, but looks like one of your girls is in trouble.'

Barney reached into his pocket taking out a crumpled letter. Seán grabbed it off him hurriedly. It was from Bridget.

Something terrible has happened to Neasa. She made me promise not to tell anyone, but I have to tell you, I saw it all, it was up at the lookout …

Bridget told the whole story in her letter, every last detail. Seán's knees went weak and he had to hold onto Barney for support.

I don't know what to do, Daddy. I know you told me to look after them, but I'm afraid. I need your help. I've heard stories at school that they send girls like Neasa away, girls who get in trouble. Some of them never come back. We can't let this happen.

'Oh Jesus, Barney. My poor baby, my little Neasa. How did this happen to her? How did I let this happen to her?' He squatted down, head in his hands, wanting to pull his hair out. 'Jesus Christ, she's just a kid. I'll fucking murder the bastard. I'll kill him. I'll kill him, whoever he is when I find him.' He turned to Barney. 'I have to get off this ship. Where are we? Where the fuck are we?' he roared.

'It's okay, guv.' Barney grabbed Seán by the forearm as if afraid he'd jump overboard. 'Me and the lads, we figured you'd want out. We've put a plan in place. We'll get you off.'

'Where are we? When do we hit land?'

'We land in Norfolk, Virginia in the States in about two weeks. We've had some repairs in South Africa and they're going to fit us with a longer runway, more guns and a new catapult for US planes. We reckon we are going to be there over a month.'

'I want off as soon as we dock,' said Seán.

171

'Easy now, Seán,' Barney said. 'We have to be careful. Stilton has it in for you. His uncle was killed by the IRA in your neck of the woods, reckons maybe you even had something to do with it. You need to keep your head down and out of his way.'

'What's your plan?'

'Right, so Stilton reckons you are going to try to skip when we land in Norfolk. One of your lads, Byrne, is his snitch. He has him lined up to watch you night and day. We figure he'll let you escape and then have you caught so that you will be tried as a deserter.'

'Byrne from Galway?' said Seán.

'That's the one. Sly little bugger, ain't he?'

'Informers!' spat Seán. 'They've always been the curse of the Irish.'

'Forget Byrne. We can use him. We're due in Norfolk on the twelfth of this month. We wait until we land. We'll have some shore leave then. In the meantime, we'll feed him wrong information, set them on a wild-goose chase and while they're waiting for you, we'll have you safely stowed away on another ship.' Barney looked to Seán for approval.

Seán nodded. 'Go on.'

'Boys have done a whip-round for you, some bribe money for a stowaway passage. Even Byrne chipped in, fancy that. Probably got reimbursed by Stilton,' said Barney winking at Seán. 'Once you get to the UK, you're on your own. Should be easy enough to get home from there, man of your resourcefulness, eh guv? What ya think?'

'You've it all worked out. I don't know what to say. How can I repay you?'

'Me and you will have a few pints in Dublin when all this is over. Buy me a few pints of Guinness, eh, and set me up with one of those red-haired feisty birds ye have over there. I like them foxy.'

'Thanks, Barney. You're a real mate.'

'Don't mention it. We all have kids. You'd do the same for any of us. Come on now and let's get some chow. Just remember, keep your head down for the next month, stick to the plan and we'll be alright.'

'One more thing, I'll need to contact home, let them know I'm coming. They haven't heard from me in months. They'll think I've forgotten about them.'

'We'll you can't do it on board here. It'll get caught in the censorship. We'll have to wait till we get ashore and then get a telegram to them.'

Forsaken flakes of ice floated in the washbasin. Bridget gathered some in her hands watching them expire in the redness of her palm, then doused her face, trying to shake the fullness from her head. Neasa was still sleeping peacefully. She wasn't curled in a ball, nor was she turned facing the wall. At least now, thought Bridget, she won't be left on her own in this storm, if they were to be tossed like leaves in the wind, she'd make sure they fell to the ground together. The kettle whistled below on the range, clatter and chatter from the kitchen rising like steam through the gaps and knots of the floorboards. A fleeting melancholy arrested Bridget. She listened to her mother's song-line, to her dreamy half-chat. How beautiful, how true, how vulnerable people are when they think nobody is listening. Then the moment was gone. Her mother had no idea what was coming. How will she take this? Best to come right out with it, no beating around the bush, no point in dressing it up. Bridget went over and shook Neasa lightly.

'Come on. Up with you, sleepyhead.'

Neasa got up, stretched languidly and reached down cupping her little bump in her hand. 'So, it really is happening,' she said resignedly, stifling a yawn. 'I had the most wonderful dream that it was all a dream, a dream within in a dream.'

'Come on over here. Wash up and get dressed. Let's brush that long hair and make you presentable. You're still the most beautiful girl in Ireland, and in a few years when all this is over, you'll still be young and beautiful and you'll meet some lucky man who'll look after you and you can get on with your life.'

'There's nobody that'll want me now. Who'd want a girl like me?'

'Oh, Neasa, don't worry. You're still the same girl you were five months ago before all this happened. Any man in the country'd give his right arm to go courting with you.'

'Well I don't want to go courting anymore. I wish I was more like you, plain and simple, then nobody would take any notice of me and I'd be left alone.'

Bridget smiled ruefully. She'd always harboured a secret jealously of Neasa's looks. Now Neasa was envious of hers. Grass is always greener for sure. Bridget sat her down on the floor in front of the mirror and knelt behind, brushing the knots out of the silky hair. Neasa's eyes were downcast, as if afraid of what she would see in the mirror. Bridget touched under Neasa's chin and gently lifted.

'Look at yourself,' Bridget said. 'Look at yourself in the mirror.'

Neasa raised her eyes.

'You are Neasa O'Donovan. You are my younger sister and I love you. Your father and mother love you and your little brother Seán Óg loves you.'

Tears streamed freely down Neasa's face.

'It was not your fault. None of this was your fault. You are not on your own. We're going to help you. We're going to get through this, do you hear me?'

'Yes,' said Neasa, smiling through the tears. She turned and hugged Bridget.

'What are we going to say to Mammy? Remember you

174

promised about the lookout. We can't tell anything about the lookout.'

'We'll just tell her straight out. I don't know how she will take it, but after she has ranted and raved, we'll just have to make a plan and get on with it. You're not the first girl in the world to have a baby. Come on let's go down. I'll do the talking, alright?'

'Wait,' said Neasa. 'Whatever happens you won't let them take me away, will you? I've heard of girls who've gotten into trouble like me, being taken away to the city to the nuns. I heard they're terrible places and some never come out. You won't let that happen to me, will you?'

'I won't, Neasa. I promise.' Bridget hoped she could keep that promise.

Maeve was putting the breakfast things on the table when the girls appeared at the doorway.

'Oh my, Neasa, you look lovely this morning. I haven't seen you in that dress in months. It's so pretty on you, and your hair lovely and straight.' Maeve reached out to stroke Neasa's hair, but Neasa inched away.

'Well, it's just nice to see you looking a bit like your old self again.'

Bridget swallowed hard and steadied herself.

'Mam, we've something to tell you. Will you sit down?' Bridget said.

'What is it, girls? I've a million and one things to do this morning.'

'Can you sit down for a minute, please? It's about Neasa. It's important.'

Maeve looked to Bridget guardedly before sitting at the end of the table, her husband's usual spot. The two girls remained standing, Bridget at the foot of the table, Neasa behind her, half in her shadow perhaps using Bridget to soften the blow of their mother's reaction.

'Well, there's no two ways about it,' Bridget said, her

mouth dry, 'so I might as well come right out with it. Neasa is pregnant, five months gone. She's going to have a baby.'

Maeve's face slid right off. She looked to the floor as if to retrieve it, then around the room like she was searching for something she'd lost. Bridget let the silence hang. She felt Neasa's hand slip into hers.

'You're not serious?' Maeve shook her head. 'You can't be serious. How? How did this happen? She's only a child, for God's sake.' Maeve turned her attention to Neasa, eyes pleading, 'Neasa, is this true? Is it true?'

Neasa nodded gravely, her eyes still downcast, heavy, weighted, worried, embarrassed. 'I'm sorry, Mammy.'

'Oh, Lord save us. Sweet divine Jesus, this isn't happening. Please tell me this isn't happening.' She went to the dresser, pulled out a bottle of brandy and poured herself a stiff measure.

'Who was it? Who did this to you? Who's the father?'

Neither girl replied. Neasa's hand tightened in Bridget's.

'Tell me now, right this minute, who was it?' Maeve hopped up from her seat, her cheeks like two beetroots.

The girls stood their ground, hardly breathing. Bridget knew this question would be asked many more times over the next few weeks and months.

'She won't say, Mammy. She says she can't tell us, says she'll never tell.'

'Won't tell us? She has to tell us, we have to know. Who was it Neasa? That's a good girl, now tell us who it was.'

'No,' Neasa said defiantly.

'It was Paudie, wasn't it? That's why he was calling around here at all hours of the night, screaming and shouting. It was Paudie, now, wasn't it?'

Neasa stayed quiet, a steely determination about her now.

'Was it Paudie, Bridget?' Their mother directed the

question to Bridget.

'I don't know, Mammy, she wouldn't tell me either. I don't know who it is. It doesn't matter now, surely. He's not going to help us now whoever he is.'

'Doesn't matter? Doesn't matter?' Maeve's voice stepped up to a higher pitch. 'Of course it bloody matters! Maybe he might marry her. I know she's only sixteen, only sixteen, oh Lord, but there are ways around it. Maybe he can help us.'

'No,' said Neasa. 'He can't help us, ever.'

'So that's it then is it? No father? What are we going to tell people? Will we tell them it was the Immaculate Conception? Oh Lord, wait till they find out. We'll be the scandal of the village. Wait till your father finds out. He'll tear the place apart.'

Bridget let her mother's tirade run. She paced, asking the same questions over and over, turning her attentions from Neasa to Bridget then Neasa again. She watched her carefully until she saw the first signs of sufferance, desperation still there but a sliver of acceptance or perhaps defeat all the same. She had to introduce her plan now before her mother talked to anyone else. It was tantamount that it be resolved here, this morning, before anyone else got involved and it got out of hand. It was the only way.

'Look, Mammy. I wrote another letter to Daddy, telling him all about it, but we don't know when he will get it, if he gets it at all, so we are going to have to work this out ourselves without him,' said Bridget.

'And what do you propose we do?' Maeve asked sceptically.

'I have a plan,' said Bridget.

'Do you now? A plan?' Her tone altered to sarcastic. 'Isn't that wonderful? Well thank God for that.'

'Just hear me out. I was up all night thinking it through. She can't have the baby here. If she stays here she will be taken to one of those institutions and the baby will be taken away. There will be a big scandal and she'll never live it down.'

'Oh, Neasa. Neasa.'

'We have to get her away, and as soon as possible before people start noticing the bump. I still have some of that money Granny left for my schooling and I know that you have been saving a little from the money coming from the Navy. We could scrape enough together for a boat to England, and enough to live on for a few weeks until I find work.'

Her mother laughed hysterically. 'England is it? As if ye aren't in enough trouble already, and what would the two of ye do in England, for God's sake?'

'I heard on the wireless they are crying out for women to work in the factories over there with the war on. We'd get a small place and I could look after Neasa until she had the baby. Nobody would take any notice of the two of us over there. We could wait there until we heard from Daddy or until he came home, and then he'd know what to do.'

Bridget paused, she looked her in the eye, could see her faltering slightly. She had no notion of how to deal with this, was terrified of having to decide.

'It's the only way. Do you want them to take our Neasa away?' she said.

'Of course I don't. It's just … it's all so sudden. I wish your father was here. Oh, I don't know what to think.'

'We need to act fast, before people start to talk, before it gets out. We haven't time to be thinking about it,' said Bridget.

She knew her mother shied from being the decision maker, always wilted when faced with something outside her control. She knew she would have to take the initiative and press on with the plan, but she needed her mother onside.

'You want me to make up my mind today?' said Maeve. 'Have you gone soft in the head? I'll have to think it over. We can't rush into this. I need to have some time to think. Now get out of my sight the both of you.'

The girls went back upstairs, Bridget satisfied the seed had been planted. Their mother would come their way. What were the alternatives? None. None she'd accept. Bridget even allowed herself to get a little excited at the prospect of the two of them moving to London, embarking on a new life.

'Oh, Bridget, you were amazing. Did you really mean it about London, about the two of us going together?'

'I did. You'll come with me then, will you?'

'Of course I will. I think it's a wonderful plan, the two of us over there together, and you helping me with the baby. Do you really think nobody will bother us over there?'

'For sure people won't judge you like people here. You'll be just another person in the crowd, free to do what you want.'

'You'll be like my husband, going out to work to support me and when you come home from work at the end of the day I'll have your dinner on the table and a bottle of stout for you.'

The two of them laughed together. For the first time in months it seemed like Neasa was looking to the future with something other than dread.

Maeve left Seán Óg with the girls and went for a walk. She had to clear her head, get her thoughts straight. How could Neasa do something like this? How could she have been so stupid? Who was the father? Could it have been Paudie? She would have to find out. Oh, so many questions. How could she not have seen this coming? How had she been so blind? Five months gone and she hadn't noticed. And the girl right under her nose! It was clear she hadn't been herself in months, then there was the sickness. Maeve put it down to a tummy bug. And Bridget, again so calm and collected, plan in place, already moving on to the next step, streets ahead of her. She couldn't even get her head around the pregnancy yet, not to mind planning how to deal with it.

Bridget is far too young, too naïve, too untried with the

world and its hardships to make earnest decisions like that, she thought. But then, what to do instead? The girls weren't old enough to be going off to England on their own. What would Seán do? How would he handle it? I need to talk to someone, need some advice. I need to get this off my chest. I can't make this decision on my own. She couldn't talk to Mary about it. Paudie could well be the father. She couldn't get her involved at this stage. She only had one other friend in the village. She and Kitty had become unexpected friends over the last few months, and Kitty had been very good to Bridget while she was studying. She was desperate, she had nowhere else to turn. The post office was closed for lunch when she arrived so she knocked on the house door.

Kitty answered, teat-towel in hand. 'Ah, Maeve, come in. I was just making a bit of lunch.'

'Sorry, Kitty, I didn't mean to disturb you.'

'Don't be silly. I'd be glad of the company. Come on in, you look like you've seen a ghost. Are you alright?'

Bridget sat at the table. Over a cup of tea she told Kitty the whole story, even the plan Bridget had hatched. She hadn't meant to say so much, but once she started talking, it all came out. Kitty had let her spill everything without a single interruption.

'I just had to tell someone,' Maeve said sobbing. 'I don't know what to do.'

'You poor thing. That wan has got you into a right mess. I always knew there was a want in her, parading herself around. It was bound to happen, carrying on like that.'

'Ah, now, Kitty, that's hardly fair.' Maeve's cup shook in her hand. No mother liked to hear their daughter accused of being a tart.

'There's nothing fair about the state she's in now, is there? She never thought about her poor mother or her sister, while she was lying on her back. That Bridget is a saint and with

180

great prospects and now she's dragged into this sordid affair. She never stopped to think about that, did she?'

'Don't you talk about my daughter like that. She's only a child. She doesn't understand. It wasn't her fault.'

'Well she was old enough to open her legs for some fella, wasn't she? Who was it anyway?'

'She won't tell us, says she can't tell. It is none of your business anyway'

'Won't tell ye? Well, I never heard the like of it. The little bitch. Does she not know how serious this is? Who does she think she is? You'll have to drag it out of her.'

'She won't tell. I know her. She's as stubborn as her father when she wants to be.'

'And what about that fella, out fighting with the auld enemy where he has no business being and his daughter running around like a tramp at home. 'Tis at home keeping an eye on his daughters he should be instead of halfway around the world on a ship fighting someone else's war.'

'That's not fair,' Maeve said. 'I'm sorry I said anything to you, I thought I could confide in you. I trusted you.'

'There's only one thing for it now,' Kitty said ignoring her. 'We'll have to go up for the priest. He'll straighten her out.'

'I'd rather not get him involved.'

'You're coming up with me right this minute, and we are going to tell him everything. The Church decides these matters, not little girls. Running off to England in her state will do no good. They'd end up prostitutes, the pair of 'em before long, servicing soldiers and sailors home on leave. How would you like that? Is that the road you want them to go down, is it? Because that's where they are going if we don't put a stop to it.'

Kitty put on her coat, grabbed her hat and gloves, Maeve's elbow, and on the way to the priest's house mumbled under her breath about that little harlot below in Kilbeg.

A sinkhole sat roundly in Maeve's chest. Bridget looked at her reproachfully, almost scornfully as the muffled conversation from the good room tried to peel through the walls. Maeve had arrived back home a half-hour ago with the priest and Kitty in tow, helpless and downtrodden, guilt gelling even before she opened the door. It was then Fr Sullivan dismissed Kitty.

'We can take it from here, Mrs Collins. Thank you for your help,' he had said, and then to Maeve, 'I think it best if I talk to her alone.'

It had now been an hour. An hour of silence on their side of the wall.

'Why did you have to go and do this? Kitty Collins, of all people. You know how she is when it comes to things like this. I've heard her a million times referring to this wan and that wan and the way this one carried herself and how this one got herself into trouble and it was all her own fault the way she was carrying on. You must have heard her go on like that. Why did you think she'd understand? Why did you think she'd help us?'

'I'm not sure—'

'She thinks she's helping herself in the eyes of God but this isn't good for us, not good for Neasa. You know if Daddy was here, he wouldn't let the Church near us.'

'I'm sorry, Bridget. I had nobody else to talk to. I didn't realise this would happen.'

Just then, the door of the front room opened and Neasa came out, her face ashen. She had been crying. She dashed like a stray cat up the stairs. Fr Sullivan appeared.

'Maeve,' he beckoned, 'let's have a chat in here. Bridget, will you get us some tea. That's a good girl.'

Bridget hurried back in with the tea, using the good china they took out anytime the priest was around. Maeve and the priest talked in hushed tones like traders at a mart. The conversation ceased. Bridget hesitated to suggest they continue, and instead, as was obviously waited for, she backed out of the room, but remained on the other side of the open door.

'She wouldn't tell me anything, Maeve,' Bridget heard the priest say. 'I'm none the wiser. She wouldn't even look at me, not to mind answering my questions, and I asked many.'

'What are we going to do with her?' said her mother.

'Well, England is out,' he said. 'That was one thing Kitty was right about. That's not the place for them at their age. The Church will look after her here. We'll help her.'

'I don't want to send her away, Father. Isn't there anyway I can keep her here? I've heard stories about the places they send these girls to.'

'All nonsense, Maeve. I've visited these places myself, said masses there and met with the girls. They are looked after very well, given the best of care. The nuns that run them are saints. You'll be able to visit her and when she has the baby, they'll give her some training and find her a job somewhere afterwards so that she will have a normal life. Doesn't sound so bad now, does it?'

'I suppose not, Father. It's just … it's just I'd hate to think of her all alone up in Cork. Wouldn't it be better if she had me or Bridget with her?'

'Which would you prefer, having the two of them over in England, where God knows what could to happen to them, or above in Cork with the Good Shepherd Sisters looking after them? At least you'd be able to look in on her and know she was safe. Besides, she wouldn't be on her own, she'd be with girls in the same boat, with the same problem. It's the best thing for her really.'

'And what about the baby? What happens to the baby?'

'You know she can't look after a baby, Maeve. She can hardly look after herself. The baby will be cared for by the nuns, or given up for adoption to a good home. There are plenty of well-to-do couples out there are unable to have children.'

'I don't know, Father. It just doesn't seem right,' Maeve

said, but her tone conceded defeat.

'Maeve, I don't see you have any other choice. Have a sleep on it tonight. We are only looking out for Neasa. I'll call back tomorrow. Let me see myself out.'

They met Bridget in the hall on the way out, it was obvious she had been eavesdropping.

'Thanks for the tea, Bridget,' Fr Sullivan said and left, flashing a smile over his shoulder.

Fr Murphy sauntered in the pristine landscape of the park, the dew sparkling on the grass in the early morning sunshine. There was a virtuosity about the terrain and the changes inside him were mirrored in the scenery that surrounded him. He found newness in things once stale, his faith fertile where once it was sterile. It would be midsummer's day in a few days, the longest day of the year, a day to honour Saint John The Baptist. A great day to start afresh, he thought.

He had been sober nearly two years. It had been a tough course of self-doubt and self-loathing, but he was a new man, a man of vigour and reaffirmed in his faith, ready to recommit to his vocation and devote himself entirely to God's work. In his former life, he simply ambled through the motions, pushed into a vocation. His heart really wasn't in it. He saw now how far he had strayed from the path. He had let the Devil tempt him, let his bodily and earthly desires overcome him. He flushed in shame when recollecting the lustful, sinful thoughts he had entertained, the dreams that would come to him at night, the whiskey that fuelled it all. At first, when they had brought him to this house, he had resisted. His inner demons were strong, his will weak, mind tempted by sensual urges. They had assigned an older priest to him, a Jesuit, Fr O'Shea. He had been hard on him, locked him in his room for months. He would never forget the loneliness and despair. Every day Fr O'Shea would visit him, castigating him, upbraiding him, telling him how worthless he was.

'You have sinned against God, defiled the cloth,' he'd said, looking more like the Devil than a man of God. Everything about him was severe and pointed. His ears, his nose, the long nails on his hands, his canine teeth. He towered over him, tall but stick-thin, his skin stretched tight over his bones, grey like the winter sky.

'Your sins are all the more serious because you are supposed to be a man of God. A special place in the hottest part of hell will be reserved for you.' The words spat from his mouth.

Fr O'Shea had terrorised him with his visions and descriptions of hell, of the torment he would endure there for eternity, no respite, no forgiveness, no reprieve, until one day he had come into the room, a red-hot poker in his hand. Fr Murphy had crept back into the corner beside the bed. Terrified, he begged to be left alone. Another priest restrained him and Fr O'Shea lifted up his shirt, exposing the white saggy flesh of his stomach, and pushed the poker into his stomach, branding him with the iron, holding it tight a few seconds, then holding it up in front of his face.

'This is your last warning, Michael,' he had said.

He always used his first name, refusing to acknowledge him as a priest.

'Remember the pain I have caused you today. I take no pleasure in this. In fact, it pains me greatly that I have to resort to these methods to save you. Remember this pain. This pain is nothing, not even a fraction of the pain you will experience in hell for eternity if you do not change your ways and come back to the Lord. Imagine this pain, this pain on every inch of your body, for every second of every minute and every hour of your time for eternity. You think about that tonight.'

They left the room, taking with them a jug of water, removing the only thing that may have brought relief to the burn.

The day after the poker, when Fr Murphy heard the key in the door, he was down on his knees, head bowed.

'Father, please save me, please help me find my way. I want to do God's work again. Will you help me, please?'

Fr O'Shea rested his hand on his head, anointing him as a chaplain blessed the troops before sending them into battle.

'I will help you, Michael. God will forgive your sins, but from this day on you must resolve to do His work and His work only. You are only an instrument through which His work is carried out. You must put aside your wants, your needs and desires, all earthly things, so that you may carry out His word.'

Fr Murphy looked up to him, like Delilah did when at his side. He missed the old dog. There was many a night he would have liked her company over the last few months.

'You must become an empty vessel so that the word of God may flow through you. And you must be strong, for the world is full of evil and evildoers. The sins of the flesh are all around us in this modern world. We must save people from themselves, for they are weak. We alone are strong. We must be beacons of purity, chastity, charity in the world. We must hold the candle in the darkness, our hands unwavering. This is a great responsibility. Do you accept this? Do you give yourself anew to God?'

'Yes, Father, yes I do,' he said, overcome with emotion. They knelt together, prayed the rosary. After the rosary Fr Murphy asked if he would take his confession.

'Rest now tonight, and sleep. You have been through the horrors of your soul but you have come out the other end. Tomorrow we begin anew. Prepare your confession thoroughly and I will hear it then. We will wipe the slate clean. God has welcomed you back into His bosom. He is indeed merciful to those who repent. You will again in time make yourself worthy of His love.'

From that night on, Fr O'Shea became a different

person. The castigations stopped, the abuse stopped, he became kindly, compassionate. He was his confidante and mentor, gave him guidance and counselling.

As he remembered those cathartic days Fr Murphy's hand went down to his stomach and he caressed the welt. How lucky I am to have been saved, he thought. With the influence of Fr O'Shea, who had the ear of the Bishop, he had been offered his old parish back. According to Fr O'Shea, there was an allegation against his replacement from a previous parish. It was said Fr Sullivan suffered a wandering eye when it came to girls, and he was being transferred to where they could keep an eye on him.

In a few days, he would be back in Union Hall, ready to begin God's work, again.

They sat on the sill in the recess of the window, cross-legged and watching the gulls swoop in over the boats landing their catch. Bridget's fingertips tapped a tune on the pane in time with the rain-shower drumming at the window, Neasa absentmindedly traced pictures on the steamed glass.

'Are you alright?' she asked.

Neasa nodded, and tried a little smile, but it died and withered like the onset of winter.

'What did he say to you?'

'It doesn't matter, it's over now. I heard the door go a while ago. Was it him? Is he gone?'

'He's gone,' said Bridget, 'for now.'

'Did he talk to Mammy?'

'Ya, they talked.'

'Did you hear them? What did they say?'

'I don't know,' Bridget lied.

'We're still going to London, though, aren't we?'

'Yes, we are, whether they like it or not. Neasa and Bridget against the rest of the world, eh?'

Bridget worked the plan over in her mind. Her mother would cave into the pressure from the priest, she knew that. She trusted the Church in most things, and the possibility of avoiding a decision would lead her that path too easily. Neasa would certainly be packed off. They needed to get out of here quick, and on that boat to England before anyone else interfered. It was time to pay a visit to Fr Sullivan. He owed her some answers, and if he wasn't forthcoming, well, her dad hadn't answered any of her letters but Fr Sullivan didn't know that. Who was to say he wasn't already on his way home?

Bridie Keohane answered the door, and looked surprised to see Bridget.

'Is Father Sullivan in, Mrs Keohane? May I see him for a few minutes? I know he is busy. I won't take much of his time, just a quick word.'

'Come in there out of the rain. Go into the parlour and I'll see if he's available.'

The parlour was a comfortable room, furnished well, one wall lined with books, cold now though, with no fire in the grate. On the table sat the Remington typewriter and user manual. A heavy coat was thrown over the chair and beside it, a paraffin lamp. Was that the lamp I saw in the forest, she wondered?

Bridie popped her head back around the door. 'He'll see you in the back room, Bridget. He has the fire on in there.'

Bridget followed Bridie down the hallway and into the smaller room, furnished much like a study. Fr Sullivan was propped in an easy chair in front of the fire, smoking a cigarette.

'Bridget,' he said, getting up. 'What a nice surprise. What can I do for you? Please, sit down.' He motioned to the chair opposite.

'I didn't know you smoked.' She remained standing.

'Oh, just the odd one. Guilty pleasure. It helps me relax.'

He flashed his toothy smile.

'I want to talk about Neasa.'

'What about Neasa?' He turned away hastily picking up coals with tongs and dropping them into the fire.

Bridget waited until he had finished with the fire and was facing her way again. She wanted to see his face.

'You were up at the lookout that night, weren't you?'

'What night?'

'The night you came back with Neasa, the night you went looking for her.'

'Yes. I met Neasa in the woods that night, walking back. I was nowhere near the lookout. What's this all about?'

'I saw a man in the woods, in front of me, with a lamp, going up towards the lookout. It was you, wasn't it?'

'Of course it was me, I was out looking for your sister. Your mother asked me to find her. But why are you asking this now? You were there, you saw me bringing her back.'

'Neasa was raped at the lookout that night. I saw it. I saw a man in the forest going up there holding a lamp. You were in the forest that night. I saw the profile of a man, dressed in black like you. I've seen the way you look at Neasa. It wasn't right, wasn't right spending all that time with her.'

Fr Sullivan was on his feet, enraged. 'How dare you?'

'Someone was writing her letters, fancy words. None of the boys around here could write letters like that. It was you, wasn't it? It was you and now you want to send her away. You want to bury it all and your child she is carrying.'

'How dare you speak such words in my house? How dare you accuse me of such a vile act? I'm a man of God. And after all I have done for your family. I promised your father I'd look in on you, and I kept my promise. But now, now I'm done with you. Done with you, I say. Please leave, leave now.'

Bridget stood her ground, she waited for his anger to subside, wanted to hear what he would say next. That would tell a lot. He remained quiet for what seemed like an age, his eyes watered as he looked into the fire.

'Is that what you think of me?' he said, wearily. 'Is that what you really think? How could you?'

'It doesn't matter now anyway, doesn't matter who done it. Maybe it wasn't you, maybe you saw who it was? Maybe I'm going mad? It's done now and whoever it was will suffer for it, in this life or the next. It happened and I can't change it. Neasa can't change it. You can't change it. We all just have to live with it.'

Fr Sullivan's stare remained with the fire. Bridget didn't know if he was even listening to her. He seemed to be in shock, shocked that a seventeen-year-old girl could march into his living room and accuse him of such a thing.

'Father, are you listening to me?' she said. He turned to face her. 'What matters to me is what happens next. I will not let Neasa be sent away. I am going to look after her.'

'It's the best thing for her, Bridget. Your mother agrees. Especially now if what you tell me about the rape is true. She will need special care. The nuns will know how to look after her.'

'I know what's best for my sister and being locked away like a criminal will certainly do her no good.'

'It's not your decision to make. You don't understand how these things work. This is the best we can do for her and that's it. It will all be arranged in the next few days and that will be the end of it.'

'It won't be me that will be calling up to you next time. It will be my father and he won't be as understanding as me, especially when I tell him I saw you in the woods that night. We got a telegram from Daddy this morning, saying he got discharged and was in London. He will be coming home in a few days,' she lied.

The colour drained from his face. 'You wouldn't tell him anything about me because you know it's not true. You know I had nothing to do with that.'

190

'I don't know what to think anymore. I'll just tell him what I told you and let him come to his own conclusions. It doesn't matter anyway because when he finds out you sent his daughter away, he'll come up here and strangle you with his bare hands.'

She could see she had him. He held on to the side of the chair to keep his hand steady.

'It doesn't matter to him that you are a priest. He has no time for priests anyway, doesn't see any difference between priests and men, and he has killed plenty of men. What's another one on the list, priest or not?'

'What would you have me do?' he said shakily.

'I want you to go down to my mother tomorrow and tell her that you have changed your mind, that you thought about it overnight and that the best solution for everyone is for Neasa and I to take the boat to England as soon as possible. She will listen to you.'

Fr Sullivan sank into his chair. He didn't look back to Bridget. She stood there waiting for an answer. He stared long and hard into the fire and eventually turned to look at Bridget as if he had forgotten she was there.

'Please leave,' he said.

Bridget moved towards him until she was inches from his face, looking him straight in the eye. 'You are just a man, wearing costumes and crosses that you think makes you God, but you are just playing God, and I won't let you play God with my sister. I don't know what happened in the lookout that night, but I can't help feeling you are in some way responsible.'

Fr Sullivan tried to interject, his anger rising again, but Bridget held up one finger. It may as well have been a sword, and she marvelled at her calm exterior considering the claws of anger that tore at her skin from within. It was like someone was talking through her, one of her mighty ancestors, one of the great O'Donovan warriors of old, who feared neither man nor God.

'You will help me fix this. If you are not down at our door in Kilbeg tomorrow morning, as God is my witness, there will be hell to pay,' she said.

The priest's lips quivered. He attempted to speak but withered under the steel of her righteous stare. She left him to the heat of his fire.

It was early the next morning when Fr Sullivan arrived back at the house asking for Maeve. He brushed past Bridget in the hall giving her no acknowledgement. They went into the good room and Bridget listened through the door as he went about explaining to Maeve his change of heart. When he had gone, Bridget joined her mother in the front room.

'What did he say?'

'He thinks maybe it's better off for everyone after all if you both take the boat to England. He said he thought about it long and hard last night and changed his mind.'

'And?'

'And what?'

'What do you think?' said Bridget impatiently.

'I suppose if Father Sullivan thinks it's a good idea, well, he should know really, and I wouldn't like to see her sent to one of those homes, so maybe it is best. I wish your father was here to help me decide.'

'Then we'll go. Go to England.'

'I'm going to miss you both so much, but I'll pray for you every day. You have a good head on your shoulders, girl. You make sure you look after Neasa now, and the baby. I'll be over to visit, of course, when your father comes home.'

'Good then. That's settled.' Bridget made for the stairs.

'When will you leave?' Maeve asked.

'The day after tomorrow. We'll sail from Cork.'

'So soon?'

'No point in hanging around. Better to get over there and get settled in properly before the baby comes.'

Bridget ran up the stairs, taking two at a time. 'Neasa, pack your bags. We're heading for London,' she said and ran into her arms.

'We're really going? When do we leave?'

'Day after tomorrow, from Cork.'

'Midsummer's day. We'll see the bonfires lit on the hills as we sail away.'

Kitty Collins was torn between excitement and indignation. She had just received a telegram from Fr Murphy. He was coming home tomorrow. She was to deliver the telegram to Fr Sullivan. It stated that he was to have his bags packed and be ready to vacate the parochial house tomorrow morning. He was being transferred to another parish in Cork City. This was what excited her. The indignation, well she never really liked Fr Sullivan and his fancy modern ways. That was grand for the city but wouldn't do down here in the country where they were true Christians. She couldn't believe it when she heard the two O'Donovan girls were off to London on the boat, and that one, only sixteen and with child, a child who would never know its father. We can't let this happen, she thought. A terrible example to be setting other girls around here. We might as well tell them to lay down and open their legs for any passer-by. You can't just go around fornicating like that and to hell with the consequences. She delivered the telegram to Fr Sullivan and waited while he read it so that she could see his reaction. His chin quivered and the corners of his mouth slid down so that she was treated with his lovely pearly smile, only the wrong way around.

'Would you like to send any reply?' Kitty said chirpily.

The priest coughed, clearing his throat. 'No, thanks, that won't be necessary.'

'I take it you'll give him a full report of the goings on around here while he was away, including the shenanigans of that O'Donovan wan below in Kilbeg. I hear she has notions of going to England on the boat. We'll see what he has to say about that.'

'You'd be better off minding your own business, Mrs Collins. Our Lord said, "And why do you look at the splinter in your brother's eye, and not notice the beam which is in your own eye?"'

'Have a nice trip, Father.' She snorted and walked away down the drive.

Neasa and Bridget chattered excitedly, packing their last few things into bags. They had told everyone they were visiting relatives for a few weeks. Kitty Collins would probably leak the true story around the village in time, but there was nothing either of them could do about that. The boat for England was scheduled to leave this evening and tomorrow morning they'd both be in England.

Bridget unexpectedly suffered a twinge of sadness. She would miss Kilbeg and Union Hall. Although things had been tarnished of late, she would hold fond memories of the place: long afternoons on the boat with her dad picking periwinkles, the evenings she spent with her grandmother in the post office, her confirmation day, even their last Christmas together as a family, sitting around listening to the King's speech. But she could take those memories with her, she supposed. Bridget thought of the pot of potatoes. It doesn't matter where in the world you are if what is inside you stays the same.

Bad memories could be discarded or ignored. Balance is necessary in life. Without bad times, there would be no good times, without evil there would be no good and so on and so forth. Her grandmother's dormant words had begun to stir themselves inside her lately like bears in a torpor sensing the thaw and preparing for spring. She hoped her mother would cope by herself. She had Seán Óg to tend to, and she could now give him her undivided attention. He would surely benefit from that. Her mother had her faults, but she was a kind and loving woman and only wanted what was best for everyone, misguided somewhat by the Church. But she did what she thought was right. All her life she was surrounded by people who were steadfast in their beliefs, immovable rocks stoically refusing to budge from their ideals. She hadn't room to forge her own way and had allowed herself to be swept up and carried along. You couldn't expect a packhorse to lead an expedition. The time alone would be good for her, thought Bridget. If only this war would end and Daddy could come home. Bridget still listened to the radio every evening. There seemed to be no let-up in the war, seemed to be no stopping the Nazis.

'Now, have we everything we need?' Bridget said to Neasa.

Neasa was swallow-like in her excitement; the old Neasa. Her eyes were full of hope, and her newly-washed and brushed hair fell luxuriously over her shoulders. Her features were trusting again. She beamed.

'Everything's packed,' Neasa said. 'Mammy even gave me some baby clothes to take.'

'It's so good to see you happy again,' said Bridget.

'Thank you for arranging everything. You know, I used to think we had nothing in common, that you were boring, head stuck in books. I thought you were so bloody sensible and grown up. It annoyed me so much, everyone saying how intelligent you are.' She took Bridget's hands in hers and held them tight. 'When people talked about you and me, it was always, "Oh, that Bridget, so mature for her age, so intelligent, she's a wonder, she'll go places, brains to burn." When they talked about me they'd say, "She's so pretty". That was it. I had no other redeeming qualities. I was known for being pretty. I was so jealous of you and so jealous of what you had with Granny. There was no point in taking any interest in school. I could never be as clever as you, so I concentrated on my looks. I thought that was the only thing going for me and I used it. Look where that got me. Anyway, I'm glad you are so sensible. I'm glad you are so mature. I'm glad you are you.'

'That's funny,' said Bridget. 'I was jealous of you, too, of the attention you got from people. I guess we need to learn to be happy in ourselves. Come on now or we'll miss that boat.'

An almighty pounding sounded at the front door. They looked at each other, startled, and headed down the stairs.

'Who on earth is making all that racket at the door?' said their mother.

She hadn't the door open an inch when Fr Murphy shoved his way in like a bull. He was bigger than Bridget remembered, massively framed in the doorway. He was seething, eyes narrowed, forehead creased above his bushy eyebrows. He looked lean and fit, much better than the last time they saw him. She could sense tension, a coil ready to spring. His eyes darted from Maeve, and then over to the girls on the stairway, sizing them up. There were no hellos or pleasantries.

'Which one is she?' he asked, spitting the words.

'Father Murphy,' Maeve said, she looked at him bewilderedly, 'welcome back. Would you like a cup of tea?'

'Which one?' he asked again, louder, more urgent this time.

'What do you mean, Father? Who are you looking for?' she said.

'You know very well who I'm looking for. I've heard all about what's been going on, and I'm back to sort it out, and just in time, too, by the looks of things.' His eyes found the suitcases in the girls' hands.

Neasa whimpered, dropped her case and ran back upstairs. Fr Murphy made for the stairs.

196

Bridget stood in his way, three steps up. 'We are going away. It's all arranged. Father Sullivan even said it's for the best.'

He moved to the bottom step. Bridget backed up, one unsteady stride.

'He did, Father. She's right,' said Maeve, desperation in her voice. 'He called to the house yesterday morning.'

'Father Sullivan is gone, and good riddance. He had no idea how to run a parish. This is now my parish, again, and by God I won't have this kind of carry on. I will drag ye kicking and screaming back to God if I have to. Now get out of my way.'

'No,' Bridget said defiantly. 'I'm taking my sister away.'

'How dare you? You'll go straight to hell with your sister if you are not careful. Get out of my way.'

Bridget summoned all her courage. 'No.'

The priest charged her like a bull, his biretta flying from his head. He grabbed her by the hair, swung her off the wall, and flung her down the stairs. Maeve screamed. Bridget crumpled in a heap on the floor. Fr Murphy didn't even look back. He carried on upstairs, bent on his mission.

Fr Murphy had arrived back in the village that morning. He had been greeted at the house by an impertinent Fr Sullivan and had taken an instant dislike to the man, and sent him off at once. He was unpacking his things when Bridie announced a visitor. Kitty Collins. Kitty had been one of his daily mass-goers, a very devout woman and generous in her devotion to the Church both in terms of time given and monetary donations.

'I'll see her in the parlour, Bridie.'

Bridie readied the room.

'Oh, Father. It's good to see you back,' said Kitty.

'Good to be back, Mrs Collins. Sit down there and take the weight off your feet.'

Fr Murphy remained standing. Kitty sat but got up again

quickly. She was in a state of some excitement, flighty as a carrier pigeon waiting to be let off.

'What can I do for you?' Fr Murphy said.

'It's about Neasa O'Donovan, Father.'

'What about her?'

'I don't like to be the one telling tales, but Father Sullivan was doing nothing about it and it isn't right. I'm so glad you are back. Nothing like this would have happened if you were here.'

'What is it?'

'She's got herself in trouble.'

'What kind of trouble?'

'Well, it was always going to happen the way she used to flaunt herself around the village. She'd been seen heading off with the boy of the McCarthys. She's with child now, won't tell who the father is. There's rumours that there was an older man involved, the whole village is talking about it.' Kitty paused.

'Go on,' he said.

'They're planning to go to England, herself and her sister Bridget, heading for Cork today. Father Sullivan sanctioned it and their mother is allowing it.'

'Are they now?' Fr Murphy began to pace the room, hands behind his back.

'Yes, Father. It's a terrible state of affairs, the whole thing. Sorry to land this on you on your first day back, but I felt you would want to know.'

'You were right to come to me. I'll look after this mess.'

He dismissed Kitty and continued pacing. What would Fr O'Shea do? This was to be his first challenge as he started anew, his first test from God. He had saved his own soul, now thanks be to God he had the opportunity to save another, a young girl fallen into the clutches of the Devil. Fr O'Shea had taught him well. He had been harsh, brutish even, but this is what it took. Sometimes people had to be saved from themselves. Didn't Our Lord himself destroy Sodom and Gomorrah in a rain of fire and brimstone?

Neasa was crouched in the corner of the bedroom when he appeared. Her bladder opened. She could feel the warmth running down her legs. He approached and stood over her.

'You have sinned gravely against God, child. But God forgives those who repent. You were tempted by the Devil and succumbed to the pleasures of the flesh, and in doing so tempted others into sin. The Church will make you pure again. You will do your penance and rid yourself of the sins of the body. Do you understand?'

Neasa didn't know what to respond.

'First, we must have the truth. Who did you lie with? What man did you drag down with you into the filth? Maybe it was more than one. Name them, speak now.'

Neasa remained in the corner, wishing she was anywhere else, anywhere but here, trapped.

'Speak! You will tell me. We will have the truth. I will not leave this room until I have the truth.'

Silence. Neasa didn't open her mouth. She stared out the window, imagining they were already on the boat, herself and Bridget, arriving into the harbour in England, gleaming modern buildings sparkling on the shoreline, smiling, happy people milling around on the dock, all so glamorous, Bridget holding her hand, smiling at her, and as they approached the shore, she could see someone gesturing wildly, jumping up and down. He stood a head above everyone else, dressed in a brilliant white navy uniform, smiling and handsome. It was Daddy waiting for them on the shore. Suddenly there was a hand on her jaw. She was jolted back to reality. The priest pulled her face close to his.

'Are you listening to me?' His breath fell hot on her face. 'Do you want to spend eternity in hell?'

'No, Father.'

'Then you need to tell me. I need to hear the truth.'

'I will never tell. I can't tell.'

'You are only making this hard on yourself.' He reached under his soutane, and pulled his belt from his trousers, wrapped the buckle around his fist, and began swinging.

An animal instinct took over Neasa. She lunged, hands flailing. Her nails caught his face and tore at him. He let out a wail and grabbed her, letting fly with the belt.

Bridget had lost consciousness briefly. She was lightly concussed and felt woozy. Her mother brought her into the kitchen and put a cold damp cloth on her forehead, Bridget pushed it away. A blackbird landed on the sill outside, it pecked at the window seeming to want to get inside.

Bridget could hear the priest, his deep voice booming. She rushed from the kitchen, her mother following. She tried to push open Neasa's door but it was locked. She pounded on it with both fists. She could hear Neasa pleading beyond, whimpering like a trapped animal.

'Let me in,' she cried. 'Leave my sister alone.'

'Fr Murphy, please, let us in,' cried her mother. 'We'll all talk this through, please.'

Their entreaties were ignored. Bridget banged on the door with her fists and when the skin on her knuckles bled, she went at it with the flat of her palms until they were numb. At the door of the lookout she'd failed Neasa, now her sister was in danger again. She'd promised her she'd look after her. She burned with a helpless rage. They'd been so close. They'd miss their boat. Kitty would have it blabbed all over the village. Behind the door Fr Murphy's voice boomed an avalanche of threats and accusations. She wheeled on her mother.

'How could you let this happen? How can you just stand there? Do something.'

Her mother opened her mouth but no words came.

Seán Óg began to cry downstairs, she looked at Bridget helplessly and scurried down to pick him up.

When at last they landed in Norfolk, Virginia, Seán felt the lake of restlessness subside. The end was in sight. He had an irresistible urge to jump overboard as soon as he saw the docks, swim for shore and run, and keep running. Since coming out of the cells, time had been a bothersome friend, one whose feet stayed under the table long after the welcome had worn out. Seán was a man of action, but he had to calm himself and bear the wait. Even now on dry land he would need to rope in his impatience, tether it until the time to act. He knew Stilton was watching him, waiting for him to slip up. They had been feeding Byrne information, drawing him into their confidence, told him the location where Seán was to meet the captain of a freighter bound for England to pay him off, told him the name of the freighter and her date and time of departure. Byrne would lead Stilton there on the day of departure. Seán knew they would leave it until the freighter had left the dock heading out to sea, then they would board the ship and search for the stowaway. Meanwhile, Seán would be safely stowed away on another boat, leaving at the same time. He would be well out to sea before they finished their futile search, and on the way home to his girls. At least they were here now, he thought, as they made ready to go ashore.

Most of the men were looking forward to some drinking and revelry. If they were lucky, some dancing with the local girls. Others thinking maybe there was a part of town they could go to where they could pay for a bit of action, nice and easy no fuss, money handed over and a bit of relief. None of the men had seen a woman in months. They weren't fussy, any bit of warm flesh would do. Many would think of their wives and girlfriends, their eyes closed as they found their rhythm. Seán's priority was to get a telegram out to the girls. He knew he would be followed by one of Stilton's men when he went ashore, knew the telegram would be read but it didn't matter. It all fitted into the plan. They knew he was going to jump ship anyway.

When they got ashore, Seán went to find the telegraph office. There was one on the main street just a few blocks from the dock. He wrote a short message:

I've seen the letters. I'm safe and well, so don't be worrying. I am in Virginia, USA on shore-leave. I will be leaving for home in a few days, taking a ship for England. I hope to be home in two months at the latest. Tell the girls and Seán Óg I will be home soon and not to worry, everything will be alright.

Seán felt a great relief once the telegram was sent. They would know he was still alive, that he received their letters and that he'd be home soon. All going well, he would be home before the baby was born. He was forming another plan in his head. Barney had plenty of connections in London. He would pack up the family and move them over there. The Navy would be looking for him as a deserter but Barney told him they would never find him in the East End. The East End looked after their own, he had said, they had a different law to everybody else. Barney said he could get him plenty of work, well-paid work.

With some of the weight taken off his shoulders, albeit only some, he went off to meet his shipmates for a drink.

Fr Murphy spent over an hour in the girls' room. He alternated between beating Neasa with the belt and attempts to cajole her with soft-spoken entreaties. She wanted to tell him, wanted the pain to be over but what could she say? How could she tell him what really happened?

'Give me a name,' he said, 'and it will all be over. It will just be between you and me. Nobody else has to know. Why are you protecting him? Where is he now that he's left you in this state? He doesn't care about you.'

Then he would get angry again, raise the belt and lash her across the legs, buttocks and back, slapping her face with the palm of his hand.

'You probably don't even know, do you? You don't know who the father is. It could have been one of many. How many did you lie with? How many times did you fornicate?'

'It was only once. Only once, Father,' she pleaded. 'Please stop. I can't tell you. I can't tell you. You wouldn't believe me anyway. Nobody would. You'd all think I'm mad.'

'Nobody will think you are mad, child. We'll believe you. You must come clean in front of God. You must trust in me, trust in God. We are only trying to save you.'

After many rounds of beatings, she broke down, no longer able to hold her will.

'I'll tell you. Just stop, please, I beg you.'

He bent towards her and inclined his face so that she could whisper into her ear. Between sobs Neasa explained what had happened up at the lookout, reliving it herself. She caught her breath.

'Go on, child, keep going. Who was it? Who was the man in the corner?'

Neasa hesitated.

'Tell me,' he said raising his hand to strike her again.

'Alright, alright, please,' she said and told him what he demanded to know.

Fr Murphy came slowly down the stairs, the steps groaning under his weight. Maeve rushed out of the kitchen when she heard his footsteps. The colour had drained from his face. A few beads of sweat had formed on his forehead and were slowly heading south, down his cheeks. He pulled a handkerchief from his pocket and dabbed at his brow and neck. He turned to Maeve. She waited for him to speak. He seemed to be trying to collect himself, form his thoughts.

'Your child is insane,' he said. 'She suffers delusions and hallucinations like someone possessed. For her own good I will be sending her to Cork to the Good Shepherd Sisters. They will look after her for the time being. We'll make sure the baby has a good home.'

'No, Father. Please, don't do this. We'll look after her here, Bridget and I,' she pleaded.

'Impossible. When a girl grows up in a Godless house, this is what happens. She has inherited the sins of her father. She needs education and guidance and discipline. The nuns will provide. She will be a different girl when they are finished with her.'

'No.' Maeve grasped Bridget's shoulder for support.

'Yes. I will advise the nuns she is to have no visitors. Your daughter is one of the most serious cases I have come across. Visitors will do her no good. After the baby is born, we will see.'

'Oh, my poor little girl,' Maeve sobbed, hands at her temples.

'Why are you crying? We are going to save your child.' He looked down at Bridget. 'You can count yourself lucky that I'm not sending her away, too, the way she defied me on the stairs. That's another one who needs discipline. I'll be keeping an eye on her.' He turned back to Maeve. 'There will be a car here for her in the morning. Have her ready. No need to bring much. The nuns will provide everything. You are not to make a fuss or a scene. I don't want to have to get the guards involved.'

Maeve nodded helplessly.

'We'll see you in the morning then, nine o'clock.' He

picked his biretta up from the floor, placed it on his head and walked towards the door.

'Father,' Bridget called after him.

He turned, Maeve was surprised by the steel in Bridget's voice.

'Was it with the Devil you were with when you went away?' The big man seemed to wilt under her gaze. 'Is it him you're working for now, because this is certainly not God's work? You say you are saving my sister. Who is it that is going to save you?'

He left without closing the door, his soutane trailing behind him in the muck.

Equinox

Months crawled by with no news of Neasa. Bridget and Maeve boarded the bus for Cork. The vehicle was half-full, farmer's wives mostly, making a trip to Cork for a bit of shopping, a rare excursion for them and they prattled witlessly. Bridget and her mother sat beside each other, stones in their throats. Hardly a word passed between them these days. After Neasa was taken, Bridget's hours passed in shadows of regret. She wrote to Neasa, but received no reply. The church, like a great whale, had swallowed her sister whole and unlike Jonah, they weren't for spewing her back out.

A telegram had arrived from her father. He was on his way, it said. Bridget tiptoed around her hope, her only hope, that warm feeling in her chest when she thought of her dad. She rationed it out in small doses lest she'd come to the bottom of the bag. In the mornings when she woke, or at night before bed, she'd dose herself with a few grains of promise just to keep going. It was running out. He should have been home by now.

The bridge across the bay was seldom out of her sight, and sat in the corner of her eye most days, she watched impatiently for a trace of his return. The afternoons were the worst, the optimism of the morning waning, light draining on another day without reunion, the barrier of night slamming down on the possibility of his return for interminable hours. In the night she dreamed the same dream over and over, the same dream every night. An army of images and emotions marauding through her sleeping mind, pillaging any peace to be won from slumber. It was the lookout, always the lookout, its stone façade innocuously washed in moonlight, lodged in Bridget's psyche like a malignant tumour. The scene set, the players would steal in from the wings, threading on the creaking boards of Bridget's memory. And so the act commences, enter the protagonist, the antagonist, the drama unfolds, reaches a climax, enter the heroine ... but wait, she's still in the wings, a leading-lady with stage-fright, her lines learnt over and over but lost to her now. The show must go on, even without the leading-lady. And so it does. And she watches on. The tragedy unfolds. The curtain falls, no applause, a silent ovation from the darkness.

The Good Shepherd Convent Asylum was built in 1881. It housed a home, a convent, a laundry and an orphanage. Originally built as a place to rescue prostitutes from a life of sin, they were given the name the Magdalene institutions after the biblical character of Mary Magdalene. More often than not, however, these institutions strayed from their original brief and widened their scope, taking in unmarried mothers, abused girls and even young girls who were considered too promiscuous or flirtatious for decent society. These girls were often signed in by their families or at the whim of their parish priest. Some of them never came out. They died there, buried in a common grave, with not even a headstone to record their time on this earth, their identity taken even in death. The building was an imposing red brick structure, built on top of a hill and curved like a fortress.

Bridget swallowed hard, dread seeming to stream down the steps towards them from the cold stone fortress. Her mother took a deep breath and lifted the cast iron knocker on the heavy wooden door. After what seemed like an age, the door was answered by a nun, tall and thin, in a white habit with a black veil. A large silver heart hung from her neck engraved with an image of the Good Shepherd, staff in hand, looking down at a lamb cradled at his bosom.

'We are here to enquire about my daughter. She was taken ... er ... sent here a few months ago and we just wanted to see if we could visit with her.'

'Have you an appointment?' There was no welcome in the stern voice.

'Well, no,' said Maeve. 'We have written a number of times requesting a visit, but we've had no reply.'

'You need permission in writing to visit. Permission is required from the Bishop.'

Maeve took a hurried half-step forward before the door could be closed. 'Please. We are so worried. She was to have a child, and the time is way past. Please, can you tell us anything at all about her? We just want to know if she is alright.'

Bridget saw a hesitance in the nun's offhanded demeanour.

'What is the child's name?'

'Neasa O'Donovan. Her name is Neasa O'Donovan.'

The door closed. They waited and waited. It started to rain, a heavy summer shower and in seconds they were soaked through. The door opened again. The same nun was back.

'Come in,' she said, ushering them in to the hall. 'Mother Superior will see you.'

They were led down a high-ceilinged corridor. Young girls, all dressed in the same long grey shapeless dress, were on their knees, not in prayer, but scrubbing the floor, bars of soap as big as themselves. Their hair was cropped the same; short as if a bowl had been put on their head as a guide and everything below cut off. The girls scuttled out of their way, allowing them to pass. They didn't look up, just kept their heads bowed. The nun ignored them completely, as if they were lambs grazing in a pasture at her feet. She opened a door at the end of the corridor and led them into an empty classroom.

'Take a seat here. Mother Superior will be with you shortly.'

They both sat in the front row, new students, afraid and alone and anonymous and in need of a friend. Another long wait, but at least they were dry. There was utter silence. Bridget listened for sounds, but found more silence, an echoing silence of abandonment. She jumped with a start when the door opened and the Reverend Mother walked in. The nun must have been in her late sixties, but the oval of her face was fresh and her eyes sharp. A large pectoral Cross rested on her bosom. Bridget felt her piercing stare as she sized her up. The woman sat behind the teacher's table. It felt eerily strange, her mother beside her at a desk, looking so small and frightened, worry etched on her forehead like a pupil who had forgotten their homework. Reverend Mother flexed her long slender fingers, before folding them and laying them to rest before her on the table.

'Now, then, who have we here?' she asked.

'I'm Maeve O'Donovan, Neasa's mother, and this is her sister Bridget.'

'I see. And what can I do for you?'

'We'd like to see Neasa, if possible,' Maeve stammered. 'Or to hear some news of her. We haven't heard anything in months.'

'I'm afraid that's not possible. Neasa will not be having any visitors for the foreseeable future. Shall I proceed to talk freely in front of the child?' Those sharp eyes cut to Bridget. 'Would you prefer she wait outside while I give you the details of Neasa's case?' The tongue spoke to Maeve, but the eyes remained on Bridget.

'No,' said Maeve, a curl of uncertainty to her reply.

'As you wish,' the nun replied brusquely. 'The girl gave birth six weeks ago in Bessborough House. It was premature but mother and baby were fine.'

'Were fine?' said Maeve.

The nun's eyelids closed slowly, a sign of impatience. 'It was a baby boy and we made the necessary arrangements.'

'What do you mean necessary arrangements?' said Maeve.

'He will be cared for by a good family. That is all I can tell you. It is best for the baby and of course, your daughter.'

'You … you sent the baby away? Already?'

'It was done with great care and sensitivity. Neasa will be staying with us here for the foreseeable future and no visitors will be permitted.'

'But why? I'm her mother?'

'The girl is in danger of submitting to temptation if allowed to resume her previous life.' Mother Superior straightened the Cross at her neck. 'To put it bluntly, she is inclined towards promiscuity. A routine of work, prayer and reflection will assist her return to the right path. When she has shown repentance, visitors may be allowed. That is all I can say on the matter.' She stood. 'The good sister will show you out.' And with that she left the room.

The young girls cleaning, neared the other end of the corridor. The floor gleamed but a dull sterility hung in the air, the aura of sanitation overpowering. A dirty cleanliness, Bridget thought, and she longed to be outside, to feast on the untainted air, rain or no rain. One of the girls risked a look upward. She couldn't have been more than fourteen, a cute, petite little thing. In the short look, Bridget recognised fear and the shame.

Outside, on the front step, the midday sun seemed blinding. The burly door banged shut behind them. Maeve walked slowly down the steps. Bridget followed a few paces behind, her legs heavy, her heart heavy. They were leaving Neasa in the bowels of what they had seen. She turned and looked back up at the building that had swallowed her sister. Would Neasa's face look down from one of the windows? Just a glimpse? Just a glimpse, please. Nothing stirred. All was still but for the tricolour hanging proudly above the door, waving in the breeze.

Seán stowed away on the US Freighter, the Jack Carnes. He and Barney had arranged it, keeping all the details to themselves. They had scoured the bars along the docks for a few nights, hoping to meet someone they could trust and do a deal with.

They had met Jim Broderick from New Jersey, captain of the freighter. Seán trusted him from the get-go.

'I've Irish blood,' he had said.

They talked of Ireland. He had two daughters of his own. Seán explained his predicament, offered the captain money which he refused, and a few days later Seán was on board. He was locked in a room below deck for a few days, but was comfortable and was brought food. Once well out to sea, he was allowed on deck and he mingled with the crew, helping wherever he could, paying his way in labour. He spent some very pleasant evenings with Jim. He was invited to eat with him most nights and they would sit and chat about their families, or tell each other stories from the past. Jim was born into an Irish-American bootlegging family. He told stories of the operation they ran during prohibition, running speak-easies and distributing liquor in New Jersey. When alcohol was legalised they had set up a shipping company. Jack ran the business for years but tired of it and took to the sea himself.

'I like the freedom of it,' he had said. However, he still longed for the glamour and excitement of the prohibition days. 'Best days of my life.'

Jim consumed copious amounts of alcohol while they talked, rum mostly, and towards the end of the night, Seán would often have to lift him over to his bed, out for the count.

The freighter was unescorted, its cargo not valuable enough to guard. It was well past midnight when the U-boat struck. It had been tracking the Jack Carnes for an hour or so before it launched the first torpedo. It tore through the hull and the freighter took on water. Seán was in his bunk when he heard the sickening thud, followed by a loud explosion. All the men rushed on deck. The ship was already listing when the second torpedo hit and the boat shook violently, knocking two men overboard. They rushed for the lifeboats. She was going down fast. Seán looked around for Captain Jim. He was nowhere to be seen.

'Anyone see the captain?' he roared competing with the alarm bells ringing out on deck.

Nobody heard. Most of the men were already in the lifeboats, or clambering in. Seán rushed below deck. The boat was listing dangerously now. Seán knew he didn't have much time.

Two of the crew rushed past him. 'Get out,' they warned him. 'She's going down quick.'

But they never made it. The bow had submerged and the ship began to sink backwards. The two men were hurled back towards Seán and he fell backwards himself, as walls suddenly became floors. Water gushed in, rising quickly. There was no way out. The water was up to his chest. Seán had faced death before but he didn't want to go, not now, not when he was heading home to see his girls. They needed him. The water was under his chin. He gasped for air.

'No,' he screamed. 'Neasa, I'm coming for you. Neasa …'

He struggled under the weight of the water, thrashing and flailing, holding his breath a long time, until eventually he could hold no more. His mouth opened and the water rushed into his lungs, filling them up. Still conscious, he experienced a moment of deep calm, his body weightless, a moment of clarity and beauty and then he was gone, soul departed. His body sank with the ship.

Neasa woke and shot bolt upright in the bed. She had heard her daddy calling in her dreams. She looked around disoriented, for a moment forgetting where she was. It took a minute for her eyes to adjust to the gloom, then seeing the metal skeletons of beds either side of her, her heart sank and she lay back down on the thin mattress. She shared the dormitory with forty girls. Girls wasn't exactly correct. Some were older than her mother, as old as her granny had been. Others were no more than twelve or thirteen. Country girls, city girls, posh girls, poor girls, farm girls, factory girls, office girls, all landed in the one pot and the nuns watching them like witches over a cauldron.

It didn't matter what age they were, all the penitents were referred to as child and they in turn referred to the nuns as mother. Not all arrived here pregnant. Some were simply unwanted by their families or husbands, and some unwanted by the parish priest. The reasons for being unwanted varied, too. Some were simple-minded or mentally ill. Some had been too frisky with the boys, some raped and abused, some orphaned. The specific reasons didn't matter. They all knew they were not wanted. They all wore the same uniform, wore the same haircut, suffered the same penance. They were all the same girl, unwanted stepdaughters in God's crowded house, they plodded the hallways now with vacant stares. If there was something missing inside them before, the nuns ensured they were completely hollowed out in this place. Empty vessels walking silent corridors, Neasa could almost hear a forsaken echo emanating from them as they went

Neasa had stopped counting the days? How long had she been locked in this prison, long shadows of the crow-like nuns looming over her at every turn? After the hospital, a daze set in. She remembered the pain of the birth. Excruciating, like nothing she had ever experienced before. Nobody had warned her, or told her what to expect. She didn't know what the contractions were when they started, then when her waters broke she cried out in panic. She thought something had burst inside her. The pains came faster and faster. She lay there on her own, watching the hands of the clock on the wall climb and slide slowly around and around. Eventually three nuns came into the room. Not one of them said a word to her. Her legs were strapped to the bed and two nuns pinned her down, while the other busied herself between her legs. She cried out for her mother, over and over, the pain growing more intense until she felt she couldn't bear it no more. A baby cried. She looked up before she passed out and saw the black cloaks of the nuns, their backs to her, huddled over her baby, wrapping it like a butcher's package before scurrying from the room, the baby's cries trailing off into the distance, somewhere very far away.

When she woke she was in another room with some ten women, all in beds. Her throat was raw and sore and she was very thirsty. She reached for the jug of water on the locker to her right, and a shot of pain ran through her. She reached down to touch herself. Her hand came back up smeared with blood. She retched violently but there was nothing to bring up. Then she remembered the pain and vaguely remembered the cries of a baby. How long ago had that been? How long had she been out? She looked around her again. The girl in the next bed smiled over at her. She was older than her and had a friendly open face.

'You've been asleep all night,' she said in a strong Cork City accent, the words at the end of her sentence stringing up in a lilt. 'They wheeled you in last night at about eight o'clock. It's ten in the morning now. Don't worry the bleeding is normal. It will go away after a few days.'

'Thanks,' Neasa said weakly.

'What'd ya have?'

'What did I have?'

'The baby. A boy or a girl?'

'I ... I don't know. I can't remember.'

'Better off, not knowing.'

'How come?'

'You can't give them a name then, can't picture them in your head or nothing. Means you'll forget them quicker. Better off.'

'Will they not let me see the baby?'

'Not on your nelly. Baby's gone, probably even in its new home as we speak. They say they sell them to rich people who can't have babies.'

Neasa went to retch again. She felt like something, an organ, had been ripped from her body and stolen in the night.

'This is my second one. They took the first one from me as well. Good riddance, I say. Can't be looking after a wee one in my line of work.'

'This is your second time in here?'

'Ya, all part of the job, you see. Happens from time to time. You come in here, get fixed up and your back out working the street again in no time, good as new.'

Neasa didn't understand what the girl meant.

It took two days for the bleeding to stop. She was walked to another part of the building, taken to a room and given a disinfectant bath which stung like Hell. The nuns held her down, she couldn't escape their grasp. They cut off her hair and gave her a shapeless dress, a pair of black hobnail boots, two pairs of underwear and two pairs of thick cotton tights. Worst of all, they gave her a calico strip which they pulled tight around her chest and knotted at one side to flatten her breasts. She was told to put the rest of the clothes on, stripping down naked in front of the two nuns giving the orders. Then she was brought to the Mother Superior. She was warned not to speak or she would be punished.

'Mother Superior will explain everything,' they said.

Neasa was led into a big office and left standing in front of a large desk, the Mother sitting behind it, writing in a voluminous ledger. She didn't look up when Neasa entered, didn't acknowledge her until ten minutes passed, when she removed her glasses, put down the pen, and closed the ledger with a thud.

'Come closer,' she ordered, 'and listen carefully to what I say. I will not repeat myself. Do not ask questions, just listen. You will nod if you understand.'

Neasa nodded, the first of many, she suspected.

'You have sinned but have been given a chance to repent. You are one of the lucky ones. You are to stay with us here until you show us that you have repented and reformed. You will take the name Fidelma. Forget Neasa. We are not concerned with that girl anymore. Through work and prayer you will atone for your sins and cleanse yourself. Do you understand?' The nun looked at her over the top of her glasses. 'Do you understand?' she repeated.

Neasa nodded.

'You will work in the laundry among other duties. Obey the vow of silence, attend services as required, keep your head down, work hard, say your prayers and forget the outside world for a time. That is my advice to you. The sisters will show you to your dorm. Tomorrow you rise at six o'clock for mass and after breakfast you will start in the sorting room.'

Days and weeks blended, none marking time, none bringing any news from home. Neasa assumed Bridget and their mother would come, take her home, rescue her. The baby was born. The baby was gone. Trouble was behind her. She was once again normal Neasa. She should be with her family. She knew it was forbidden but in a moment of despair she whispered a question to one of the nuns, the one who supervised her section, the less fearful one.

'Your family are functioning without you. They no longer want you. Would you be here if it was otherwise?'

The work was exhausting. Tending the linen wasn't so bad, but some of the clothes and underwear were beyond filthy. Dirty laundry landed daily from all over the city, from priests, bachelors, butchers, chefs, prisons, orphanages, hotels and hospitals. Shit and blood, vomit and piss, yesterday's food and wine, semen and spit and snot. They handled it all, bare hands sorting and cleaning, girls whose souls had been sullied, unsoiling the city. No hands were to be washed until the evening when the chores were completed. Then there was the detergent that burned the skin and the bleach that stung the eyes. They hauled huge amounts of turf with barrows in out of the garden to fuel the laundry because of the shortage of oil due to the war. The work was physical and tiring and oftentimes dangerous. The first week she was there a woman lost all the fingers on one hand in a spinner. The linen was destroyed and the nuns were furious. Everything had to be washed again and they were kept back late until not a trace of blood remained. She had heard another lady lost an arm not so long ago.

She could have coped with the work, gotten used to it, but she couldn't get over the emotional pain of being constantly put down, told she was no good, that her family had abandoned her, that she was a sinner and must do penance. It was made very plain that she was a low-life. And she believed it. It was easier that way. Then there was the loneliness. They weren't allowed to talk to each other, they weren't left idle for a moment. There were always chores even after the day's work in the laundry was done. It was an endless cycle of scrubbing, cleaning, tidying, bleaching, prayers, forever down on her knees, her sore knees, red-raw from crawling on the floors. For recreation they would do needlework or make rosary beads, and even then, one of the older penitents, was put between them so they couldn't talk. Some of the older women were worse than the nuns. They were called auxiliaries. They'd stayed on after their time was finished, becoming institutionalised, with most having nowhere else to go. They'd attempt to catch the younger ones out and report them. At night, the dormitory door would be locked, and in the morning they'd have to listen for the key turning in the door and be up and out of bed before the nun came in.

One night, when the loneliness was the weight of a lead blanket, Neasa attempted a conversation with the girl in the bed beside hers. She just wanted to hear her own voice, wanted to remind herself that she still existed. It was a one-way conversation. The other girl dared not respond. One of the auxiliaries reported the attempt to a nun, who dragged her out of bed and made her kneel in the middle of the dormitory. She was left there the entire night, her back on fire, her calves cramping. In the morning, it was bread and dripping as usual, but every morning for the rest of the week she was made to eat her ration off the floor, while the dormitory watched on, a nun looking down on her, making sure that when finished she repeated the same prayer over and over.

'I beg almighty God's pardon, Our Lady's pardon for the bad example I have shown.'

When she couldn't sleep, she would sneak into the small lavatory. There was a skylight above and she would sit there looking up at the moon and the stars, wondering about the outside world and her family at home getting on without her. Had they forgotten her? Did they not want her anymore? With eyes to the sky, she couldn't possibly believe it to be true. She pictured Bridget and her mother and Seán Óg and her father, all clearly, somewhere out there under that same sky. Sometimes a bird landed on the window, a blackbird and she'd whisper up to it, sending messages out into the world.

Then one night, Neasa was caught staring to the sky above her, humming a lullaby she used to sing to Seán Óg, humming it also for her little baby that had been taken. They boarded up the skylight.

Like coming to believe she was a low-life, Neasa came to believe that her family had forgotten her, forgotten about the middle child, the child that used to be called Neasa, the middle child that committed sin and brought misery to the family, to the village. There was something gravely wrong with the Neasa that had arrived at the doors of this place. Reprobate and unclean. She accepted the work and the penance and prayed for forgiveness. She dared not dream or hope or even think of the future, or of the past.

The day the telegraph arrived Bridget was on the pier with Seán

221

Óg. He loved watching the boats and the birds. His little finger pointed up to the clouds and followed the circling and the glide of the seagulls. The first signs of autumn were beginning to appear. The breeze had a slight chill to it in the evening as it meandered through the trees in Kilbeg Wood, worrying a leaf here and a leaf there until one fell from its branch to the forest floor where it would decay and return to the earth, giving life anew to the trees above.

She saw the telegraph being delivered, the knock on the door, her mother answering, accepting the telegraph. She saw her open it, reading it briefly and then crumple like one of the leaves to her knees in the doorway. Bridget knew then. She had long since prepared herself for this. It seemed a natural progression, following on from all that had happened. She had long since given up the notion that there would be a happy ending, her father, the white knight of the fairytales, riding into town on his stead, Neasa behind him holding on to his waist. She had felt in her heart awhile now that he was gone. She picked up Seán Óg and walked slowly back towards the house. Her mother looked up at her as she approached. She held out the telegram balled up in her hand.

'He's gone, Bridget. Your father's gone.'

'I know, Mammy. I know,' she said taking the telegram. 'Come on inside.'

Bridget closed the door behind them and read the telegram. It was from Barney. The telegram said simply that Seán had been lost at sea, went down with a ship, torpedoed by a German U-boat in the North Atlantic. He'd been making his way home to his family, it said. That's it then, thought Bridget, that's the end of it now. Just to see him one more time before he was taken, just one more hug from him, would have been enough. Even a body, even if his body came home, she would have been able to say goodbye to him. She had been robbed even of this, just like Mary and Paudie. Neasa's fate sealed now as well, no way. If the nuns hadn't broken her yet, the news would certainly finish her off.

Bridget grieved selfishly as if it was the only thing she had left. She took to the bed for days on end, not leaving the room, not eating. Was there anything left to live for now, she thought? Her mother was no better, for weeks walking the house in her bedclothes not knowing if it was night or day. Mary next door took Seán Óg into her care, as Maeve wasn't capable of looking after him. There was no funeral service. There was no body and no official confirmation of Seán's death. His name wasn't on the crew list of the Jack Carnes.

Bridget's nightmares became worse. She had trouble sleeping. Soon she became delirious and caught a fever. For days she slipped in and out of consciousness, her temperature soaring. Sweats and shivers. The doctor was called. Her mother came out of her own grief and stayed by her bedside day and night, nursing her, terrified she would lose another. The doctor said he didn't know if Bridget would pull through. There wasn't much he could do for her. It was up to the girl, he said. She either wanted to live or wanted to die.

Bridget drifted between worlds. She lay on the grass on Rabbit Island, watching the clouds float by overhead, her father beside her whistling a tune. Then she was up in the lookout, a man in dark clothing standing over her, his face in the shadows. She was in Kilbeg Wood. A boy hung from the end of a rope, swinging in front of her, his features twisted into a gruesome smile. She ran on until she was in Daly's field. There she came across her family huddled in the corner of the field, emaciated, like the living dead, their mouths green from eating the grass. They moved and blocked her way, but she cast them aside and hurried on. Then she was at Trá Na Wadla, sitting on the stony beach. It was dark and suddenly from all around she heard music, beautiful music, music so sad it almost stopped her heart. The music came to an end, played itself out and then there was silence. Out in the sea in front of her, a vision rose, the most beautiful maiden she had ever seen, dressed in brilliant white robes, golden hair flowing out behind her in the wind. She opened her mouth and let out the most soulful, sorrowful wail, as if it had come from the depths of the sea at the beginning of time. The maiden called to Bridget. She got up from the ground and walked towards the sea, seduced, drawn to the light. She let herself go and she closed her eyes. She felt all the pain, all the regret, all the guilt leave her body. She was floating, drawn into the water, longing for its silky fingers to reach out and caress every part of her, embrace her, swallow her up. Then she heard a voice call in the distance, a familiar voice. She wanted it to go away, to be left alone but the voice sliced through the keening of the maiden and the call of the sea and then the maiden was gone.

Bridget blinked and looked around. She was sitting on the floor of the post office. Pipe smoke drifted on the air and danced around the rays of the summer sun that pierced the gloom through the window. Her grandmother stared down at her, shaking her head in disapproval.

'For the love of God, Bridget, where were you off to with that wan? 'Tis lucky I came along when I did or you would have went off with your wan, and what would you have then but moaning and wailing all the days of your life? 'Tis grand for a while, but you wouldn't be long getting sick of Clíona and her misery.'

'I'm so tired, Granny, I just want to go to sleep. I want to go where my dreams can't find me, somewhere safe and warm to lie down.'

'Will you get out of that, now, once and for all. You're worse than that Clíona one out there in the bay. Do you want to end up like her moaning and weeping for centuries?' she said with a snort. 'Pick yourself up now and dust yourself off and get on with it. Do you think you are the only one who has ever suffered? God almighty, I could tell you stories.'

Bridget open her mouth to reply but words wouldn't come.

'You have been through much, Bridget, and there will be more to come. You have seen much that is bad about people, but not all people are bad. There is good in all people. We are all born innocents. It is how we treat each other that makes the world. Do not let your suffering and experiences go to waste. If you do then all will have been for nothing, all your suffering, all of Neasa's suffering, your father's, Danny's and all the people before you, right down to the beginning of time, it will all have been for nothing. Suffering is how the world is built, how the world moves, how our race learns. We are all moving towards something, Bridget. The whole world is moving towards something, all inextricably linked. Every little thing has a purpose. We are all part of something bigger. We don't see it of course, in the way the wave thinks it acts alone and that its time is over when it crashes to the shore. But the wave is just part of a vast ocean, and when it breaks on the shoreline it is pulled back again to play some other part. Rise above the suffering. Remember, your world is your actions. Make use of your life for good, learn from the mistakes the rest of us made and remember,' her granny reached out her hand and placed it on her breast, 'God is in here,' she said and moved her hand to her forehead, 'and in here. God is in you. Bring Him with you everywhere.'

Then Bridget was back in her bed in Kilbeg. Her mother stood over her, warm hand on her forehead.

'You're awake, thank God. For a while we thought we were going to lose you, with that bad fever, but your temperature is normal now. The doctor said you should be fine.'

Bridget smiled and reached up, took her mother's hand and squeezed tight.

They had no body to bury but they had some things that

reminded them of him. His old oilskins, his tobacco tin, and his favourite geansaí and cap. He didn't own much else anyway, was never much of a man for possessions.

They walked hand in hand out towards the old *cillín*. The first frost had come in this morning and Bridget hoped the ground wouldn't be too hard. This had been her idea. It was the Samhain, a time to honour the dead. Bridget suggested it fitting to create a memorial to their father, somewhere they could visit. She had always liked the old *cillín* and remembered Christmas Day a few years back when she had followed her father instead of going to mass.

She lifted her father's woollen *geansaí* to her face, breathing in his scent one last time before burying the few things beside his brother Danny and his mother. Maeve and Bridget knelt down to say a prayer while Seán Óg chased a robin through the trees. Bridget didn't know who to direct her prayer to, she thought on it awhile and settled on her namesake, the Goddess her father had named her for.

Brigid, bride of the earth,
Sister of the Sluaigh Sidhe
Daughter of the Tuatha de Danann
Take my father into your eternal flame
Let his fire add to your fires
Bringing flames back into our hearths
Bringing life back to us once more
Winter is brief, but life is forever
May he find peace on your shore

They walked back the road towards the village, arm in arm, Seán Óg running along in front of them. The door of the church was open as they passed. Bridget let go of her mother's arm.

'You go ahead, Mammy. I'll be along soon.'

226

Bridget moved into a pew at the back, and knelt. She prayed for them all, that they all might find peace, for Danny, for Paudie, for Fr Sullivan, Fr Murphy, for her mother, for Kitty Collins, for Neasa, for the nuns, for her granny and for Seán Óg, for the men fighting in the war all over Europe. She prayed for them all, over and over.

She didn't know how long she had being praying but sat back up in her pew letting the peace and stillness of the church settle on her. She looked up at the wooden effigy of Jesus on the Cross that hung from the ceiling over the altar. It reminded her of the Cross that hung from the Mother Superior's neck. It wasn't him she had been praying to. It wasn't anyone in particular. She'd just been praying, putting it out there. That was all. She didn't expect an answer. Who was the man on that cross anyway? What was he? The crucified figure looked back down at her as if asking her, as if she had the answer.

'You are only us,' she said aloud, her voice sounding like someone else's in the silence of the church. 'You are only us. You've always been us. You don't exist without us.'

She rose slowly, straightening her skirts and walked down the aisle, the afternoon sun like molten gold leaching under the door. She knew then what she was going to do with her life.

Fáinne

As the car turned left at Leap, Bridget began to feel the same mixed emotions she always felt when she came home. She was a girl again and she felt herself shrinking in the back of the Toyota. Anticipation, excitement, dread, guilt. The water was a deep green where the sea snaked to touch the village. On the other side of the road a rock face rose up topped by trees and the road twisted and turned hugging the stone faces, making its way to Poulgorm Bridge.

Three generations sat in the car: Bridget, her nephew James — Seán Óg's eldest — his wife Carmel, and their children.

James said to the children, 'A pound for the first to spot the bridge.'

Silence for a minute or two as the kids in the back craned their necks. They furrowed their brows in concentration. Bridget wondered if she was included in this.

'I see it, I see it!' shrieked young Cian, thrusting his hand across the back of the driver's seat for his prize, the other two moaning in disappointment at losing out.

James turned and smiled.

Bridget settled back into her seat. A car approached from the other way so they pulled in at the widened space in the middle of the bridge and let it pass. She glanced over at Kilbeg Pier and picked out the old family home. She turned her attention to the kids, who seemed a little in awe at this old woman sitting with them in the back. They'd probably heard the fuss all week, witnessed the house being scrubbed from top to bottom, the good room would have been painted of course, the garden weeded, all the talk would have been about her arrival, their granny and granddad on edge as they awaited the arrival of the nun.

Bridget winced as she thought of the trouble they had gone to. It was always the same every time she came home. Her brother Seán Óg and his wife Anne tiptoeing around her, in truth a little scared of her. She didn't give off an authoritative impression herself, it was just the habit. Amazing how a piece of material could put such a barrier between people. At least this time she had the kids. She would spend the few weeks getting to know them and could keep out of the adults' way. Nothing worse than walking into a room and inducing silence.

'We're going to have a great few weeks, kids,' she said. 'Have ye ever been to Trá Na Wadla, the secret beach?'

'Secret beach!' they gasped.

'Yes, only I know the way to it.'

Their eyes opened wide. 'Where is it?'

'Shh,' Bridget said, raising a finger to her lips and motioning with her eyes towards the front seat. 'Just for kids, no adults.' She winked. 'We'll go there tomorrow, if I can find the map.'

She caught Donagh's eye. He was the eldest, his face a frenzy of freckles and when he smiled she saw the gap between his teeth. He was regarding her closely. There was something in his gaze that she recognised, a curiosity, a thirst. She could see he was holding back, that there were questions ready to roll off his tongue.

As they passed through the village of Union Hall, Bridget marvelled at how little had changed from her last visit ten years ago, and how little it had changed really since she was a girl. Some of the houses were now painted in bright colours. Pinks, greens, blues, all side by side. A kaleidoscope of colour as they cruised up the slope of the village. The same names hung over the doors of the pubs. Casey's on the corner, Nolan's squeezed in between two townhouses on the other side of the street, Fuller's general store, undertaker, hardware shop, fuel merchant – whatever you required in life and death, Fuller provided. They passed the Black Field and the church on the left. To the right the road sloped up Doctor's Hill and into Skibbereen, the grotto of Our Lady across the road, the statute facing the door of the church. Everyone in the car blessed themselves. Was that rehearsed for her benefit?

The lake was covered in lily pads, strewn over the surface like the aftermath of a messy picnic. Two swans glided through the mess and left a wake of clear water, the June sun making their trail sparkle. They turned left at the Cross and up the hill towards Ballincola where Bridget's brother had made his home for the last forty years, the potholed road juggling the kids in the back, until at last they turned in at the top of the lane and got out of the car.

Seán Óg and Anne were waiting outside. Seán Óg shifted from foot to foot, uncomfortable in his new shirt and trousers. The old outhouses opposite, overgrown now for years, had been completely overrun by wild roses and their busy pink flowers contrasted nicely with the plain white houses on the bane. She never knew how to greet Seán Óg. A handshake, a hug, a kiss? She settled for a handshake. No point in trying to force intimacy after all these years. She had never really gotten to know Seán Óg. He was so young when she went away. She gave Anne a warm embrace. They had looked after their mother over the years and she had moved in with them when he married Anne. Grandchildren aplenty arrived and this had kept her busy. She had been very happy with them here, in her last years.

Tea was served in the front room, the smell of fresh paint still evident and the upholstery on the couches still a little damp from the cleaners. She noticed Anne had used her mother's good china, still doing the rounds after all these years, reserved for her now, rather than the parish priest. She wondered if she was drinking out of the same cup Fr Sullivan had used in the front room in Kilbeg all those years ago.

'Ye have the place kept lovely,' Bridget said.

She heard the kids squealing and playing outside, their good clothes thrown off, now free to enjoy the rest of the afternoon in the sun.

'She's the whole week trying to keep the kids out of it,' said Carmel.

Anne looked out the window towards the front field. 'Era, they'd no interest in it until they weren't allowed in.'

James sat stiffly, squeezed in beside her on the small settee. 'At least it's fine weather. Keeps them out from underneath our feet.'

Conversation was strained. Seán Óg never said much anyway. He leaned forward in his chair, rocking, his head down, staring into his cup.

'I suppose it's hot in Rome these times?' Anne said.

''Tis,' Bridget replied. 'You wouldn't step outside the door between twelve and four.'

Silence again.

'Right,' said Seán, 'I'm up North to look in on the cattle,' and with that he disappeared upstairs, changed and was out the door in a flash.

James and Carmel soon followed, leaving Anne and Bridget in the room.

'What are the arrangements then?' Bridget said.

'The body is in the funeral home in Leap. She came home yesterday from England,' said Anne. 'The removal will be Wednesday evening and the requiem mass at twelve the day after.'

'Everything okay with the grave?' said Bridget.

'It's all fine. She'll be laid to rest beside her mother and grandmother, just like she asked.'

'Thank you for arranging everything. You're very good.'

'It's nothing. She had a hard old life, poor Neasa. It's

only right that she should be laid to rest back with her own.'

After breakfast the next morning Bridget drew a hasty map, spilt some of her tea on the paper, used the range to burn one of the edges, and went off to round up the kids who were already up and playing football down the garden.

'I've found it,' Bridget exclaimed as she made her way towards them, holding the map aloft with her right hand.

The three crowded around, breathless with anticipation as she knelt in the garden and spread out the map on the ground. She traced the route for them with a finger.

'Now it could be dangerous, so if anyone wants to stay behind, that's fine.'

They ran off to ask their mother's permission to join the hunt. Bridget stood for a while enjoying the stillness of the garden in the morning sun. Three small fields ran down to the lake and she spotted Seán Óg in the last one, building a wall. He was stooped over a pile of stone, picking one up, turning it in his hands, putting it down, selecting another until he found the right one, slowly building stone upon stone with as much care and love as if he was building a cathedral. Many people searched for peace and redemption in convents and churches, as nuns, priests and missionaries in foreign lands, in prayer and contemplation, silence, fast and abstinence, sacrifice. Seán Óg didn't have to search. He found it here, inside himself, stooped over a wall, wiping the sweat from his brow, lost in the unrecognised bliss of doing something completely.

Donagh looked up at the face of the nun as they made their way up the back lane towards the big hill. Her skin was tanned and leathery after many years in the sun in foreign lands. Her face was embossed with lines and told a story in Braille that could be read under fingertip, an adventure in ridges, crow's-feet and furrows. Her navy pinafore dropped straight down. She didn't fill her clothes at all. She wore those brown tights that all older woman wore and they were bunched up around her ankles. He didn't know if she had hair or not under her habit. She had a very clean smell like soap and there was music in her voice as she told stories of her travels in Africa. She had a kindness in her eyes that he was drawn to. They were of the lightest shade of blue, and sparkled like a young girl's, but a sadness lurked behind them and when she thought nobody was looking she'd often stare into the distance as if there was something there that pained her. As she spoke, the world around came alive, mounds in fields becoming fairy palaces, woods transformed into enchanted forests, beaches into otherworldly amphitheatres. She told them of wars and famines, ghosts and banshees, *púcas* and sluagh sidhe and their ancestors tied up in it all as if everything in the world was connected by a great web, the seen and the unseen, and all of it leading back to them, the O'Donovans involved in it all. Donagh looked forward to the long summer ahead and the trove of stories he'd reap from the old nun's company.

They reached the top of the big hill, its rise like the beam of an old plough and the blade dropping steeply towards the village. From here they could see the little inlet of Carrigilihy to the west, High Island, like a burly sentry guarding the entrance to the bay. To the north was the village of Castletownsend. They could see the colourful houses stacked on the hill and the vague threat of the jagged stags peering over the village's shoulder from the sea. Below them to the other side was Poulgorm Bridge, wading on its long legs in the shallows of low-tide as if it were an angler waiting for a bite.

'Now we're heading off the road,' said Bridget. 'Stay close to me. There are a lot of angry bulls around here.'

Caitlin shrank back, a little apprehensive.

'Don't be such a sissy,' Donagh said, feigning bravado.

'They're hardly going to attack a nun, are they?'

They headed off over the fields. The day was beginning to heat up as the sun climbed in the sky. There was a stillness in the air, nothing stirred, not a leaf or a blade of grass. Cows stood motionless as they passed, chewing suspended. They eyed them sullenly as if blaming them for their lot. It hadn't rained in weeks and the ground was hard under their feet. The land was poor, hilly and covered in gorse bushes and briars. It was tough going for the kids, but they were excited at the prospect of the secret beach.

Just before they reached the beach, Bridget pulled up. 'We're nearly there. Now, before we go down I need you to make me a promise. This is a special place. Sometimes, just before nightfall, you can hear music coming from the beach, the most beautiful music you could ever hear, like all the birds from all the countries in the world were part of the same choir and singing in harmony. People stayed away. They knew it was the fairies coming out to dance.'

'Fairies!' said Cian. 'I don't believe in fairies.'

Bridget looked him straight in the eye. 'Neither did Dan Driscoll and look what happened to him.'

'What happened to Dan Driscoll?' Donagh said.

'You didn't hear?' Bridget said. 'Oh good Lord, poor old Dan, he was below in Nolan's one night, full to the brim with porter.'

'What's porter?' said Caitlin.

'Guinness, darling, or Murphy's or it could have been Beamish. Whatever it was anyway, he was full of it. Talk came to Trá Na Wadla. He was full of brave talk, said he didn't believe in fairies, and for a bet he said he would spend the night down there, and what's more, he said he would do it that very night. He set off with a blanket borrowed from Nolan and a shoulder of whiskey under his harm. That was the last anyone saw of poor Dan Driscoll.'

237

The three were staring at her open-mouthed.

'What happened to him?' Cian said.

'Well,' Bridget said, and paused, 'it's not for sure but, it was certainly no coincidence. Days passed and there was no sign of poor old Dan, and that was strange as he never missed a night in Nolan's. Nolan himself was getting worried for he had given the shoulder of whiskey on tick and was losing his best customer. Anyway, Jimmy Collins was out walking the land one day and he came to this little hollow in the ground with a few trees where the cows used to shelter in the rain. Now, what he saw under one of the trees gave him a start. He rubbed his eyes and looked again. There under the tree was the whitest donkey he had ever seen in his life, and he lying on Nolan's blanket, an empty shoulder of whiskey beside him.'

'They turned him into a donkey?' said Caitlin.

'Well, we can't be sure, but there was neither sight nor sound of Dan Driscoll from that night on.'

'Granddad has a white donkey,' gasped Donagh.

'That he does,' said Bridget. 'Jimmy Collins was scared stiff of that donkey and didn't want him on his land. Bad luck, he said, so your granddad took him off his hands and has had him ever since. That must be thirty year ago now.'

'Granddad's donkey is Dan Driscoll!' said Cian.

'Well, at first he wasn't sure whether it was Dan Driscoll or not, so one Sunday your granddad filled a bucket up with porter brought it out the back field, left it under the big tree in the corner, and hid behind the ditch. Sure enough, it wasn't long before the donkey sauntered over. His nose disappeared into the bucket and he didn't stop until he had the whole lot drank. He took a step back from the bucket, let out a loud belch, and a deep sigh of appreciation as your granddad had seen Dan do a hundred times leaning against the bar in Nolan's.'

The kids were dumbfounded.

'Now, so ye have to promise me, you don't tell any of the

adults you were here. The fairies won't like that and the beach will disappear forever. This place is just for kids. Never come here after dark and never on your own.'

'But you are an adult,' Cian said.

'I'm not,' says Bridget. 'I'm a nun, a child of God. The fairies know that. Now all together, we promise.'

'We promise,' the children said in unison.

Trá Na Wadla was covered in flat grey stones, perfect for skimming. The kids passed the time in competition. Cian, as usual, was winning. The water stretched without a ripple across the bay like a sheet pulled taut. Bridget sat on a rock to the side, resting after the long walk. It was just how she remembered but much smaller. It had seemed so big when she was a child. Impenetrable, surrounded on three sides by rock face and hemmed in by the sea.

'Sister Bridget, can we go swimming?' Donagh was standing beside her.

'Of course you can, pet,' she said.

Cian had carried their togs and towels in his back sack and Bridget watched them change, towels wrapped around themselves, protecting their modesty. They wiggled and wormed their way out of their clothes. One hand on the towel, the other pulling and dragging, they kicked their clothes off. Cian dipped his toe in the water, ever cautious as Donagh ran past him with a whoop and dived straight in, screaming hysterically as the impact of the cold water hit his body. Bridget reached into her bag and took out a small glass bottle and a piece of paper. She read over the words on the paper, and satisfied, rolled it up and stuffed it into the bottle, replacing the cap. When she thought nobody was looking she went to the edge of the beach and threw the bottle as far as she could, well away from where the boys were swimming. She felt a tug at her sleeve.

'What's in the bottle?' It was Caitlin, little blue eyes staring up at her above a freckled button nose.

'It's a message, dear.'

'A message for who?'

'Did your parents ever tell you about your great-grandfather? My father?'

'I have a great-grandfather?' she asked.

'You did, my dear. He's in heaven now, but that's a story for another day. Go call your brothers, we'll have to be getting back for lunch. Good girl.'

The bottle was nowhere to be seen. Bridget hoped the sea would take it to where she wanted it to go.

The house was quiet as Seán Óg took the stairs to his bedroom, tired after his day's work, a glass of Paddy in his hand. The floorboards creaked under his feet like an old friend saying good night. Anne and Bridget sat in the kitchen, Anne with her hair in curlers sitting under the purr of the hairdryer. Anne's daughter came up from the village every month to re-do her perm, and she sat now waiting for it to set.

'You wouldn't get us a drop of Hennessey from the dresser, Sister? I can't move here,' Anne said.

Bridget fetched the bottle of brandy and two glasses, returned to the table and poured two large measures.

'I didn't know you took a drop,' said Anne.

'Didn't the Lord himself turn water into wine at the feast of Cana?' Bridget said. 'And, I'm on holidays.'

It was late but the evenings were luxuriously long. Bridget sat facing the window, the hills outside bathed in half-light. The landscape had an otherworldly feel. It was the longest day of the year and, close to midnight, there was still light in the sky. The conversation ebbed and flowed, and another drop was poured. She had always felt more at ease with Anne than with her own brother. Anne possessed a plump kindly face, soft features and a rosy glow to her cheeks. Everything about her radiated homeliness and comfort from her soft permed curls to her rounded ample bosom. But she had a sharp mind, a keen wit, an ability to see the best in everyone and draw it out. Her grandkids adored her, and she ruled the roost, not through fear or threat but because a compliment, gesture or kind word from Granny created a delicious warmth in their bellies. They were addicted and had to have it. Bridget thought of her own grandmother, in her last days, sitting in her rocking chair, in the shadows of the back room in the old post office, book open on her lap, the fire dancing on the wall behind. How she would have loved Anne. She would have loved the man Seán Óg grew into. She would have loved the family they reared and the life they furrowed out for themselves on the side of this hill in Ballincola, surrounded by their kids and grandkids.

'Did you ever hear much from Neasa?' said Anne.

'I used to get a letter once or twice a year.'

'Did she ever mention coming home?'

'Sure, she'd say it every year, but there was always something. Then she left it so long, I knew she'd never come. But she knew who she had here. Only Seán Óg, and he wouldn't remember her at all.'

'I remember her growing up,' said Anne, who was a few years older than Seán Óg. 'I was much younger. I started school the year she went away. She was the most beautiful girl I had ever seen, and the way she carried herself, all the boys were after her. One smile from her and they would have followed her over a cliff.'

'Does Seán Óg ever talk about her?'

'Never' said Anne. 'I tried to ask him about her a few times when we were first married, but you know Seán, he's not the talking type. I even suggested visiting her when we were in England, but he wouldn't have it. It's like he is ashamed or embarrassed. I often thought of her, poor girl, and prayed for her every Sunday in mass, and prayed for the poor baby. You know we were always warned when we were growing up to behave and stay away from the boys, or we'd be taken away like Neasa O'Donovan and never be seen again. It's so strange that she never came home.'

'Well, she's home now,' Bridget said.

Bridget lay awake in her bed that night, focusing on the crucifix on the wall, rolling the beads of her rosary through her fingers, reciting her mantra. In those first years in the convent, that ritual got her through many a night, working her way through the joyful, the luminous, the sorrowful and the glorious mysteries. In her thoughts she would travel back to Union Hall and pick the house at the end of the village. The O'Leary's were there at the time. She would work her way through each household, up and down the village street, dedicating a decade of the rosary to each person within, some of them long dead, until she had the whole village done, then she would start again, back at the first house. That was a time when the dreams came every night. As the years went by she dreamt less, worn out every night by her work in the missions and coming to the realisation that there were plenty of people in the world more in need of prayer. Now she was back in Union Hall. Neasa was back as well. She'd be at the undertakers now, getting dolled up for the last time. Strange that she would have asked to be buried at home. She hadn't been back to Union Hall since the black car took her away all those years ago, now she'd be coming back over Poulgorm Bridge in another black car. It was fifty years since Bridget had entered the order, fifty years also since she had seen Neasa for the last time. They had written to each other and Bridget had tried to meet up with her many times, even travelling to Birmingham on one occasion, only for Neasa not to show. Neasa had eventually been let out of the laundry after about ten years. She had gone to England and had worked at a big hotel in Birmingham. She was still young and pretty and had many relationships, but none of them lasted. She had been married twice, but had never had any other children. She suffered from periods of depression and battled with alcohol addiction all her life. In the last year, her son managed to track her down and they wrote often. He was forty before he discovered, by accident, that he was adopted. Neasa had written all about him to Bridget and they had made plans to meet up in London. However, as was the pattern in Neasa's life where tragedy was a daily occurrence, Neasa died before they got a chance to meet. She had never mentioned it in her letter but Neasa had cancer. She died in a hospice in London, on her own.

Bridget couldn't remember the last time she dreamt. The dream was always the same. She was a girl again back up at the lookout, peeping through the door. The scene in the lookout came at her all night. Again and again she saw Neasa on the ground, her underwear torn, discarded in the corner among the old glass bottles, her dress hitched up around her waist. First she was crying out, tears streaming down her cheeks, protesting, then her cries faded into a whimper, and a gasp every time he entered her. Then she was silent, her face sideways, mouth open, eyes blazing, defiant. She saw the white flesh of his buttocks as he thrust into her, his black trousers down around his knees. She heard his groans as he began to find his rhythm, his hurried anguish as if he knew the guilt that would come and wanted to hasten it. Afterwards when he had finished, he turned his head away, his body slackened and he rolled off her. Neasa just lay there like she was dead, her face turned looking at the wall, her toes twitching. There was something familiar about his movements as he dressed in the light of the moon, and in her dream, the dread built up to this point, until it became unbearable. He pulled his trousers up and inclined his head so that Bridget caught his profile in the light of the door, and she saw his face. Every time it was different, always familiar as if it was an old classmate she couldn't place, a friend from early childhood or a relation she hadn't met. Each time she nearly recognised him, felt it was just going to come to her, the name on the tip of her tongue. She would open her mouth to call out and wake up gasping, her breath gone and her heart panicking in her chest.

There weren't many people at the funeral, just family. There was nobody else that knew her or remembered her in the area. Even Seán Óg's children, her nieces and nephews, didn't know they had another aunt. Seán Óg had never mentioned her. Then suddenly they had an aunt and her body was being brought home to be buried. They were full of questions and Bridget filled them in, leaving out the scene in the lookout. When they asked about the father, Bridget told them that nobody knew. It was a secret Neasa had chosen to take to the grave.

'How could such things happen?' they'd said.

Bridget had heard this question many times down through the years. She had heard it after the war when the concentration camps were discovered. How could this happen? Every time there was a massacre, every time a child was killed or raped, serial killers, ethnic cleansing, genocide, she had witnessed it all and people always acted surprised. How did this happen? She had worked with the poor and downtrodden in many countries around the world: Africa, India, The Philippines. People didn't realise that it was people just like them who carried out these unspeakable acts, that all of us are capable of doing the same, that inside all of us there is the capacity for evil and the capacity for good. We have only one freedom in life, really, one choice. How much of the evil do we bury? How much of the good? There is a pit in each of our souls if we wish to start digging. It's there in each of us waiting to be exhumed. We think it's buried deep but once we break the first sod we find it's surprisingly close to the surface.

As they waited for the priest to enter, the door at the back of the church opened. Bridget turned to see who it was. A man stood awkwardly at the back of the church. Her eyesight wasn't the best these days, but for all the world she could have sworn it was her father standing there; the same build, same big shock of sandy hair, he even moved like her father as he slipped, nimbly for such a big man, into one of the pews at the back. Bridget couldn't stop looking over her shoulder during the service. When called as a minister of the Eucharist for Holy Communion, she saw him waiting in the line to receive. She had difficulty looking up when he stood in front of her, towering over her. Her hand shook as she reached up and placed Our Lord on his tongue.

Outside afterwards, he was standing chatting with Anne and Carmel. He turned and smiled over at her, a smile that warmed her heart, made her feel like a child again. Anne beckoned her over. She resisted the urge to run and jump into his arms.

'This is Daniel, Bridget, Neasa's son. He's over from England for the funeral,' Anne said.

'Hello, Sister,' he said, his blue eyes dancing and sparkling in his head. 'I've heard so much about you. Neasa used to write about you all the time. She was so proud of you.'

Bridget was filled with joy, elated he was here with them now, that a piece of her father and a piece of Neasa was living on. She had so much to tell him, so much to show him. She reached out and hugged him.

'It's so good to meet you, Daniel. Are you home for long?'

Daniel smiled. He was an O'Donovan alright. Smart enough to recognise the welcome and the apology in the word home.

'I have the week,' he said. 'My wife and kids are going to join me tomorrow. We've taken a house in the village.'

'I'd love to show you around, if you'd like,' she said.

'I'd like that very much.'

Neasa was housed in the ground beside her mother and grandmother. The gravediggers flattened sods of earth skinned from a neighbouring field with the back of their shovels, then retreated a few steps. A dark line of mourners traipsed out of the graveyard onto the lane like cattle leaving the field for the milking parlour, anxious not to betray an impression of haste. They donned their caps and mumbled their respects as they filed past. Anne lingered at her side, but Bridget sent her off, wanting to be alone for a while. Bridget removed her habit and shook her hair out, let the breeze take it. Her mind went back to Kilbeg all those years ago, sitting on the pier with Neasa, watching the sunset, waiting for their father to come in on the boat. Last night in the funeral home, she had seen Neasa for the first time since she had watched her leaving in the back of that car all those years ago. She was tiny in the coffin, the cancer having laid waste to her body, and the face could have belonged to any old woman in the street. There was no resemblance to the Neasa she once knew.

'I'm sorry, Neasa,' she said out loud. 'I'm sorry for everything.'

She turned and walked back through the graves to the gate, but something stopped her dead. He was here, she could feel it. She turned around and sure enough there was a man the far side of the ruined church. He was dressed in black smoking a cigarette, staring out to sea. She walked up to him, unafraid now. He turned to face her.

'Hello, Bridget,' he said. 'Do you remember me now?'

He was dark, sallow skinned, a red scar ringed his neck, his eyes burned malevolently, his teeth yellow, his fingers long and gnarled, nails curled out at the end where he held a cigarette. The smell assaulted her.

'It was you, wasn't it? Up at the lookout that night. It was you who raped Neasa. I saw you there. I remember now. You looked over straight at me as you dressed, and that's when I ran. I was so frightened I ran.'

The man just laughed, mocking her.

'Who are you?' she said.

The man laughed again.

'Tell me who you are!' Bridget screamed.

'Who am I?' he said, feigning surprise at the question. 'You know who I am. You all knew who I was. It's not like anyone hadn't seen me before. I wasn't sneaking around. Everyone saw me, everyone was warned but chose to ignore me. You saw me. Who am I? I am that which the world has forgotten. I am that which is inside each and every one of you, that which you bury. You see my work all around you but deny it has anything to do with you. You ask me, was it you? It's better that you look to yourself. Who is responsible you all say? Who has done this terrible thing? Who am I? I am Danny, I am Father Sullivan, I am Paudie, I am Kitty, I am your father, your mother, I am Father Murphy, I am Neasa, I am in the hearts of all men, of all women. I am you!'

He paused. His facial expression changed. The cigarette was gone. The years fell off him, his boyish face now glowed, handsome and healthy. He smiled compassionately and radiated kindness. He reached out and with soft hands touched her cheek, his eyes shining with beauty and truth. He leaned down to whisper softly into her ear.

'That which you bury, doesn't go away. Do you see me?'

'Yes,' she said.

'Do you understand?'

'Yes,' she said, lowering her eyes. 'You are us, it is always us. There is nothing but us.'

She raised her head in time to see a blackbird flying off back towards the village, the man was gone and she was alone again. A white butterfly fluttered by, and landed on the fresh earth of Neasa's grave, rested for a moment then danced off on the wind out over the ocean.

Indigo Dreams Publishing
24 Forest Houses
Halwill
Beaworthy
Devon
EX21 5UU